The Religious Hysteria of Doctor Humphrey Humperdinck

THE RELIGIOUS HYSTERIA
OF DOCTOR HUMPHREY HUMPERDINCK

The Phoenix and the Chimera: A Seriocomic Romance

JOHN TAN

PARTRIDGE
A Penguin Random House Company

To order additional copies of this book, contact
Toll Free 800 101 2657 (Singapore)
Toll Free 1 800 81 7340 (Malaysia)
orders.singapore@partridgepublishing.com

www.partridgepublishing.com/singapore

'The roots of education are bitter, but the fruit is sweet.'
Aristotle, (Diogenes Laertius)

Chapter One

ADVENTURE OF THE POSTHUMOUS DETECTIVE: A DUEL WI' DA DEBBIL

JUST AS CLAUDE MONET lived in a picture (in Giverny, France) Mrs. Umney came out of a picture in Canterville Chase. This last incidence proved somewhat of interest: because, when Doctor Humphrey Humperdinck purchased Canterville Chase:—it was she that was on hand to welcome him:—for she was his housekeeper (dressed in heavy, black cretonne and wearing medium heels) all the time he was there;—until the unfortunate event of his breakdown, six months later. Humphrey had always had great interest in old buildings, ancient specter-haunted edifices and moldy rooms; the prophesy in the library window, especially (an advice to da larned) which, he held in high regard, wonder and esteem:

'When a golden child can win
Prayer from the lips of sin,
When the barrenly shy lass bears.
And the little one gives away its tears,
Then shall all the house be still
And PEACE come to OUR COMMONWEAL.'

Humphrey Humperdinck was a man that the Other-worldly had placed a mark upon; and even in his Mother's womb he responded to the spiritual and psychic phenomena, with an intensity that few unborn babies was known to respond. He participated in Sumptin, a communion, which few or even none of the common clod, knew about. He was informed about rightness and wrongness at a young age, the intrinsic beauty of decency and gentility, and nobleness of mind. Gain of fame, or money wasn't what led him to the Ghaistsweepin' business. Be that as it may, in medias res, I shall begin these tales, with an incident, happening, in Humphrey's hometown, just outside Philly. It took place while he was at the recovery stage after the horrendous crisis in Somerset, England—to wit,—a nervous breakdown (under mysterious circumstance),—that occurred in the cellar in Canterville Mansion, where the ghaist-containment units were housed—but about this, much more later! With something tantamount to a violent effort, almost—he was, at that time, trying to come to terms with his illness, by salvaging what was healthily rooted in the past; retracing his origins—revisiting paths taken in his early life; so that he might be graced with an enhanced self-understanding,—if naught else, in the light of his situation. He was receiving care; and some measure of care he had. The root word, of which, the Gothic KARA,—meaning, "to lament (with) . . ." He had been only too happy to accept this, if I could discern rightly, as his friend, who would wish to relate to you his allowing for this possibility—in sharing all his too acute pains, so that I could experience his sorrow, grieve with, and, cry out with him! Anyway, he felt an impulsion, he said, to go back to Philly, to see his Father's old house another time:—and this has something to do with issues and unresolved conflicts still embedded in the man's childhood past . . .

No 344-A Little Main Street looked like any old Colonial, American familial establishment on the East Coast, with its typical English influence. The mansion-like house stood a little way off the artery of the town, on solid, higher grounds, where both leaves and the grass was greener—lusher,—owning to a beck running behind the building. A double-storied, fivebedroom'd one, with white lace curtains, and pink porches and gables; da shades of apples brindling, darting and bobbing here and there,—today, at any rate, there was a good deal o' atmosphere an' nostalgia of homecomin';—a return to solid qualities, and attitudes, and class values:—mayhap, o' sumptin that made this country greater than every other in da whole wide wurl. The garden was redolent with blooms, and the family there now had a new tree-loft,—and in vain did Humphrey look for his old garden seat, which was a rubber tire hanging from a nut-tree branch. branch. Growing up a small town boy, and raised there, it was not until he was sixteen that he studied in Baltimore; and later, in New York State University. Most people wouldn't dream he should turn out to be anythin' but an Average Joe of Middle Income America, as it was only during the last few years in 'varsity that he really excelled, and exceeded, himself,—and everybody else for that matter,—and, graduated summa cum laude, which was nothing short of miraculous; and so,—accolades naturally followed!—Instead of becoming an insurance salesman like this father, he became an eminent scientist. There was another boy from this same small town, a Bob Bunyan, of contemporaneous age, who could be considered a childhood "friend", of sorts. The savant had not seen this Bobby Bunyan since "the parting of the west" when that person went to California over twenty years ago,—but, today,—he ran into him in Town—coming out of the local drugstore. Humphrey noted he was carrying a box of surgical gloves, and putting surgical scrub inside his coat, and he was lisping, 'Well, I didn't bring my valise and I refuse to git 'em into their polka-dot paper bag! So there!'—it seemed—without recognizing Humphrey at first, whispering low, immaculately precise, and businesslike;— da precision and efficiency of a house spider;—as if, to suggest, he normally answered to a stranger's unspoken question. Bobby Bunyan seemed to have come home to roost in his own backyard; but, when Humphrey recognized him, they began to say, "Well-be-met!" and all that school-chum stuff. Bobby Samson Bunyan could not be more different, and certainly, there was no reason why Humphrey should recognize him, or why, the before-mentioned person, should be coming out of a drugstore, at that very moment, in front of Humphrey's path or sparking the latter's recognition. We shall not speculate. Bob's attire, his mannered tilt of the hat,—egg-stain on his waistcoat—and style of ambulating, and, elbow-patch—all attested to the Private Detective, of the type, we meet hard-boiled, or, watch on our wonderful Telefunken Tee-vee or sumptin. Mostly, perhaps, that beaked snot o' his never more keenly aquiline; and his lips, aniline, as though he had stepped off a movie-set. With deep-set, owlish eyes, and a strange, hurried, ingratiating manner, he said, 'Egad, oh,

I'm bona fide . . . ! a Bona fide sleuth!' His eyes riveted Humphrey Humperdinck to the spot, yet, never eyeball to eyeball fer more than a few seconds,—he repeated with a grating, unamusing chuckle,—'I am a licensed P. I.!' giving our savant his typically obnoxious Buyanian once-over; a deep stare, and, gurgle in his throat, that was calculated to measure you by the modern standards of the wurl;—in addition, to your own frail estimation you had of yourself when he and you last met. Bobby had indulged in a liddle bullyin' or vicios leg-pullin' of the savant, whom he nicknamed "Mosquito Spaghetti" needless to say, an appellation, the then taunted Humphrey much detested; and this nomenclature he used now;—bringing Humphrey to remember the same old heartbreakin' feelin' that children are liable unmercifully—naturally, to capitalize on the weakness of others who are weaker than themselves . . . Bobby Bunyan intimated he had recently been promoted to Head Detective, which post he had been reticent to accept; but which he took anyway because the pay packet was pleasantly remunerative. "The League of American Gentlemen" was an agency out of Quebec; and coincidentally, he had come back to Julesville to recuperate after a colon operation that summer. At the same time, he was running a little unofficial operation for a local client, which, he remarked, would involve—at the most—a few days' work. With dolorous, wingeing accents, he hinted that he didn't mind the extra cash, because of the very excellent pay, and, being an experienced operative in the industry, he might get to fire his special licensed issue, and crack a few ribs, ha, ha! into the bargain,—which he was prepared to throw in fer free, old son! Bob Bunyan was a tall man, tanned darkishly,—in fact, so embrown'd, that the shadow of his hooked nose looked blue, and when he took off his hat (to indent the crown), you saw he had short-cropped wire-like hair. His shoulders were strangely angular, drawn up at an acute angle—elsewhere, there was not a shred of hair on his body. Either a glistening, slug-like shininess (resembling an Olympic trial swimmer),—hung about him or he regularly shaved and perpetually stropped his obsessive razor; nor was theer an inch of excess fat upon him. His fingers were wrapped with sticking plaster; and similarly, on his chin, so that a glimpse of his face made one breed a chill in the nape of one's neck, especially—in this fairly fair weather. They reluctantly shook hands; and, as the detective opened his grim mouth, Humphrey flinched. For Bobby's gums were pinkish-gray, and out came a nasty smell an' a high, falsetto, fruity guffaw! Faugh! It was so caricaturish that the savant seemed to have seen him from someplace before;—I mean, this Bobby,—at the man's juncture of his life, but where, for the life of him, he couldn't remember. At once, the savant caught himself thinking that he didn't like Bobby Samson Bunyan, no-how; niver did liked him, in actual fact—and, 'Meetin' Bobby Bunyan is far—far from my wish today!' he was thinking.

But, the detective stuck in an elbow upon Humphrey's thoughtful preoccupations—and in a loose way, started to be chatty, and trying to throw up epithets and anecdotes, all fitful, violent, and suggestive;—insulting to women-kind,—insults and insinuating comments. Then, smiling thinly, he dropped a hint here and there he was ready to do Humphrey a service—showing himself to be a man of the world; and he placed a playful hand,—freightedly, on the savant's shoulder. The moment it rested theer, it felt like a paperweight! And just as with the handshake previously, it made a spine-tingly impression upon Humphrey! 'Oh, I wish I could extricate myself right here and right now; but that would not be very seemly nor polite,' thought the savant; but the other only guffawed louder and suggested, 'Go and have fun with Lisa! Hev a look around town, and after you hev paid your score; ha-ha, you can git out feelin' reelly KKREeenNNNN! Yep, 'tis an interestin' place, this new place, "The Cock and the Plough": a double entendre,—and soon 'ee will lose yer deadness over a bottl' o' dark-color'd sherry, an' spiced cold bird! What do you expeect? Fer others, life's a bitch! Ye can see dat sunscape in darkness that bares all o' itself to th' naked eye—Wot? All reet, Mister Humperdinck . . . no harm . . . meant or done . . . !'

'Still the snivelin' darty liddle scumbag,—aren't ye!'

There was a mortally terrified disgust in the savant's voice; and so, unable to make any headway, sullenly, with a half-mouthed oath and mumbling darkly some trenchant remark about "Infernal spies"—the head detective quitted his long-time acquaintance . . . Amid a rolling cloud of dust-balls, which had sprung upon 'em from who knows where; and, Bobby Bunyan was blown westward and disappeared for a time.

'Was this really my childhood friend, Little Bobby Samson Bunyan?' As Humphrey strolled underneath the steel bridge and up towards the stunted, entwining lime-trees and the children's playground,—he seemed to remember the taste of apples, and of apple cider in his mouth. He suddenly heard the cracking of a branch or large twig underfoot and he seemed to catch a glimpse of Bobby Bunyan's trench coat, but, once again, it disappeared round a corner. As the narrator of these tales I won't dilate details;—but Doctor Humphrey Humperdinck's very words were, '. . . #@& . . . in tarnation!'—when, near his instep,—he saw an uncrumpled, crisp bus-ticket that he nearly trod underfoot. He could just make out the words, ". . . to b. b: meet H.H. outside drugstore, or wait till he passes. XYZ."

A tinge of unexpected fear, passing through his lanky frame, Humphrey was rooted to the spot;—trying to make sense of it. The ticket had been purchased somewhere down south, and the point of departure was Reno. Was it Bobby's, and that message meant for him? Was Bunyan a liar and what he told him (Humphrey)—a bunch of cock-a-mammy fibs, that could only have proceeded from the mouth of sich a one? Handwriting: squalid: a legible scrawl done and underscored by a black felt-tipped pen. Any sorta pen. Was H.H. himself? How about XYZ? Who was he? The message seemed from someone, a high-dizened anonymous boss, pulling the strings of the convalescent (if he was that?)—but, still, menacing detective!— Someone had taken grave pains to arrange this meeting an hour ago—whose identity he didn't know—but what was his stake in this? Who seemed to have been interested in him;—and what did they intend with him? Had he been poking his nose in somebody else's business for ever so long—without ever knowing it? Something that suggested itself forcibly in Humphrey's mind was a theory of a conspiracy that had been dogging him; ever since he entered, mind, body and soul into da ghaist-spifflicatin' business. Humphrey went back to the streets, looking 'em up and down, with feelings of rising, then utter confusion. The chanced find—though it might also be rationalized as fortuitous,—had the resultant effect of putting him cagily on his guard. He was now strolling under an overcast sky, and all at once, something hazed from some point in the past, cloaked him from what was familiar and well-loved, in town: so it had seemed,—to the savant; but after a while, a dizzying and acute light-headedness overcame him. His soul anguished over, and for no reason at all— what might have flavored a pleasurable reminisce was wiped away too quickly. Doctor Humphrey Humperdinck had to overcome his sudden distress; being the tenacious streak of that old gamecock (himself),—that mental prostration o' his, and irrespectively, began to assess and reassess his situation. The upshot was, he resolved to take a risk, if he could, to try to investigate the alleged private investigator more closely. Thus, here, his spirit came to a valley of darkness, one amongst his many,—in the life of our august an' extraordinary savant. It was to equip Doctor Humphrey with the knowledge that the choice of the Spirit was not biased in nature; notwithstanding—what was to ensue between the two, Bobby and Humphrey, and he was hurt once more;—and more seriously this time! Losing not an hour in trying to make enquiries about Mister Bunyan, he telephoned his old friends and mutual acquaintances, people who had known Bobby very well at school, he telephoned Quebec, Vancouver, Reno, San Francisco, Las Vegas, Portland, Albuquerque, and probed the man's past, and his history, so that he might have some idea of what was going on in Julesville at this rate. An assistant editor, Andy McGreevy L'Estrange, entertained him when he called a newspaper office in Reno, and said he knew Bobby well; and he said his paper had carried an obituary notice about him:—which he himself wrote out—bec'os the notorious Bobby Bunyan, P.I. was dead. But Humphrey had other conflicting reports as well, with reportages of the man, as far as an Ashram in Mumbai, India, and in South Africa or Botswana; and so, Humphrey had to piece out his checkered career from many differing sources. Meantime, he was prepared to wait—staying at home as much as possible;—keeping an active weather-eye and sharp-lookout for Bobby, in case he runs into him in some dark unfriendly corner . . . !!! Despite taking his medication, Humphrey's nerve was on edge, and he seemed to feel there were eyes about lookin' at him when he was not looking.—Tortured, by a naggin' thought that someone somewhere was laughing at him! It was now Saturday. It was six days since he "accidentally" met Bobby Bunyan. He had been in Julesville for a week already; and, the stay he had planned was an indefinite one.

Today, being the day the savant would like to see the faces of his relation's children, to wit, his Maternal Uncle;—for 'twas a treat he had been saving himself up; for, having told himself: ("not until I feel up to it and my mind is reely stable, would I take an hour and half's ride to Red Fern.")—there seemed to be an additional babe or tot, besides the older children, the latter of whom were sitting at table,—when he got there. A girlish face, with one missing tooth, smiled up at him; and, with keen delightful recognition, he saw his uncle's puffy eyelids; and shook hands with Uncle Ben and Auntie May, and planted kisses on the children's head. The effect on the group he created was gratifying,—quite a commotion: and his uncle, a man with clean-shaven jowls, but big hairy hands, said, 'Have a cup of coffee and compose yourself easily, my dear young fellow!' There might have been some seedling of friction that might have peeped through inside that smoke-filled room from da past, but this, Humphrey dismissed . . .

'Sit! Sit!' declared the savant's comfortable Auntie May, who was rubbing her callused hands with evident joy at seeing her nephew; busy with the old-fashioned tea cosy, as usual.

'Ah—many thanks!' Humphrey replied self-effacingly, as the coffee appealed to his senses and palate;—lost for language: 'Excuse moi—I must say muh words, words, words don't sparkle dandy today, but I must declare I'm reet glad to be here. I am digging in my mind eternally for the reet words to say, but I must say I am feelin' muddled and mined onlee feeble gold—to-day!'

Suddenly, there was a burst of pattering little feet—either walking on straw or wearing stockings—and a little boy, sandy-haired and angelic-looking, appeared, having come down the auld oak staircase, the savant caught him up and lifted him high—so high, that Humphrey's elbows clicked and locked. The boy's name was Abel, and he was a deaf-mute:—Humphrey's beloved cousin. The savant had been the first to realize his impaired physiological condition when

Abel was in his toddlerhood, but still loved him above the rest. All the while, the child, nine years old now,—if he could, Humphrey knew,—would be gushing over him, by now! How he knew the visitor would turn up at that moment was beyond surmise, bec'os, as his uncle said, Abel had been sleeping; but now, the entire family took it upon themselves to give Humphrey a rousing welcome with one united will: their darling prodigal, with all their heart! And this, despite being forewarned something was not right with the savant's mind . . . !

'Doff off that jacket o' yours, will you, dear Humphrey?' said his Aunt May; and after that, she showed him a few drawings of Abel's; with crayoned captions which read, 'Creepy durt bags!' (concerning ghouls), 'I want to be just like Humphrey!' and 'Numero Uno!' and Humphrey engaged her in conversations about what Abel had been up to, and what he studied in school; as a consequence. An instant later, a lively talk sprang up, and, as they talked it grew amply evident that, at any rate, this family was still very proud of him, and his scientific achievements: no change discernible substantially,—in their relationship with him. He was still Doctor Humphrey Humperdinck; the One and Only! The fine flowerlike lines on his aunt's beautiful face grew soft under her chin as she recounted his achievements to him—upon which the savant prest her hand; and caressed and kissed the children all over again twice more. He was glad that they, too, had been grieving with and for him. And, within this intimate circle which he felt he was a member of, there and then, a space for grieving for himself started to elongate—as regards to what had been lost—so that,—when he recovered—he could rejoice, later, by so much he had gained in da exchange. In da bright and sunny smiles of this family, he felt the different parts that were shattered inside him were given a chance to mend:—in a flood of positive and affirming emotions . . .

'Thanks for the compliment, dearest Abel!' he said brightly with a warm smile.

'Are 'ee all right now, Humphrey?' said his Uncle Ben, lighting up an enormous black root and staring down at the linoleum that, still, in places remained unpatched up.

'Er—yes, sir—but I'm not strong enough yet—yet!' replied the other, avoiding his eye at all costs . . .

'Stay here by all means. Stay here with us for a few days! Despite the eleven of us, there is always still room for one more. We can always make do.'

'Thanks. I think I will.'

'For a few days you can have the "best bedroom" as they say it in England,—what 'tis called; though Red Fern is an unlucky suburb fer 'ee—Humphrey! My brother's best friend's son died shortly after you went to high school. Dreadful accident! Have you met anyone from your childhood days in Julesville, Humphrey, which you used to know—and hobnobbed with?'

Somehow, due to the forgoing incident that I had described earlier, Humphrey could not bring himself to answer, (which his aunt thought was strange) although Humphrey had compiled many shadowy details about Bobby Bunyan. Still, he wasn't a veracious tattler by nature;—he didn't want to say anything about Bobby, if he could,—and so, he just sat there on the sofa near the solid, ancient staircase, and looked uncomfortable and sheepish. He smiled ambiguously, and shook his white, bald head.

'Good afternoon, then! I will go and feather duster under your bed,' said his aunt, getting up.

'No; it isn't that—! It's all very well to say that: and I am for—' Humphrey started to say; but Uncle Ben interrupted him by saying, 'Well, as I recall, rascals you were an' rascals you still are, all o' you, and whether you see any o' 'em or not is the blessed same to me . . . the lot o' you, havin' burned my favorite cat's tail twenty-five years ago, 'tis yer friends, I set the least store for . . .'

It astounded Humphrey that his pang of guilt was still extant; and he suddenly stood up as though he was impelled (by sumptin) and he said,—'I have seen nobaddy in town but Little Old Bobby Bunyan!

At this, hereupon, as Humphrey looked over to his Aunt May, he was surprised to see her putting her hand to her mouth with her white lace hanky, as though she had involuntarily given a little jump; and then, tried to cover this by smiling facetiously at him, as though he was yet another still-life linocut print that had been hanging in that sitting room for over twenty-five odd years!!!

'Ah, the very boy!' blurted his uncle with severity; and, there was a curious look in his gray-blue eyes. Humphrey grew more surprised as the two covered him up and down with uneasy glances;—the uncle passed his hands over his streaked hair and auntie adjusted her bobbins; as the children were ordered to leave the adults alone, while they talked over the business. 'Boy, my mind's completely a-whirl; what's goin' on; what's afoot?'—murmured Humphrey.

The two, Uncle Ben and Aunt May, still looked hesitant and troubled:—unsure how to proceed.

'What's da matter? Just let me know: in your very own words say why both of you should be so quaintly fearful—jus like dat—at a drop of a name? Tell me, what happened to young Bob-bee?'

His aunt laughed nervously: 'Nuffin' Humphrey! Don't ask too many questions . . . But, anyways, the fact of da matter is, is that 'ee canna have met Bobby Bunyan in town . . . !'

'Why—why? Why can't I have . . . met . . . Bob-bee?'

His uncle, being a man of no subtlety, said at last, softly,—in a fierce drawl, 'because the last we 'eard o' him was he was dead! 'EAD! Doornail-dead, comprende? Ech, May? In the newspapers last fall, there was an article that said he died of cancer; and how he had ow'd lotsa money to folks up north, not nice, obese ones, reely . . . and that he was involved in various wild-catting scams and greedy double-dealin'; and was constantly on da take! He was entangled with hustlers fer a fast buck—dat good ole, aristocratic-nosed George Washington, arter all was Bobby! 'Ee was into drugs and implicated in the death of a young girl, but he could not stand trial because his own prevented it. Bobby was a rotter, as I once thought, he would turn out, although you might have not believed possible, when you were young like him once . . .'

'Then, it must of course, mean,—'twas a case of mutual or double mistaken identity . . .' muttered Humphrey with a puzzled frown, and putting his hands into his pockets; and, he began to throw out the whole idea that the man was still alive. But—was he—a spook? This dem blast from da past; what had he to do wi' him that he should raise outta da grave . . . and why should he want to meet up with him and incite him . . . ? He wanted to put the whole matter out of his mystified brain; and from vexatious consideration. 'Is that all—?'

'I will desist the vagaries of my Olympian will, and allow you to romp and play wi' the children to your heart's desire,—by all means, but don't burn the whole house down,' said his uncle evasively,— 'Ha-ha! Stay for dinner, but let's talk about sumptin' else, sumptin' more cheerful, this Julesville outskirts is not such a dreadful or dreary place. Take the old jalopy, the British-make, and go fer a spin . . . new suburbs are springing up like cauliflowers and cabbages, an', do you still remember your favorite water-willow near da old abandon'd mill-house? Reminisce with it, how your life has been, and how its life has been, and all dat kinda stuff! See dat old Ferris wheer dat dark Hungarian bookie was found dead under (—you still remember?) well,—it is now da dump; and then, you come back here. Your round trip will take you just in time fer dinner. It's at seven-thirty sharp.'

'Very well, I will start at two. After I had my bath, and have taken a little time to recollect my thoughts . . . I think, I will have my usual nap first, as it is only a quarter to one o' clock. Wake me up at two, Aunt. And, oh, please, tell the children I do so need the rest; a little peace and quiet, and wouldn't they pipe down a little? Just a lit—'

'Are you telling me to pipe down, young man?' said his uncle mildly, (chuckling, but he was the only one), as he knocked out the dottle onto the ashtray . . .

And so,—the savant played the part he envisioned and set himself out to play; never more glad was he, in so hospitable a surrounding; in the midst o' the incessant laughter that was part and parcel of the children's play and gaiety, which, nevertheless, irked his nerves, sometimes! The wurl, for him had become a big, untidy and noisy place; too much so, to his liking, bec'os of his shattered nerves. The Family was always talking shop and chatting and exchanging news; and he privately thought, he must have the good will to endure them,—not least, because he dearly loved these treasured ones . . . ! It was graced living, so evidently abundant, in what this was all about! Grace wasn't something that gives with one hand while it takes with the other another time; it is open-handed and isn't mercenary!

Grace, thought he, niver betrays the receiver, nor is it niggardly, and, blows hot or cold! Grace seeks,—and looks after the welfare, good, health and desires—of its recipients! Kindly, gently and consoling is Grace, and as Humphrey let this sink in, he has borne the brunt, and overcame some of his earlier inner turmoil. Grace—imparts a quality of bliss and permanence: it gives gratuitously whatever is needed to complement the true and righteous knowledge of God . . . This Superior Being Himself is revealed by His Grace . . . Humphrey had been thinking,—if one is livin' a graced existence, living in Him,—he couldn't be disappointed for long in life (bec'os an undisappointed spirit resides in him: for struggles spiritual, that yield up dead sea fruit, is a sheer impossibility for that one),—in the last analysis! After all, hadn't we been told advisedly, "SEEK AND YOU SHALL FIND; ASK—RECEIVE." Something of this, the savant was beginning to recognize intimately; bestirring, by its workings inside him. He had much ground to regain and reclaim; but I draw his reflection to a close here, and bespeak not now about God's Graciousness—bec'os, I must on with my narrative—which is a lengthy one:

After they had partaken of their meat, fowl, turnips, and greens, suddenly, there was a barking of a dog,—the sound coming from the back way, which Humphrey had not gone round to inspect. There must be a kennel there, and as he put his neck through the kitchen window, which swung on its rusty hinges, he saw it was a white Labrador. His uncle's wife was letting it out from where it had been kenneled. And, the aunt's and the nephew's conversation ensued in the following manner:

'A very bad and dangerous dog—that—Aunt May?'

'I do think—not very; for you to say!' she replied, holding its leash, 'yet he's a real brute to people who have no business here, and he is very cleaver too; an intellectual mutt—that knows precisely how to keep burglars and any undesirables away from here . . . !'

'It looks fierce and pampered of mien at the same time!' muttered our savant, ruefully. 'Are . . . they a lot of undesirable people in the suburbs, nowadays,—besides the usual derelicts an' drunks?'

'Sometimes—there are! I shall keep Five-rovers unchained tonight night, just in case, and also while you are here, just in case, you know;

on the off-chance . . . any eventuality,—you know? So that, you don't take to no harm! He likes you, the old boy, and you seem to have no fear of him! Well, I must exclaim! I reelly must declare, dat you have made a friend here, my boy!'

'Like a cool-headed mastiff, it is yelping a facetious liddle yelp— rising to a series o' superb liddle squeals, ho-ho! Seriously, Aunt May, are there still a lot of bills unpaid like the last time?'

'Yes, Humphrey. I mean, any amount o' 'em, still too much bills left unsettled; until your uncle settles 'em. An avalanche of them is still lying on the top of the dressing table, muh dear!'

'Here, Aunt May . . .' said Humphrey. And he looked away, while she pocketed a thick, rubber banded wad o' hundred dollar bills, he'd shoved into her hands. 'There is more if you need more,' he said.

Hereon, let us hear from Humphrey himself all that occurred to him at eight-fifty that very night, the 22nd August,—when he was taking the air and having lemon-coke inside his uncle's toolshed (that middle-aged relative had been fond of tinkering with bits of dis and dat here), this shed, round da back, which jutted at an angle, from the stone wall, that was away from any interconnecting structure;—except the walkway's roof,—the nearside of which, was the kitchen door. This back part, behind the house, was dressed neatly with simple tiles rather than the usual grass. The dog was on the prowl (for any stranger or idiot) and though, the backyard was only somewhat spacious, his aunt's assiduous industry had resulted in boxes of geraniums, chrysanthemums antirrhinums, alyssum, phlox, cornflower, gypsophila, larkspur, various herbs and dahlias growing there:—and a chuck wagon gotten from a fair, all a-rust, was standing, purely ornamental now, havin' being laid out for that specific purpose.

'It was a hot night,' began the savant; addressing his words to me, advancing his right hand towards his right and touching and indicating to me his lower abdomen near his left pelvic area . . . 'I had been sitting quietly alone on a kind of striped cloth chair, and enjoyin' my drink when I heard a noise near my ear;—a sudden, low whining sound—da kind 'ee know, when a dog bristles up, and has sniffed the scent of someone he doesn't particularly care for—but which maddens him, bec'os, he's afraid? It lasted briefly, maybe a minute or so. I thought it must be the Labrador but he wasn't very near . . . but, suddenly theer was a blud-curdlin' yelp, just once, that betokened the mortal terror of some mortal enemy!—Spun me around, it did, for it gave me quite a turn. I tell you, at that moment, I had no idea what was about to befall. Do you hear Professor Wyndham Tanischi? John, d' ye hear? Well, I niver get to hear another yell from that purty dog ag'in; and, after a while, though the silence was most foreboding of danger (a most sickening feeling) I reasoned it was all right,—then. The dog had probably gone off to sleep. I needn't tell you I am a fearless man, comparatively, to most men, by even your standards;— and in match-ups with thugs, hoodlums and ghaists, I can hold my own. Reckoning by time, some minutes must have elapsed after dat last howl, but, that night, I felt a creepy feelin', a right creepy feelin' that seemed to hover at the back of my skull,—as though someone was looking right down to my nape, where my collars were. No wonder, I kept looking at the door of the shed,—as if sensing or waiting fer somebody to put in a sudden appearance. Someone did come through there—as the minutes ticked away. The muscles in my thighs, calves and lower abdomen, as if someone had waved a magic wand, had become frozenly tense, and my chest, knotted up, and sweat dripped from my brow. Something was coming to get at me, I thought. I had tried to move the instant he appeared, but my limbs were manacled by an unaccountable paralysis, and I tried to utter something to reassure myself, but nothing issued from my voice-box. There was not a breath of air stirring, no wind, in this dead calm o' night, and I was caught out in an uncomfortable, sitting position; feeling like a stone statue. I couldn't move the whole time; as though, having become bewitched! My thoughts and perception seemed to have been in slow-mode and, my eyes, unseeing: it was a befuddled state of mind,—as if that moment I was experiencing adverse reaction, after taking my psychotropic medication, due to some kinda contraindications . . .'

('Then, what happened, Humphrey?' I, Professor John Wyndham Tanischi said, looking at him at length, with simpatico . . .)

'No sound of footfall nor tread of feet, but a faint shadow passed over my shoulder—the left one, I think. At that moment, something shot back the bolt inside o' me, and my tongue was loosened at once, and, as I startled into a shout, the light bulb that was dangling from some kinda groin in the roof exploded,—and I was plunged into darkness. It was a very loud pop! My strange passage into even stranger seas and dreadful things I had felt when I saw—out of the mundane shapes of flowers, and furniture, car fronts, and even old stains of leakages on roofs and walls, and such-like suggestive two-dimensional delusions, that had become my idee fixe that never ceased from tormenting with Sisyphean regularity for a long time—became trice-intensified. Although, I had tried scraping the ugliness from these airy nothings, but they now recurred, in the half-moonlight. Now, as the pop sounded, my guts felt dragged out and salt thrown over my raw wounds, like salad. In addition, I thought my Uncle Ben and Auntie May would have heard either sounds—and so, I was comforted by that thought—but nobody came! I was about to rise to my feet, and go to the shed's door for help, when I saw that the door was now shut. I thought my uncle, sipping his cappuccino coffee, had come in and shut the door behind him, while trying to get to the bottom of the mystery. There was moonlight streaming in through the window. I thought I heard a creaking mouse, someone's dog barkin' a few houses away, and I saw the headlights along the Interstate and the particolored ones of Julesville; dotting all the way up the black hills beyond. I thought if I could only rest quietly here with my iced drink, which was still in my hand, and recuperate; but the party-pooper had come in! Framed against the backdrop of the window's pretzel-thin moonlit rusty bars, silvered with a slice of moonlight, was a figure—the figure of a man, contrasting with the deeper shadows in the darker corners;—standing in a posture that I clearly remembered seeing him a few days ago! He was still wearing his same fedora and coat, in three-quarters profile. I recognized the contorted, unpleasant face, leering at me,—with convulsive revulsion and despicable excitement—it was Bobby Bunyan.'

(Some few moments must have passed, but now as Humphrey's eyes grew again accustomed to the darkness, in the pale, opalescent moonlight when suddenly the Shade, darker than the rest, spoke.)

'Boo! Pardon me, a thousand pardons fer bursting' myself' in 'ere! Since you possess not a few quirks to your personality, is it A PARTICULAR PECULIARITY IN YOU to recline alone in so dark a niche? Are you not afraid—of GHOASTS? It seems you are Humphrey—but I am now a Lamprey.'

'It's you, Bobby Samson Bunyan?' I said, plethoric ally; stifling some unaccountable rising tide o' panic behind my voice. He was one o' da few, indeed, who could have one over me whenever he chose, and this had been Lang-established since we were children. Eye sockets: too hollow, cheekbones, too prominent, jaw too square-cut, his shoulders, padded,—he looked eerie, and as unsuitable to be 'ere;— just like a vinegar bottle, that was difficult thing to stick a candle on.

'The one and the only!' and, he made reply, 'Doan you know me, Spaghetti Humph? Doncha like da sight o' my shabby canines in dis palpable moonshine? I 'ope you don't mind muh lettin' mysel' in . . .' he continued, enjoying, to see my disconcertment.—'And, mee . . . shuttin' . . . da door behind mee—mee—mee . . . !!'

Pausing to consider for a moment,—for, by this time he had ceased to speak, I said—stentorian-like: 'You are dead! DEAD! Why, if da newspaper reportage is true, and what you have done be accurate—you should . . . be . . . well, in hell I'm afraid, rightfully, Bob . . . ! Are ye a ghoast?'

'Not quite. I can onlee p'rhaps claim some little resemblance in regard to a misinformed 'ppellation—as regard to that crew.'

'Bobby—you ar' a freakin' Zombie, aren't you? You are a baloney!'

'Yeep—on velveteen; reet you are on the money—fer, lately, I have become sich a one after a sudden demise . . .' he said, licking his holmberry lips;—twisting his neck this way and that.

'How's life treating you as a zombie, Bobby . . . ???'

'O! Excellent! It mends:—as a lamprey! Beware! things can be ghastly yet for you—ghastlier and ghoulish yet!' and so, saying, with the quickness of moonlight shifting in the mist, he unleashed a brutal attack on my life with his Rambo-knife. As he did so, he muttered with a snarl (confound him!), 'I was taken ill at the Municipal Library car park . . . and died two weeks later. Take that, for the troublesome clod that you are! Oh, did I git you there—and then,—AG'IN?

Too bad, Rin-tin-tin, is not here to help you to even the odds! Bye, Humphrey! I will wait for you in the churchyard, and you can shed a tear fer me, when you are food fer worms, like me. My friends doan like you! Dey doan like 'ee at all!' he chuckled,—and his chuckling then turned into a definite roar. With a mortified expression, I saw warm rivulets of prune-colored blood—seeping out onto my clothes; and he still went on, 'What I need is a little expertise! I doan want to use da licensed Magnum bec'os it would be too loud a reportage that Bobby Bunyan again walks abroad the world of men as a ghoul: a zombie!—Well, my niche job I was paid for is nearly done, and 'tis time to put on a pair o' wings. You have made yourself a general nuisance while we are apart; and, did you hear the light bulb going out—ha? That was the school bell—and da Black Maister has come to teach you a very black an' magisterial lesson!' The walkin' corpse, Bobby Bunyan, had struck me on my thighs and the last time in the abdomen; and the last thing I remembered seeing before I blacked out was the nasty evil form of the late Bobby spinning, and the furniture, and the window-sill,—where the moonlight was,—vibrating violently; and, there was a low hum, a spluttering and a hissin' . . . and when I open'd my eyes again, someone had given me a sip of water; for someone had made the decisive experiment to come here and help me. On that same ground where Bobby had lately been standing, something invisible seemed to have been rammed into that zombie or ghoul;—and pummeling him all over: for Bob's shape was melting like wax and turning runny,—into a foul, disgusting, and evil-smellin', revoltin' pool—of puke and shit. In an instant, I realized that my heaven-sent, Abel, with holy water, in a bucket, had doused the fellow and given him Hell's greatest pain, fer this its hellish denizen! My head was still throbbing and reeling, and my pain was so great, it made me groan out. Abel pulled me up to raise me, with the same expression of resolute calm—the hallmark of the brave. I did not speak, for there was no need: 'twas a product expressive o' the same uncanny instinctive understanding and mutual sympathy betwixt us! Now, since the zombie was prologue and no more than a black, satiny, stain on the threadbare carpet and evaporating fast, we stepped o'er it as one would over some dead, contemptuous snake. This evil an' licentious snake's coxcombry had come to an end! Thanks to my cousin, Abel, the Valiant! The Intrepid! The twice-dead man, having lost all vestiges of color, had turned white;—finally, melting away like a spider's gossamer web. (However, it had been a wordless scream o' da zombie that had pierced through me earlier; and methought, Bobby's eyes had a surprised look, a look of hateful disbelief: crazed eyes, which were rollin' in da depths o' their individual hollow sockets!) Then, widening my own, to my surprise, I could see Abel was silently praying for me and, while he was kneeling down, I felt the cuts on my palms, and my wounds where that shithead knifed me,—and these wounds began to close: with incredible rate not thought possible! But, no prosaic fact! What with the pageantry of wild, relieved thoughts, that ever and anon were whirling across da auditorium of my mind, I rose mutely, staggered to my feet.

Evidently, Abel had espied the zombie amongst his Mom's flower boxes (with the moonlight feathering the clouds and touching the fences) and somehow disappearing into the toolshed, he had fled fer da 'oly Water: bekearse he had some immediate and intuitive inkling what was afoot; and his mind, bec'os of his profound faith, saw where the remedy lay (like his Mom's, his faith was Catholic).

'Oh, my! Dat demoniacal soul!' I cried aloud, when I realized that those on the good side had won this duel with the devil. 'Oh, my!' For, it was sheerly a sigh of monstrous relief; and, in my heart of hearts I did not hate Bobby Bunyan—and by not hating I had turned something potentially disastrous to the good. And so, I struck a blow against evil.'

Suddenly, three familiar figures came along the covered path where we were now both walking along; a short distance away from the kitchen door. These were: my Uncle Ben and Aunt May and their oldest daughter, a girl of eighteen years of age.

'My Uncle was businesslike, with an air of a garrulous old dog, and he said, 'Did or didn't I hear sumptin' go pop?' He had come downstairs in his sweatshirt and held a firearm in his wet palm; which was waving like a limp cabbage leaf stalk, or an under-ripe banana . . . He must now have come to realize that I was trembling and very distraught; for he had earlier heard my scream . . . That wonderful man put his gun away, put his arms around me and supported my weight: as we marched gingerly to the house—with him propping me up, for my knees were still weak. He waited and waived away my explanations with which I tried to entertain him, as we walked. We came inside, and I was solicitously set down on the sofa. Then, he likewise sat down, and looked me up and down, as he lighted his old pipe. The other daughters also flew down, and the younger children, fluttering like curious butterflies, were trying to have me in their full view, but being shooed and hushed away. As for Abel, he was the only one who maintained an impassive as well as resolute expression: I pulled his sleeve and hugged him, as if he, not I, that was the one in need of consolation . . . ! His eyes remained upon my face and lingered there and still he betrayed not the least tinge of fear when this thing was now surely over. Perhaps, when I recount his deed, it was for his sake more than my own, that I pray I might quickly put my evil past behind me. For, even now, the steadfast love of this young boy dances before my eyes—one so innocent, good and so pure—and I thank Him, the One, for creating him in his Mother's womb and being a part o' my own life. I caressed his hair and suddenly with a rapidity of boyish movement he had suddenly pulled off his socks— ones he loved very much—and smiled; amid peals of laughter from the other children; for he wanted to give 'em to me as a keepsake. He smiled at the others sheepishly when I shook my head and, then, seriousness made its way back into my Uncle Ben's frowzy brows, and he spoke for the first time concerning tonight's strange business. The 'uns were all ordered up, except Abel; with the tempting promise of Ma's treat of gingersnaps, hot plate, ice-cream soda and cookies on the morrow; and then, my Aunt May said, 'Was some no good influences bestirrin' jus now? Tell me that was it; wasn't it? Did something hurt 'ee?'

'Yes, something or someone did try to . . . I think I oughtn't to tell you . . . it's in my line of business, anyhow; that's all I care to say. Yep, I am slightly hurt, but I'm all reet now, after Abel prayed fer me . . . you did, didna 'ee, Abel? Did sumptin' 'appened to Five-rovers?—Give us a hand up, Uncle Ben; for I would like to go to sleep now!'

'Well, we will not intrude on your privacy; but do you think it should be reported to da police, by da way? But, say, has it got anythin' to do with your breakdow—in England?' said my astute and intelligent Aunt May.

'This is all very—a very disenchanting business,' complained my uncle moodily . . . 'You are suddenly very unconscionably introverted, my dear son! My! My! My!'

And I said:

'Maybe,—I don't know—but that was to make my mind, soul and body uniformly comatose, I think.'

'You looked as though you had it in da rough, Humphrey; and, your clothes is besmeared, and is dat bloodstains on your clothes? Look at your trouser-legs! Yet,—yes, there is sumptin wonderful to see what is superscribed in the neighborhood of your temples!' said my uncle. 'Now, listen, you have surmounted sumptin; a mystery, still, to your Aunt and mysel' but da poor mutt, the brave, poor Labrador is dead! Yes, sumptin had attacked it and broke its neck! Poor dog! Five-rovers, snapped in two! You should have seen it scuffling up the tarmac after creepy durt-bags! Bad luck seemed have pursued you here, my dear Humphrey! Isn't it so Maylie, dear? Bad luck! Yet, his aspect bears a triumphant mark; the imprint of a laurel wreath;—as though—'

'Very well,—well then, Humphrey,' said my aunt, the baby puking into its bib, and Humphrey looked at the child with mock-serious eyes. 'Since, your nephew, Mr. Benjamin Strait, don't wanna talk, we will let Abel to show us later, I think he was there . . . ???' she gave him a hinted warning.

However, so far, to my knowledge, the boy niver did so; leastways Humphrey's uncle never wrote him anything that made the slightest allusion or reference to the unfortunate night's incident on that 22nd,—and they, in Red Fern, might have forgotten it, by now, Well, perhaps, not Abel! Not him!

'Say nighty-night to your cousins, Humphrey, children, give your Mommy a quick kiss before you run up to your beds,' said their Father. (This, bec'os two little urchins had sneaked downstairs, these two young ones also puckered up their lips.) The adults, taking charge of me in the meantime, had put me in the Master-bedroom. They stayed beside me the whole night, keeping watch while I slept. My uncle and aunt were nothing if not generous and kind': this was the savant's little tale.

Humphrey intimated shyly to me they were massaging his knee and stroking his head that night. He had once wrote about this to thank 'em; but they declared flatly 'twas too insignificant a service that didn't deserved to be mentioned in a letter. And he told me, when he awoke the next day at eleven AM he felt quite better. There was no tremors, not da tell-tale doddering twitches, and he said he was mightily relieved, bec'os he felt no more pain. He was quite jocund, in fact; he ate a light, hearty breakfast of four hard-boiled eggs, and a niver more contented Humphrey opened up and told them about something of the latest work of a psychologist friend of his, who lived up in Long Island . . . For a long time, Humphrey never dream of Bobby Bunyan, and the late P. I. was confirmed to have died in October o' da year, previously. However, the bond between Humphrey and Abel grew stronger with time's passage and is still strong as ever—I heard. They had used Pinkerton's Champion Stain Remover (still goin' strong, too) to try to get rid of the stain in da moldy carpet—but this proved unsuccessful, the whole thing was ripped up, nails an' all and consigned to the rubbish heap, and then it was burnt. Five-rovers was replaced soon enough with a fierce and inexpensive pit-bull they bought from the local animal shelter. But, on one occasion, while Humphrey was holidaying in Rome, he did dream the dead man sitting astride on his chest, like a nightmare; but that was later . . . However, the spot where the posthumous detective met his last end was rumored to have a promiscuous smell of moonlight nights in late summer.

Chapter Two

DA EVENTS SURROUNDING
A MISSING FOREFINGER

It was already related how Humphrey had a close brush with death at the hands of Bobby Bunyan, whom, though he saw no more of him, drest in his rotting flesh, nevertheless, still, on odd occasions, haunted him:—in his nighttime dreams. But now, a 'ooman of slight form, a bare five feet two inches tall, shall be the theme of this chapter. Her brunette hair, done high up above her nape behind her head gave him a feelin' of awed wonder as regards her: da instigator. But, that second time he saw her: 'twas as though she was riding high on the wings o' love. She was a purty, porcelain figurine; who seemed always to be draped in white or titillating black lace; heightened by sich a softness of da facial features; the result of living it high and rolling in wealth and luxury:—yet, somehow spoiling that freshness of that look;—that serenity in her forehead so pleasing, notwithstanding, to behold! Looked at, laterally, if she chose to twitch her posterior— you got hot flashes that made you blush to the roots o' yer hair: because she had the prettiest, cutest fundament, bottom, or nates, which, you'd at once be convinced—any wench o' high breeding was e'er blessed with! Doctor Humphrey Humperdinck had seen her in her two opposing moods.—Once, it was when she was shakin' her wobbly neck—her mouth, dribblin' a liddle; with a pale, ashen face.— Another time, 'twas in the middle o' a dream, and she was laughing a little, when she was possessed of a good-natured tranquility, which, one would tend to think, is congruent with the blest. On both occasions, it was a neat décolletage though of opposing colors that she wore that fitted her shape to perfection.—That was, with cheeky little collars, of trim lace, and flowing dress that was the work of some foreign dressmaker, that showed her fine sex to da best advantage.

It was ever since the Ghaistsweepers: comprising o' Doctor Humphrey Humperdinck, Doctor Stanislaus Owen, Doctor Darius Mortimer and Mr. Ronnie Roper were formed, their agency, dealin' with the paranormal and based on sound scientific methodologies and high-tech equipment, had propelled 'em to near celebrity status. ('Twas Humphrey who had invented the apparatus for catchin' 'em and lockin' em up; but later, it was a joint development affair in partnership wi' Doctors Owen and Mortimer, both from U.C.L.A.!) In the early eighties, the public's love affair with these sorta heroes o' modern times niver really dissipated; because reliving distraught clients of spiritual encroachments o' da diabolical kind was more than ever greatly required:—It was an invaluable public service. The following incidents happened within an interval of 'bout two years in the late eighties.—That last, was the year they, the other members of da team, wanted Humphrey Humperdinck back . . .

The 'ooman we are a-speaking of was Lady Catherine Howard, or her sperrit, and she was instrumental in getting Humphrey's life back on track, with his ruminations on her advice and instructions she had given him; on account of the good turn he had once done her; as I shall recount to you, now.

It happened at the time when (as had been mentioned sorta in the last chapter) Humphrey was still in a hospitalized condition. He was staying in a nursing home near the New Jersey shoreline. One night, he was awakened by a dream which to all purposes and intents, when he considered it, seemed to be the sequel of his earlier adventures in New York City; involving Lady Catherine Howard's ghost—the lady who was the fifth wife of Henry VIII of the House of Tudor—who had sat for a brief space as Queen of England beside that Dread Personage, the King. He woke up convinced that he had received a message from heaven—so intense the experience was for him. Sitting up in bed, he drew up his knees; trying to recollect carefully the chain or sequence of dream-images and also—the events that had led from his receiving a parcel from a member of da peerage in England, two years back. This exalted person had many property scattered all over

Europe, in Belgium, Monte Carlo, Switzerland and France, besides many others, elsewhere; and at that time, it seemed that something had been found in one o' his estates in Normandy; and this was sent to the savant for analysis and psychic evaluation. Switching on his bedside lamp, Humphrey had looked dazedly about him, breathing in the cold vaporous air, which entered his room through the open sash-window. He began to recollect . . .

One July morning, in the mid-eighties, while Humphrey was on sabbatical, a strange parcel arrived. The man from the courier company handed the paperwork to Joanni, wisecrackin' secretary to da Ghaistsweepin' team, who, when scrawled her John Henry, noticed it was from someone who was known as Lord Bartholomew Lonrot's Personal Secretary. The main address of the sender was put down as De Vauxhall Estate, Yorkshire, England . . . Humphrey remembered the whiff of his secretary's cheap perfume as he came by her desk, and she automatically dumped the chicken rolls, coke, café au lait, Greek salad, and raisin-an'-nut cake on him that afternoon; which foods n' drinks were to be his brunch. Then, she gave him the parcel, which felt like a bottle. Humphrey stood alternately on one foot and then the other, as this was his peculiar habit to inspect the premises this way, especially, the darker corners of the refurbished library,—as if waiting for some unexpected company to materialize out of the chimneys or dank floorboards. He supposed a look of intense concentration came over him, in trying to discern the recentness of any ectoplasmic prints. He re-examined the water cooler in the corner, the rolodex and the filing cabinets, and a copy of a Picasso painting done by yours truly, on the wall,—and a calendar showing da snow-capped Alps, next to it.

'Borrow me some strawberry jam?—fer da cake?—I mean, Joanni?' he said, looking up at last; 'Hey, here's a 'ungry hant crawlin' up my buff overalls.

'Doan forgit to examine the loo, Humphrey,' said Mrs. Selkirk, 'loike, for instance, there are enough germs there to set my temperature rising and your gizmos a-tingling.'

'Take off your dark glasses, Joanni! You could cut down the New York glare by drawing up the plush violet curtains.'

'No way, boss! The heat outside today has been enough to fry an egg silly.'

'Come again? I give up,' Humphrey burped into his fingers.

The secretary, needless to say, was all agog to know what the new parcel just being delivered contained,—but, for a full five minutes or so Humphrey who was watching her for any signs of exasperation, thought:—'She might at any moment now make a comment: but I'll pretend to be aloof until she gives up askin' me directly about it.' At last, however, she said, 'A most extraordinary ting! Humphrey, I have been havin' da most curious feelin' all over ever since dat strange parcel arrived! Broken a nail, felt me own fine hairs splitting; and now hives breakin' out over every part of me own body! Poo! Foo! Look, this lump, heer! Hailed from Yorkesheer, Hingland—it, Suh!'

Swallowing his last bite o' rolls and lettuce, and looking at her appraisingly—Humphrey smilingly said, 'Dat certainly ring-sa bell, I tink I know what's it about. Ding-dong! There had been a prior communication from a gentleman about its delivery; and ah! here's the letter—that's still inside my wallet—which was received from him last week; but which, ha-ha! Joanni Lorraine Selkirk, I haven't had time to read! Could you do me da honor, Joanni, loudly, si vous plez! In any case we are going to hear what Lord Bartholomew Lonrot has to say.'

'Who's this Lordy What's-his-name? Sum kinda wrestlin' commentator chum on Tee-vee?'

He let her know in a guttural muttered reply who he was . . .

'Heard o' him through the Psychic Grapevine?'

'A veree agitated phone call from his Private Secretary, to be exact! Well, Mrs. Selkirk, won't you begin to read the missive now, without further gibbering?'

'Shore! Anythin' to keep muh bosses happy all day long, especially you, dearie . . .'

So, she read . . .

De Vauxhall Hall Estates,
Little Dorrit Jules Park,
Yorkshire, England . . .

23rd June, 19—.

My Dear Doctor Humperdinck,

If—as it is greatly hoped you can help my employer in any way you can—you would be glad of it; for money is no object. To unburden my mind—write us if you can; and later I shall send you proofs of paranormal activity and the existence of ghosts, which I have reliably furnished with details that would keenly interest you. I need hardly emphasize, how deeply gracious the Lonrot Family would appreciate any kind help,—should you feel able to accede to my employer's request to loan him your invaluable assistance in this grave matter. His Lordship has instructed me to lay before you the facts material to the case: since you are known to be the foremost specialist & expert in the field. Therefore, it is hoped you might be able to solve our big mystery.

For twenty years or more, the Lonrots had taken to collecting antiques in England and abroad; as far as Greece and Italy. I am afraid, I might be taking up much of your time by saying this, and placing more demands upon it—however to continue: without further ado:

It concerned a woman, the fact of the matter, being, ever since she arrived on the scene, the peace in the Lonrot Estate, in Normandy, where they are currently domiciled has been shattered! (Forfeited!) It happened after Easter, at their Castle called M—. (Is forfeited, the proper, or too strong, a term?) You see, she is a ghost, which has encroached on their serenity of mind: and their patience! Especially, ever since that night she was spotted by the Lordship's eldest daughter; wringing its moldy and translucent hands about the tiltyard, a-wandering; and then, casting a lantern-like glow on the stony ramparts. Milly is a naturally shy and a timid girl, you see, and his Lordship was naturally furious that such a thing should happen. Then, the conservatory had been into; and the budding musician's music score crossed out . . . It has been into my Master's study of late and making a ruckus, and the place, all topsy-turvy the next morning. The servants also complained of disconcerting rackets, tap-dancing music, fife-playing, and the clank-clank of heavy chains being dragged outside their bedrooms. How the ghost is attired, you might well ask. Dressed in black. With sequined sparkling stanes. Close fitting cap, sometimes. Else—brunette hair, well-braided. Obvious to us an Elizabethan or a Tudor ghost, from across da waters; that is, from England. So, if you please sir, find out who she was and what she meant by disturbing the house. My heart feels faint, if I have to give Lord Lonrot more information, which, I thought, in his best interest—to be withheld from his current knowledge, at the moment, but which might shed a light for you: something to do with, I mean, that oblong bottle,—dug up from Castle's rose garden where they found the dead otter two months previously.—It had been kept locked up in my private locker, until I took it to England last week—and this, I have enclosed together with this letter. It is hoped that it would not cause you to lay half tossing in the night and no bed rest!

Do you think I did the right thing? I would like to hear your opinion in regards what looked like a stump inside the bottle—with the faded gilt inscription;—plus your assurance to his Lordship, if you will undertake to do all you can for us at once.

I remain, once again, Sir,
Your most obedient Servant,

Capt. Roald N. Motherwell (retired)
(Personal Secretary)

Encl. One medium vial bottle with something black inside . . .

'Doan dat pique yer interest, eh, Joanni, doan it?'
'Shores as shores, it does, you doan say! My, my! 'Ee can say dat agin!'
'I think it's a live one, oh, Joanni. You might say 'twas nuffin' moore than a bit of caramelized bone, or sumptin . . . but 'tis . . . !!!'

And, sitting up in his linen bed in the nursing home, Humphrey recollected how he had whipped out his newly-designed, shock-proof psychic barometer, on that occasion—with one smooth flowing motion. His rapid sensor-beeps showed there was enough raw psychic energy to send showers o' ripples to inundate the New York City undergrounds, from Albany to Yonkers: Manhattan, Bronx, Queens, Brooklyn, Richmond and o'er to da Jersey side . . .

'Spiritual manifestations probable?' proffered the blond-haired plump part-time secretary; letting her tarantula spectacles slip down; giving her professional take on the situation. 'Oh! Humphrey, there's a sale at KT-Mart and I wanna hev muh buy! But whaddayegonnado . . . Humphrey Humperdinck? Humphrey, what d' you intend to do?' Fifty-three hours or so later, face flushed and in a high state of nervous excitement, the savant, because he had been able to ascertain the age of da bottle, and examined the contents in it by using forensics, he knew the black thing was a finger, and it belonged to a woman! A Princeton colleague, a good friend of his, Doctor Karl Dangerfield had helped him with the chemical analyses, the meticulous dating, the discovery, and extracting its DNA; so, Humphrey's researches was as thorough as possible. Humphrey was oozing confidence, his enthusiasm, exuberant; and so, 'twas just to say, he had spent almost three days profitably. He was full with the glow of inner satisfaction that was home to the Extremely Competent. He thought he might even be able to wrap up the case, without even stepping on French soil, within the next twenty-four hours. Maybe, even before the sun pierced through the venetian blinds of his own office window:—on the morrow!

Grabbing a quick dinner he'd ordered up, the daily chore of thumbing through the most important newspapers had been his ritual bec'os Humphrey liked to do things simultaneously; and, his eyes scanned through the articles—like a schoolboy was wont to, in the days of yore,—the logarithm tables; and then—it was back to battlestations in da Enterprise, and his blinkin' consoles. The New York dusk settling an' seen through the window—like some murky, fairy grape—was moist and damp and misty.

When ten o' clock struck, Humphrey had just finished inching da dials and miniscule gears of his instrument, and was prepared at last to receive his special guest. He was used to the Bohemian nature of his occupation,—Bohemian, because of its outré nature:—yet, without prior warning, he was startled by an upsurge of charges that sent the needles of his most sophisticated recording machine clattering. Scratch, scratch, scratch, they were penciling marks, as the drums began rolling! The specter indicator jumped two notches and da special Fulkville-Humperdinck indices soared! Up and up it went! Yet up again! Humphrey stood up, as if,—in a trance! Simultaneous to this, the rooms had experienced a drastic drop in temperature; and 'twas a moment as though there would be a lump stuck in his throat—as if at the onset of a severe cold. He glanced again at the various angled mirrors that were arranged like pivoted metal plates and he thought to himself, 'I would like to discuss wi' mysel', shore, and, meditate, on the varying cheeses I had eaten for lunch or dinner, but not now—not now!' Then, all at once, not more than three feet away, he saw her. He was ready to catch her if it need be, at a press of a button; and to aim his vacuum's nozzle at the ghost . . . Yet, he hesitated and waited, until and unless, he should have found himself in dire jeopardy.

He heard the click of the voice-recorder-cum-camera that began to record on ultra-sensitive tapes high speed, slow motion pictures; which were coated with special chemical compounds he'd invented himself, which had proved effective in the past. The deep silence that ensued arter this was, simply put—electrifying! Humphrey, once again, began to fine-tune his equipment and soon he could see the apparition clearly; though, it seemed to be in a perpetual motion:

like a hummingbird's mid-flight. His heated machine now coughed out a thin chiding steam like vexed gusts of vapor; and, likewise, the humming drone got distinctly louder. 'Twas greenish-glowin': this was an entity, that showed no dangerous proclivities;—but now, emanating from it under stronger light (an intensified, molecular bombardment within a field of two highly energized, rotatin' helix streamlets . . .) Humphrey saw it had round cheeks, and face which were palpably white,—for the first time. He saw her eyes were two pinpricks of yellow, a sickly hue, and her head, seemed to be attached to her body at a slightly odd angle: which needed some little adjustment by someone kind enough to help her—mayhap! But, her lips, half-parted, compressed into a thin line, were bluish and bloodless, like someone that was suffering from some pulmonary disease! There was something of the passive female about her, with near manikin-likeness. But something, too—of disturbed, restless femininity (which, the savant, in pulling the flip-flop, saw)— equivocal to da moral law, yet well-nigh highbred, and haughty, as one featured in a failed or unsuccessful marriage, might look.

'Say your name . . . tell us what ails you, to forsake your peaceful rest to walk in the world of living men . . .' said Humphrey, using the ancient formula.

It began hesitantly: "Faith, sir, I am gravely troubled: but I shall be inducting you to the knowledge of my name;—though 'twas lang since it was on people's lips, a lang time agone! Once, I was enfleshed in a mortal body; but, tell me, are you not afraid? Am I not a trifle disconcerting to you, standing here before you: who was a sometime Queen, but now a disembodied spirit? But—since you have asked: I must reply! I am Lady Howard, (she gave her birthplace and the date of her birth and also her baptism), spouse of Henry the Eighth of England, who ascended the Throne in the year Anno Domini . . .' Thus she spoke in very sweet, accented quaint English, very different from da usual New York burr.

'No, I'm not afraid of you. Of you,—no!'

'Indeed!'

'You said you have been disturbed, perhaps? So a bon chat bon rat you played havoc wi' the Lonrot's home, eh?'

'Suffice it to say; failing to understand me, I have to make sure that they do!'

'Well—in brief, Madam: I suppose, I do?'

'At any rate thou art not afraid; say what thou wilt, thou will be civil, and I will see thee paid out fer thy trouble. But I shall say my piece, and hence the world of living men! 'Twas the missing forefinger that has become a conduit channeling me into this present dimension. It's my last and only chance—my last—'

'Go ahead! Shoot! Aw, I'm awful sorry: I mean, say what you need to say!'

'D' ye know that ever since my Faithless Harry ordered my execution, which was carried out in Anno Domini 1541, when I braved the execution block, I have been trapped with a foot in both worlds, and belonging to none? 'Twas on New Year's Day, when, my earthly life, he took; a day when people are out rejoicing and celebrating! Take no unkindness of my words, if I would prove to thee my innocence or guilt, and my husband's coxcombry and treachery! The conceit,—that had remained within me henceforth,—when I was pierced with the knowledge—God-a-mercy!—was, Sir Francis liest! He was tortured so that he might testify against me. Young Derham made himself into a preposterous ass, to have lied so; and so, his honor eclipsed in mine eyes! But—did it save him from sharing the same fate? O, fie, fie, fie!—Know you, sir knight of a nobler realm, also, that my earthly triumph was so pitifully short-lived? I had taken my Mistress's high position, knowing full well, what sort of villainy Harry's adamantine will made him capable of, but I had entertained fond—Yes, fond!—hopes, that I could tune his instruments for my own use. In return, for his favors, I wanted habiliments that befitted my beauty, which I sold to the highest bidder at usury; for Henry's manner was proud, and his feathers, were they not beautiful, though, also,—tarnished? Foolish, foolish, Kate! 'Twas too late! And, ay, what else; did I hear you say?—But I cannot renege on what I had done. As his docile play-thing, I did not too much accounted it a shame to pander to his every motion and his fair-weather parts: e'en his insatiable stomach! And, never to be ill-seeming and cold in maintaining his big heathenish body!—He was out courting someone else—ere the axe whistled close behind my ears—I saw the wench! That wretched husband o' mine, graceless traitor, was wearing the green sleeves I had taken much trouble to sew for him and he was playing with her hand! It was too much for a woman to stomach! My heart uttered a rash curse against him, and the rest you know, I think, because I ended up in a twilight world, craving for understanding from Man! Mercy, from the Just Judge, I would have to wait till later . . . For I have, in my impetuosity, rebelled against Him, because of my fate; and needs must confess my sin of rebellion . . . we had been married, a paltry six months, and so swiftly, after that, had his affections warmed towards that prattlin' Mooncalf, Parr!—I had cursed her bitterly wi' all my soul, too; and, a rueful tear stuck to my eyelids as I thought she should be his next queen ere my fair body was cold! Bitterly: did I know amorous Harry's false ways! That was why—I'm afraid—I swore sotto voce, and cursed da both . . . of them . . . !'

'Did the executioner, ineptly, somehow sever your left forefinger that I can see is still missing?'

'No! I was dressed in my freshest and cleanest that I was allowed to wear on that somber occasion. My French valet—a Breton, was standing in the midst o' the crowd, and though he was a faulty, ugly toad of a human being, dark of hue, and array; with long swept-back black hair and a square beard: either he was too good to rescue his Mistress, or too weak, to leave empty-headed what he had come for.— Neither a lamb or a dove—a fierce inhabitant from a town in Brittany, there had been a mutual sympathy, between our two natures; and in prison, when he was allowed, he always took pains to supply my needs with a collation of refreshments—wine, fruit, dates, sherbet and goat's milk; and I think he was sorely in love with me! He was the only one who remained secretly faithful to me after my arrest.—Talking earnestly about some hinted affaire d'amour, he had approached to the scaffolding, as near as possible to where I was.—When he saw, indeed, the sharp axe was poised to strike off Madame Howard's lithe neck, I heard a voice shouted a haute voix, with a crying sob, that I immediately recognized. Then, the little man's cry, "Aide-toi, le ceil t'aidera! (God helps those who helped themselves)" and then nothing,'—said the ghoast; looking at da mirrors as though these were closing in on her. 'After he had drunk his favorite Chateaux o' Burgundy, King Henry the Eighth, my widower husband, ordered them to give me back my detached head: the head o' his fifth wife, which was, then, to be buried . . . !!'

'I understand now—ah,—I think!' Humphrey said with a shudder: for he had pieced together some of which that must have taken place shortly after. This moribund French valet, it was, that had dismembered her corpse on the sly, by bribing some of the rascally guards, who were on official duty, before it was placed inside its wooden shell, and entombed. Then, fleeing back to France, he possessed his treasured prize—a token to remember with affection the dead English Queen—and the fetish was kept and poured over and fondled until he died; and the bottle was lost to posterity, until recently. This all, the ghost affirmed, by saying, 'Sometimes, I confess I wished I had married him, instead; for he was a devout man. My member was preserved in the finest Burgundy cognac, which he liked to think as a testament of everlasting love for me; and he had many Requiems said for me. Thank you for your patient listening—I have suffered for long centuries though these Masses have helped; but the hollowness in my guilty heart will not be satisfied wi' itself . . . till someone comes along . . . and let me tell my cautionary tale! I have to confess my sins to a living human person, and so, I now ask you, if you were Harry and Catherine Parr, would you forgive Kate Howard?'

'Readily: with all my heart! If I can do so, by proxy! Shall you attain and find true peace henceforth now? Go in peace, then . . . !!'

''Tis nearly over, this sore trial; someone has heard me out from beginning to end! Can ye see yon portals opening and this great light? Hark, yes, they are coming for me! I am climbing the air to fall into the tender arms of the embracing One! And thanks to Alphonse's prayers and his Requiems, I am free, finally . . . at last, at last . . . ! And especially, I must thank you, sir! What is your name, sir? Pray, tell me!'

'Plain ole Humphrey Humperdinck, a commoner,—your majesty . . . !' said the savant, his forehead bathed in a dram of sweat, and, his lanky frame shook not a little.

'Now!—but remember my parting words! Keep 'em locked, and imprimis in your heart. It will be my prerogative to seek your constant welfare, should I be needed, as indeed, I do hope, to do you a return service. Sweet, my Lord! Farewell! Rememberest thou! O! my soul! Soon you shall need some pieces of sweet refreshment from me! Mark me!'

Such were here parting words; and she began to glow with an inward and beautiful light, so beautiful, that it beggars description. Her eyes were affixed straight up, and there seemed to rise to Humphrey, da sight o' her eyes and lips, now, having a sweetness of expression that was supernatural. Writ large on her forehead were fulfillment and contentment! Her sweetness was the sweetness of heaven. This was the sum total of Doctor Humphrey Humperdinck's recollections of the events of two years ago that night; after his dream. Because of its vivid quality, 'twas as if the whole thing had occurred only just yesterday, he thought.

In the nursing home, they had been playing cards and scrabble: they were in the vintage and gala room, of Poole's Sanatorium and Humphrey was beatin' 'em flat every time, when the clock struck nine PM. A Mr. Sanhurst with his black caterpillar moustache, a former civil servant, from Washington, D.C., was smiling from ear to ear at the next table, thumping his feisty fists, with a little miffed, 'Ah, Mingoes! Dis are da people I want!—Mingoes, you know'd? The other is a Nape! Le-nape!' (Sounding thus, very mysteriously . . .) Some complainant grumbled uneasily, 'What's dat about, Larry?' And he said, 'It's in The Last of the Mohicans: da tattered copy is here! Read and weep!' And, he began croonin' snatches o' a made-up song, into which he inserted the words 'Lenape' and 'Mingoes' which was tantamount to riling 'em, purposely. And, with evident relish, too. Mr. Sandhurst's forever-restless eyes were forever restless, bec'os they were seldom satisfied, and shifty, moreover. He was putting on weight, and he knew the effect of his sexy voice—sexy bec'os it was superior as most of da other inmates could not even utter a sustained note. Next to him, was a black-ringed, hulking giant of a man,—of irascible temper, who suddenly got up in a huff; and Humphrey had ruefully observed that, usually, the wrong guys it was that made a big splash, or impressions fer da wrong reasons. Another said, 'Sing all you want, Larry; flattery is not my forte, it takes a lot to see through da good ole boys! So, la!' Here was a strawberry-pink tongued little red terrier o' a man, wi' his brain chemistry strangely mixed up; and he was talking into a coke bottle, as if it were a telephone, turning it right and left. Sitting on the sofa furthest away was a Krool-kat character, six of the first and half a dozen of da others; and, he was universally acknowledged da specialist in startin' food-fights. At the girls' or ladies table across, a Miss Lobelia Belafonte, former National Athlete, and professional show jumper, was knitting a sweater for her dead parakeet, and expounding the virtues of birdseed in her wee, high-pitched voice! There was a cracker-barrel philosophizing man, full of books in his head and he was the saddest of them all. The old Steinway, was being carelessly played by a pair of green moldy-looking hands, and, of course, it was some sweaty auld, saccharine nocturne, by Chopin. The vintage room was a different place when the lights were out. It was not a place to wander carelessly into.

'Goodnight, Humphrey!' they called out, at last; and our savant, respecting the nurses' wishes, began rummaging for something in his duffel bag and suddenly he remembered not the English Queen, but Alphonse, because the word "TROUBADOUR" was too long and he couldn't make "TROUVERE". Now, Alphonse, Humphrey, recallin' his researches about him, had been something of both: and, just then, the clock was striking nine. Then, holding his toothbrush and his mug, he was led on to remember her, as sometime of an evening; and she must be looking down at him from her high place; yet he has never called out her name even in his direst straits. Tonight, however, her name was on his lips; and he tried to compose a prayer around it but he felt so sleepy, without making any headway. Anyway, about to drop off to sleep, under the influence of sedatives, he imagined catching her distant glimpsed-at form: and whispered: 'Haunt me, Kate!' In his sleep, he dreamt, in the middle of a rainstorm, he had been caught napping,—when it finally banked, on the institution's park-like grounds. He was wearing a singlet and togs, drenched to the skin, before he could make his way inside the door. Next, he saw his childhood sweetheart in the morgue, lying on the slab and then she woke up, and spoke intimately and familiarly with him. Then, no sooner, had he pulled his blanket away when he thought he saw a shadow with a white forehead and brunette hair: the same sweet face he had seen two years ago.—But, more refreshing to the eye than that last time. There was no rustle of feet nor the switch of her skirt. It did not resemble the previous creature—that pale, shrinking figure that he saw at the beginning—who could only boast a comely rear. This time, there seemed to be moonbeams and starlight caught in her folds of hair; and dazzling sunlight, in her white teeth and ruby lips. Her lips crinkled with effusive pleasure; as though she had delicately bitten into chocolate; which the best chocolatier has ever dreamt o' making, or, eating burnt maple sugar or pistachio ice-cream. She was nearly, so nearly, a creature of flesh as was ever dreamt of this side of paradise; and, caught by a spell, Humphrey Humperdinck wanted the dream to continue interminably; for, he knew he was only dreaming. Yet, it was all the sweeter because it would soon pass and daylight would come again.

The wraith, or visitant angel, in his dream spake out, pitifully, 'What Humphrey—So soon?'

And at this the savant (in his dream) answered, 'Yes, Katie!'

'Are you entangled in difficulties?'

'For starters: I have blasphemed: I feel I am lost!'

'Know you, that I was much guiltier and received less punishment that what should have been justly meted out to me? He is really TRULY MERCIFUL! I'm not ashamed to talk, and let me, ah, say, I did not measure up to the true measure of a decent human being. I tell you, because, I can see glimmerings o' hope that I might fan into a fire. I was not severely judged, and, were I thus so, the criterion with which I judge others might have been not so mild. 'Twas my pride of heart, my greed for fame, and for gain, and my unbitten lust, which all pointed an INDICTING FINGER at me; for, hadn't I asked from Henry, Lady Seymour's property and Thomas Cromwell's, as well: Hampton Court,—for instance!'

'But of course—you are entitled to these by your own—rights . . .'

'No, no! You don't know what you are saying! Listen! Listen! You are in for the long haul—even you, must stay here for a while—but

I will learn you to be kind and joyful, to rejoice in the goodness and mercies meted out to you. You have asked your Nurse, Helen to be your girlfriend! And you have felt she really loves you! And, more importantly, you are in love with her! You think she has rebuffed you—bec'os she keeps her distance: listen! You have been sorely tempted to curse Him in your heart. Perhaps, you have vowed never to repeat that ever since! But, I tell you, no matter how tiresome and depressing the going gets, I MUST say, COURAGE! Trust in Him still! Rome, as they say, is not built in a day! You must not press da matter with da Nurse, just yet: I think you already know that, inside of you, Humphrey! She is a heaven-sent, but the timing is bad! If a person you love loves you back, well and good. But, if your Beloved—has inward spiritual disposition to please you; to give to you in every sense of what is proper and vice versa, you are truly blessed! Truly blessed with a Heavenly chemistry! The right and real kind of loving . . . does not let his own love redound on himself . . . can you understand this a little?'

'Wow! But! Though I can sense the possibilities betwixt Miss Rolland and myself, yet I am down in the dumps, and in the dust most of the time; in a very strange frame of mind! Downcast! Very near to despairing! I have a disturbance, in my visual field. The diagnosis they gave has been what is called schizophrenia . . . There is no way I can reciprocate her love; as mental illness is not sexy. Yes, I am in for it; a long haul! But I am Humphrey Humperdinck and it would be pure double-fantasy to want to be somebody else, say a movie star or a real celebrity. I cannot wish my troubles on somebody else; and wish their joys to be mine. There is no helping it—I can only do the best I can, and one day at a time. It is something I hate, that I can plan no further ahead. Drugs, counseling and psychotherapy, group-sessions and moderate reading, swimming, gymkhana and a little socializing, with the other inmates! I know the routine here by rote! You know?—pinochle, poker, scrabble and trivial pursuit? How I long to hold Helen by the waist as there seem to be a radar-like regular understanding o' hearts between us! For example, I have just come out of my room and was feeling hungry and thirsty, and with just one look, she said, "Hello, sweet! You look hungry an' thirsty. Let us fix up something wonderful and hot for you, what do we say to some warm cocoa butter and buttermilk?" And, that is precisely what I had in mind. She must, somehow, have known I would be coming through the Tee-vee lounge, and she would meet me there; and knowing I was hungry and thirsty, she would know how to satisfy my needs! Get it? She anticipates your needs, is serious and intends to fulfill 'em the moment you desires her to! That is how my Helen is with me! Furthermore, besides being sexual in feelin', there is something holistic about it, too, bec'os it's also spiritual: that she makes me feel so good to be understood! The world hates me bec'os the world hates Christ, just as Christ has warned his friends about it, very lang ago, and as I belong to no one but Christ,—by extension, the wurl and the debbils hate me,—too! But it's so different with Helen Rolland! She is the only exception . . .'

Humphrey choked back his tears and sighed a long drawn sigh and in his dream he said: 'I don't care what happens to me anymore! Or what will happen to me. I know Helen and I have no hope of a future together. I am afraid that if I lift her skirt she is soon going to tire of me! I have nothing good to offer her! I am not the same man I used to be; and she is not going to get fired or risk the disapproval of her family . . . it's—at this point in time—simply askin' too much! And in the dead of night, sometimes, I git da feelin' that someone is sockin' it to me inside my brains, and a panic attack, a-breakin' out! It is a calm exterior that I maintained,—that enabled me to keep things under wraps. Yet, sumptin' might BREAK LOOSE and there are still dreadful things lurkin' inside o' me, chuckling like chuckleheads and having a ball inside my head. These be my enemies—and they have won! I feel a sense of desolate emptiness, like unto 'em in deadness, now . . . My Father niver comes to see me. My stars have been put out; they are dead! How heavy time hangs on my hands! What now, Humphrey, I ask mysel'? There is still much anger; perhaps, at being duped; but they tell me, anger is good! I must own it claim responsibility and work with my own feelings. They are not completely deadened, yet—you know dead?—Dead? Why, I am on the verge of chuckin' it in, throw in da towel, call it quits here—you get the picture? There is no more fighting spirit left in Doctor Humphrey Humperdinck, Ghaistsweeper-extraordinaire anymore! That's why! If Helen is not working here, I would not know how I could stand it. Still, she's my leading-lady (L. Ritchie's Three Times A Lady). There is no finer girl in the whole wide world for me! But she can't be mine, though what both of us need is love. Yet, she is here; when I needed her help. When I am down for the standing count! With other women it might be mere bodily desires, because they look very good and cute in uniform but, ah, Helen my Joan of Arc, my Aphrodite, an' most of all, my petite, darlin' little Florence Nightingale! Florence Nightingale—what a beautiful splendiferous name! I just kill myself when I think there is such a person, such a refulgent Spirit in the world. But, do I kid myself, that sich a person is for me? Sometimes, in a muddled sort o' way I would think, "O, God! Tell the debbil that not everybody is like that. Not everybaddy is a pushover! Even if my days end abruptly, I will never cease fighting him!"—Then, my heart's blood quickens and thunderously roars! I pray for a chance to git even wi' da debbil! Then, I am surging with my own innate energy.—But, it has been a dark end after da road to Canterville Chase. My illustrious career—!'

'Lord knows—my poor dear, how you've suffered terribly! It must all be six's and seven's inside o' you, all at once, without any way to sort yourself out! Catastrophic! A ruinous mess! In its aftermath, to know,—that the worst might still be yet to come! Seize your habitual thoughts, sir, and get out of the rut! Courage still, I say! Squander not your days!'

So saying, the wraith—the savant saw, stretched out her limber hands and he saw her left forefinger was missing no longer. She raised her eyes upwards and whispered something to someone in quaint French: 'Conseil d'Etat: que voulez-vous? What would you have me say, my lord counselor? O! Gloria Patri! Cada uno es hijo de sus obras ! Humphrey, I have been given to tell you, that, Agape Love is the greatest love a human being can radiate: a love like Helen's! Not lukewarm or calculating, as—well, let's not go into that: Agape is a consuming fire, a heart's itch, straining to run the race to the finish, of which the goal is the good—the emotion and spiritual wellbeing of your neighbor! Do you know He became man to save Mankind from their sins? Think: where we would all be without the event of the Incarnation; and later, the guarantees of a Heaven, stamped with "Bought for—and Paid IN FULL!' Do not seek self-aggrandizement after His many examples of meekness an' charity; turn your back to the lash now, my lad! See!—'Tis like unto Himself, always self-emptying, to be one of us!'

'The reason of emptying myself is Agape Love?

'Always, ay! You shall be filled to the fullest measure too in the end; be daring in Agape Love. Abandon yourself into His hands! The giving up of rights, privileges, and claims, and relinquishing that which might cause us pains and accepting troubles, persecutions, discomforts and losses in return! Our treasures, we must be ready to give up, for even bigger fish.'

'No holds barred? Is that what you are saying?'

'Yes! Then, there is universality: the universality of real self-giving, sacrificial and holy, to perpetuity! Everyone in your Milieu must be in communion with you, and if you consciously seek to effect this often enough, you shall have the world along with you sooner or later, even if it hates you, still! You have shown 'em your real front; and while many people might still dislike you, you shall continue to inspire 'em!

'That's big fish,—and rolls over faster even than monetary gains, and returns on investments, even if I can't cash in on it. Yes,—I must learn to grow!'

'Yes, grow, grow, Humphrey. Next is reconciliation: Trespass is as unavoidable as eating and drinking. We omit or we sinned by commission! Yet even if we have Him in us, we still commit trespass! Reconciliation is the key! Stop what you are doing, and think of the people you need to be reconciled with. So that smooth relations are reestablished between the parties. A person can take the attitude, "If my wrist is broken, I just cut off my hand! If my leg is causin' me pain, I amputate it! What does it matter? I can just sit 'ere—read the dailies at the breakfast table or listen to the power stereo in my room and be what I WANT TO BE!" Isn't that self-consuming and selfish? No, no! Seek to be reconciled, and if there is a heart out here that knocks, be opened to it! That is life! Seize every opportunity! Then, Agape will come back again!'

'And—what else? I can smell the dawn and the cold air breeds a chill in my bones and wetting my hair. Quick!—I fear I am almost awake, bec'os I can't see you clearly anymore,—I see strings of mist and blurred colored streaks o' light; and also, I fear, I chanced might be allowing Fear to come back—as he is always watchin' me, like a bird of prey. So pray you, Katie, sweet Katie: snowy white turtledove, whisper one word before you fade away!'

'Ay, love,' said the wraith. And lo and behold! Her face was no more Katie Howard's but Helen Rolland; and she kissed him on the lips saying, "Agape love means also communion: wellbeing for yourself an' for the other. For others! Actually, I set my self-love at a lower premium than my other-love. Then, it's really real!' And she kissed him again, just as tenderly, but on his forehead this time, a reverent, prolonged "smack!" 'That is what all of us should be aiming for: communion!' she breathed.

Helen's face to Humphrey's mind was fresh and oval, and her earrings flashed, as if some pent-up emotion was about to burst through the floodgates in her . . . bec'os da tantalizing prospect of holding her in his arms was the most delicious of sweets! Indeed, he saw himself catching at her but she slipped away from his arms, and vanished, leaving him surprised and burning with heartfelt longing; and a dull headache, that was very intolerable in its very persistence. He had come awake and he noticed at once, the drapes of his chamber was billowy and a certain shower of divine, spheric sparks, a-meltin';—then, the surrounding furniture were dark silhouettes and then he saw his suitcases and in a moment of calm he seemed to be infused with satisfaction that set his soul joyfully aglow! For the first time for a very long time he was glad: really glad!—besides, having Miss Rolland working in Poole Sanatorium. He kissed his pillow and turned his radio on. It was playing Stupid Cupid, by Connie Francis; then, We're All Alone, by Rita Coolidge. A weak smile came across his features, and he turned it up. It was a small radio, with not enough power to make any inmate complain that the volume might be too loud. He tumbled out of his bed and heard its bedsprings groan. The darkness was less threatening now; and he cried, 'I love you! O Katie! Katie! Thank you! I feel I already miss you! I will be missing you till the song in my life is over,—my own dear heart—Helen!—thank you, for walking into my life! I am dying inside to talk to you this very moment! You do not know how much I see in your eyes, and wi' 'ee by my side! Oh:—thank you! Thank you for precious Female Humankind! How can we ever get along without you? I shall praise Him, even when it is hard; and my heart falters!'

Suddenly, feeling a heartburn coming on, having dined at suppertime a quantity of broiled ham and consommé, Humphrey shrugged off his usual worries, and, he felt he just might make it and was more competent now to deal with the fallout of that disaster in Somerset, England, by which, I mean, Canterville Chase. Until that was done, he cannot resume the role as a useful member of society, which he had contributed so much in the past he ruefully noted . . .

Owen, Mortimer and Roper were delighted as evidences of his steady recuperation mounted and he gained in self-possession. In the sanatorium, he was always many cuts above the rest. Head and shoulders above da rest! He was at once the most observant: the most cautiously curious and by far the most sanely sociable. Still, the split inside o' him needed time to heal. At times, he was moody and impulsive. Eight months and six days later he was finally allowed to leave. He said a sorrowful goodbye to Miss Rolland; and he took a drive back through Philly to his childhood hometown where he was born. He went back home! Striking a nodding and one sentence acquaintance with his Father, this time around seemed strange;—but, the Old Man was the same as he was before. He stayed two weeks and decamped, and then back to New York City, and revisited his old University. He was regularly taking his medication which was supervised by eminent doctors, and he read psychoanalytic literature extensively, religious books, such as theology,—and philosophy, from a Christian perspective. He also read widely, hoping to piece together anything that might explain what happened to him; and, in due course, he came an' looked me up. One of the psychiatrists had recommended me when he was hospitalized in England; and, as it happened that, about that time, I recently married a thirty-five year old American, with two children, and moved, to Glen Cove, Nassau, Long Island,—he consulted me in my office in a fashionable professional quarter in the city's center, in Eighth Avenue. My practice was picking up steadily, and at first, I initially referred him to my partner, having on my plate some work of some small value. Suddenly, these regularly scheduled visits to my office soon began to engage my attention like no other, and soon he was slowly, and hesitantly, and gently, opening up to me upon my custom-made black upholstery: da trusty couch!

One day, in the fall of 19—, he said suddenly, 'Look, Professor! The curtains are drawn on the day, and the stars, faint ones, are out in their numbers through the paling light. O! How beautiful! I never saw that before up here! The faint shine revives and take center stage in da heavens as the light of da sun fades over the Manhattan skyline. D' ye think, it's goin' to be a mundane day tomorrow?'

'Each day is never mundane for genuine caregivers—Humphrey!'

'Why not?'

'Bec'os the elements that cause mundaneness, irritability and unwillingness, are not present the moment we begin our chosen task.'

'Can I be like that again?'

'Say, imagine a perfect day! Night folding up its wings and moving off to some other place, like a fakir taking his coconut mat with him. What would that day be?'

'Easter morning, sir! There is no finer dawn like that Morning, and if one goes back two thousand years, the First One. It is infinitely rich in its implications and its truth is staggering and incomprehensible . . . It has infinite treasures!'

'Answered well, you have. Your mental faculties are getting better n' better! Come and talk to me again, and I shall listen to you bec'os its time's up now, and it's also my wife's birthday. May God bless you, and keep you. I am Catholic, you know, and if there is anything you would like to discuss wi' me you can talk to me over the phone, or walk in anytime, and we shall see if I can fit you in, and thank you for coming, Mr. Humperdinck. Thank you, and all the best. Goodbye, Humphrey! Take some much required rest.' And with that, I bowled him out. Then, taking the elevator down, I thought: 'It would be at least eight fifty-five before I reached da plaza on da opposite side for another appointment; a domestic one—for my gentlemen friends and my gentle young boys are throwing a party for da birthday girl, muh darlin' wife.'

Chapter Three

CONSEQUENCE OF DA HUBRIS OF DOCTOR HUMPHREY HUMPERDINCK

'You have prepared a banquet for my foes in my presence.'

This is holy ground because in this chapter what we are in the main concerned about is human suffering. Therefore, in leafing through my notes of the savant's past, and proceeding wi' the story, it is with fear and trembling:—thus respect, that I do so . . . The nearest thing to AWE, when I am done writing, it is this—that I had hoped to find: that Doctor Humperdinck had acquitted himself of any serious fault or culpability of what befell him in Canterville Chase. In letting the dust of the accumulated years settle, I was able to bring to focus an' find enough reasons for the savant, in doing what he did,—and the events leading up to the moment of crisis—a moment of dread import, in regard to what happened after that. And, taking heed o' what he told me at least twice, 'When we meet God, we meet Him in a crowd, but yet, if we meet the debbil, as sometimes we do, we often meet him alone.'—Yet, how did the specter eliminator fall victim of spooks himself? By his own jaundiced and cynical hands, to be strangely hoisted, as it were, by his own petard, Humphrey had been trying to pull the plug of his madness about his worldly success, and what all these constituted! But, long before he held a grudge against spooks—it was his relationship with his parents that made him plunge headlong into da HURT TRAP! Humphrey Humperdinck had felt often he was so hurt by his parents that he couldn't possibly recover; and because of this, he could find no way to unburden his mind and soul. Everything—that he felt that is neither right nor proper, anywhere at all, and disasters even in faraway countries,—produced a great hurt in him: he had a heart and soul that attracted hurt from every corner like a magnet! And he felt, it is up to himself,—to redress this outer and very real situation. That was why, he told me, he became da Spook Eliminator Par Excellence: he was really and incredibly afraid, that he might become a spiritual bankrupt—like his Father. Thus, Humphrey set himself up as a target—asking da wurl (which was a hurtful place to him), 'Do 'ee really want to hurt me? Do yer worst!' At the same time, he had had no satisfying relationship with any significant other of da opposite sex; being, often, habitually afraid o' makin' himself vulnerable in social situations (although he had no lack o' admirers, it seemed!)—for, he was an extremely shy an' sensitive man. About his Father, peace! I say: because the man is now dead, and hence I will hold my peace . . .

During one early evening of incomparable tedium in autumn's quiet, Doctor Humphrey Humperdinck was ruminating before a fire in his newly purchased house in Somerset, reflecting on his life, and what it meant to him up until that moment. It was a moment—when alone—and sitting by the fender—the mood of isolation and the seasonal dreariness seemed to have taken its toll on him. There—what with the perverse vicissitudes of his career, the leader considered how far in ten years he had zapped and slammed and smacked and down'd ghaists: how, he had held his own in dangerous physical tasks, with its exposure to monumental psychic perils,—which came with pulling his own weight in these matters. Though, I am hesitant to call him antaean-like, and bifurcated at the end of his chin (the beginnings of a double one), he had no blade o' hair on his 'ead, as, reflecting the un-archetypal savant, constantly deep in, and wearing himself out with, his studies:—he had, also, brawn—to shore up his taste for the outdoors and tough physical activities, for—there was also something of the accomplished athlete about him. He was stirring da coals with the poker, and he remembered, it was shortly before a storm broke in the dark sky above his house . . . ! As I look through what I had written, it reminded me of Mr. Neil Diamond's song that ran with the words, 'I am, I said . . .'

Doctor Humphrey Humperdinck's collection of books was a fine one, and for upwards of two hours now he had been constantly on and off reading Borges's books, especially, Labyrinths, a book that had now lain ensconced between Roget's Thesaurus and Quicherat's, until he picked it up, and began to flip over the pages lazily with his fingers. This book was one of his perverse favorites—and, in one of the pages there had lain two entries or quotes: which sounded to him like a repository of accumulated years of another man's experience . . . he was feeling sore, and sensitive as a pin-cushion,—that the next thing that happened, anything at all,—might set his nerves and heart sore and a-tingling, with pain to an unbearable degree, yet again . . . ! He left his coupe (his champagne glass) unfilled and pondered his niche; and what mark he was to leave upon the world.

> . . . Truth, whose mother is history, rival of time, depository of deeds, witness of the past, exemplar and advisor of the present, and future's counselor . . .
>
> Cervantes

> Time discovers truth.
>
> Seneca

Why wasn't there any consolation for Doctor Humphrey Humperdinck as he wallowed in a welter of pain: his chest a-pounding: and, if Jorge. L. Borges words, seeming very clever and very plausible, as they were,—why did they leave him feeling stupid an' empty? And, why was he caught up and held by their mesmerizing quality and quantity? As of late, Humphrey's appraisal of the modern world in the eighties was like Dickens's, in the increasing secular eighteenth century; especially, in his A Tale of Two Cities, which were begun with, 'It was the best of times, it was the worst of times . . . We had everything before us, we had nothing before us, we were going direct to heaven, we were going the other way . . . ', as—ever since his childhood, because of his relationship with his parents:—he had learnt and taught himself to take hurts—and eventually to take more and more hurts by inviting the bad 'uns in the universe to take potshots at him:—to put himself through hell's treadmill. Because he was damaged goods: he had thought, as a result, he might gain admittance to Heaven, thereof: his unconscious rationale being, if he suffered more than he could ever suffer he might be blessed by God or be spared suffering when he was dead or later on in his life, at the end. And so, sitting here, biting his dry lips, he was frowning vindictively; as he thought of da spooks held and imprisoned downstairs, and elsewhere; and why was his life still not vindicated—as he had wanted—in this depressed and desperate state o' mind? Was he tryin' to force a situation in a world dat is nuffin' but a showcase of vanity; in which a downfall due to pride followed? The day was the latter half of October, and as he cast his bitter eyes over the window-scene before him, he saw the declining light disappearing over the hills, and the dark trees stripped o' their foliage or verdure that used to mass against the wind-driven, inky, skies: pondering the two above-quoted sentences by the two famous writers which had lent to it, a special sense of its negative pertinacity. The looseness o' da moment, without any present engagement, had left him in a state of disquieting boredom and due to his cold temperament—contemptuous of his life. He did not finish his drink, this being unsuccessful—and, he thought, 'Will I have the courage to suffer this lassitude agin the whole night through? Suffer my ENNUI, INSIGNIFICANCE and MEANINGLESSNESS my whole life to the very end? Suffer till the end of my days? I doan tink our jugulating of ghoasts or the purgin' o' the psychic realm did anything significant in changing the topography o' da world in regard to its real desideratum! The only tink it does is lining our purses—'

As the light began to retreat, and full-scale darkness breached the room from the wet diamond-shaped-paned windows, the savant let his eyes scanned the swimming words on the pages once again and as fate, or chance would have it, he began to read a story he had never read before (so it seemed to him), entitled Three Versions of Judas which made his already teetering mind to boggle: (and Borges' words, were said to be the words, in the short-story—Humperdinck had thought, albeit, blasphemous ones!—of the Swedish theologian, Nils Runeberg:) 'To save us, he could choose any of the destinies, which make up the complete web of history; He could be Alexander of Pythagoras or Rurik or Jesus; He chose the vilest destinies of all. He was Judas.'

Humphrey was so enthralled, nevertheless, that his mind carved away. Seen and read in the cold light of day, on a warm or hot summer day, of course, it could only be nonsense. He tasted the rawness of this new orientation that flavored his despondency and pain, now; making him reckless, and mad, in this wild and insane claim! So reckless and despairing, had he been,—that he wanted to do sumptin stoopid, an' dangerous, so that he was swept away by an idea, which, he was scarcely aware, was there, until it exploded his neurons, like some burning planet right before an amazed stargazer's ken. He felt, suddenly, it was true: and he, Humphrey, was swallowed up by an overpowering and all-pervading sense of evil in da universe that can only be undone by a strange, perverted an' twisted hope . . . And this hope being his being another Jesus, for Doctor Humphrey Humperdinck's pain-gripped heart was a-bleedin' for all humanity, just then . . . ! Was Nietzsche like that?

However, the algid feeling grew as the moments passed . . . He began to reel off insights that he never thought of before, coming to him pat, just like that: evil has its own pseudo-logic, a formidable array of it: power and momentum, to advance its plains and projects . . . Evil binds, and enchains, and when it comes loose, it's also chain by chain, link by link . . . evil enslaves and binds our will, and takes away our freedom by tellin' us it's all a delusion! And so on, and because of the delightful sensuousness of these revelations, he thought he was ready to be at the real service of humankind. Here, was something new; and he thought, 'Christ is a work-description . . . Christianity is also one. You, too, Humphrey, he thought, together the rest of humankind are going to hell; unless you bring evil to its denouement . . . That is, nominate yourself to save the wurl . . .'

Humphrey saw beyond the conventional—the commonplace.— Up he got, at once, and left the comfort of the warm room which fire blazed up at his shutting of the door. The pine resin'd logs had sparked, and it seemed that some irregular lumps glowed red; and from the fireplace there rose a motley procession of souls that he had encountered in his few years last past, looking at his retreatin' footsteps with grave looks; to smile at him sweetly, and pitifully if they could, amid the chiaroscuro, (for these were those he had helped during his career . . .) The first of these were Capt. Zurubabbel McCloskey, the Twenty-third Laird o' Kirk Hallows, in life—who was released from his guilty secret; Josef Smits, a bankrupt mill owner, during Americas's war of Independence (who was hung for desertion); Wylie Burlington, a London matchboy who starved to death;—and most notably, the English Queen, whose story involving Humphrey was lately told in the last chapter. The savant did not see their saddened visages and their looks of entreaty, or honest plea:—for Humphrey, to regain his self-possession:—and the moment passed! In his mounting delirium and madding and maniacal excitement, even if he did, he would not recognize 'em; for evil has its own defense mechanism; and hence, it rallied around itself, by a counterblast, sending wet leaves and debris to be dislodged from the insides o' da chimney;—and hence—causing the sparks to hiss the moment the savant might have been careful enough to take notice. In the cellar inside the ghaist-containment tanks, they began to sense sumptin' o' da operative whose very shadow was anathema to 'em . . . ! Without knowing its consequences, somehow, it seemed, his decision to do what he intended was preordained from long ago . . . and Humphrey Humperdinck understood, they were cherishing an inclement chance at revenge to smother him in their hellish embrace . . . But, Doctor Humphrey Humperdinck, on an impulse, was resolved to see it through even if it were to have intolerable consequences, later on, (talk about headstrong, idiocy, you know?) but this might be an eidolon! He seemed to descend dark, vertiginous stairs, amid a thin horned darkness which was likely to induce vertigo; like Sherlock Holmes tottering on the brink o' da Reichenbach Falls; at the brink of destruction an' death! He was sweatin' in globules by then; which ran off his back and the palms of his hands. The light seemed misty and swanky, and the room, cold and clammy. He came to a pressurized containment tank. One of the two larger ones in the room. This was where some of the kelps, sprites, fetches, banshees and ghouls were kept:—in a word, in which demonical spirits and diabolical entity or things that go bump in da night were imprisoned. But, tonight, he was going to let a whole legion of spirits to pass through his body and soul: the reverse of the process of a highly technical and sophisticated exorcism. As the needlepoint touched his body, he doubly shuddered and felt a mishmash of strangely incongruous emotions; and—for the first few seconds, it was like pure oxygen. He thought, 'I've become Pure Love!' then, a voice said, 'Let's do him over' and then, he remembered,—'In Aleppo once, where a malignant and a turban'd Turk . . . and smote him thus!' (A quote from Shakespeare, which he knew very well). What seemed like a foretaste of heaven, an' all achieved, was, all the more galling and humiliating—bec'os it had made him feel so confounding high . . . !!! His housekeeper, Mrs. Umney, sensing something was wrong, came down the long traverse to see if he was all right; her clattering medium heels leading her to him and her shadow fell across da prostrate form of our unconscious savant. She had been drinking her bitter teas and smart tonics; and she had been somewhat alarmed by the nifty drumming of the high, peltin' raindrops against her windowpanes in her room, as well as da howlin' winds outside . . . ! In spiritual matters, bec'os she was not wholly ignorant—she immediately became cognizant she was being summoned bec'os sumptin was afoot. She arrived none too soon for she got Humphrey immediately sent to a local county hospital by the gardener and the local parson who was visiting the latter, to the tune of Stevie Wonder's Yester Me, Yester You . . . playin' on the car stereo . . . Humphrey, nevertheless, woke up two days later in a delirium, ranting and raving in a peculiar way, and he was transferred to a psychiatric hospital in Allenby, which was twelve miles from da Chase. His friends and colleagues could not figure out what had happened to their leader, the man they admired most, Humphrey Humperdinck, who was, at once, so levelheaded, and so on top of it all . . . They wanted to know why: What could have possessed Humphrey to do it? Yes, things were niver going to be the same again: goodbye success, fame and money! Doctor Mortimer's engaging smile tightened into a lariat, and looked at him as though he would like to gouch a cat's eye out at the shocking news, or an old lady had nailed him roundly over the head with her Christian Dior handbag, multiple times,—but all the Ghaistsweepers stuck by him and they would talk to the insensible man and feed him and help to change his clothes (when they visited him) till at last he got better—due to their tender, loving care, and before it was three months, he could talk a little brokenly and smile weakly at them. He had lost his imbecile way o' speakin' and he began indulgin' in taking short walks around the institution's grounds and gardens. But, still, he had a long way to go, through intensive therapy, and counseling, and medication—to get him back on his feet; therefore, so as not to be as incapacitated—as he was at the beginning. The shell of his ego and heart had cracked, pecked to smithereens by what happened in Canterville Chase, and something very nasty was still for a time a-hanging about. But, Humphrey had an inbuilt shit detector and a rigorously disciplined intellect, so that, even then, there was a possibility that he might birth a hidden self, grown strong . . . and when sich was known to his friends, they will rejoice with him with gladdened hearts and cheerful voice:—for they would have realized what in Doctor Humphrey Humperdinck's heart of hearts:—he had been precisely fighting for!

Chapter Four

HUMPHREY HUMPERDINCK
ATTEMPTS TO FIND A GIRLFRIEND

After that catastrophe in England, Humphrey's heart niver used to palpitate as before anymore. It was frozen stiff, and hardly stirred with heartfelt joy at life's wonderful experiences; seldom glad—that some unexpected good had come someone else's way— for he was swallowed up by his own pain (like a slow hourly burn by da barrelful!) and always anticipatin' the worst to come at each moment . . . Dread always came back with the inevitability of a homing pigeon; and like the Ancient Mariner with the dead albatross hanging across his neck, all but invisible, except to his inward eye. An icy barnacle seemed to seized him up, as it were,—he was living in the land of shadows,—and cut off from real living. His heart wheezed, murmured, and pumped the blood, in a most squeamish manner possible; and his anxiety of late had taken on a monotonous turn that made the colors in his life gray. It was a wet afternoon over Manhattan and as Humphrey Humperdinck took the lift to get out of my office, his head was reeling. The rain was dinging like fake gold coins on the expensive Italian tiles outside the building and he adjusted his eyes to the pale light amid the hazy Avenue of the Americas as he turned into it. Reflected back in the tinted glass partitions, he saw the orangey clouds squeezing out the gray ones, and then the light shot luminous for a moment and then the sun faded again. Nobody recognized him, and, he was glad of that, as, everybaddy going out into the New York streets was anonymous, a large crowd bustling about, it was—and, this pleased him momentarily. To all outward appearances, he was just like everybody else. Suddenly, deciding to go home, he hailed a bust-up New York cab. All at once, he felt in the thrall of a double-mindedness, as was da case in most impersonal situations, while he was being driven downtown; though he had liked the idea that he had made some progress, especially,—this particular session. He and the beret-wearing cabbie chatted inconsequentially, and he thought, he might have given da game away; though, he knew, in da Big Apple nobaddy would've cared less n' two cents . . . ! However, he was acutely sensitive, and thought he looked spaced out and could not bear much inspection or close scrutiny . . . 'Bah, nobaddy cares! My Old Man doan give a HOOT!' Nevertheless, he thought: his unhealthy vibes, would not people have picked these up—somehow?—But everybaddy in New York is also slightly crazy or a lot crazier—or more sane than him too, bain't it? However, this was small comfort, thought he, to himself—

They talked about their problems and the insolubility o' most: Humphrey remembered he had suddenly remarked, 'Wait until I get home! Then, it gits even worse!' and the cabbie observed, sympathetically, 'Well a-lack-a day! The Missus, I s'ppose?—Tt-tt!' Humphrey replied, 'I'm not married.' Thereupon, the fellow said, 'Lucky fer you!' And Humphrey said glumly, 'Listen guy, I doan even have a girlfriend!' And the man, sounding as if it was as easy as getting a pet: advised laconically:—'Go home and get yoursel' one!'— which exasperated the already incensed and depressed Humphrey, very much. Humphrey Humperdinck thought: 'I'm a loony-bin,—a quadruple loser! Better to be aloof and stay clear, Humphrey . . . safer—safer! Da debbil has purloin'd his soul, da debbil has purloin'd his soul,—it's in the place of holocaust,' he found himself biting his lip and chanting, 'Oh, oh, oh! In dis wurl everybaddy's bald and constantly falling apart it seems to me.'

'Here's da house?' asked the taxi driver looking at him oddly, nodding towards him at last.

'That's right; dump me here.'

When he had unlocked the door of his temporary apartment and peeled off his outer clothing, he thought of his current boss— two Vietnamese brothers who owned a restaurant that made its own noodles, which was called S'anyone Specialist Noodles. This was an employment he had chosen himself so that he would have something constructive to do; and poundin' da secret flour dough was therapeutic as it needed a modicum of concentration—so that time didn't have time to play havoc with his mind . . . It was an hourly paid job, and, as the arrangement was a loose one, he called them on the phone saying, he won't be coming in today. Then he rang off, with the telephone rattling off the hook. In his flat was a sofa, his much-loved bookcase, and on the mantelpiece were photographs of his high school graduation and his undergraduate one, da Summa cum laude mugshot . . . He brushed the dust off this one with his shirt, and stared at the gawky tall fellow with deep-set eyes and a determined jaw, and he thought of the fantastic job offers he had from two hundred prestigious institutions and private companies that he had turned them down, when decided to do his postgraduate studies in Psychic Phenomena at Yale . . . As he stared at the photographs, he flipped off the cap of a cooler, and guzzled down deep . . . Having dozed off, a little later, he woke up at nine PM and ordered pizza from the deli round da block; quickly showered and changed his clothes, bec'os he decided he was going to work, after all. He walked past a Seafood restaurant, which he often frequented, called 'The Fishy Fisherman's Fried-fish Shoppe.'

Once at the factory, he sweated like any other blue-collar laborer; and Humphrey relished the tough, physical workout because he could keep his mind off focusing on himself when the shadows are long an' about—I mean, every night. He didn't like turnin' up at nightspots because many ghouls inhabit the woodwork of these dank an' smelly places and here the place is well lighted; though the smell be quaint and Oriental and exotic, for he liked just listen to Vietnamese folk songs about country girls trying to find husbands, coming from a blarin' stereo. He heard popular Hong Kong, Taiwanese and Singaporean starlets whose songs were only known to few Westerners outside the Chinese community in America. This would immediately reminded him of a certain lass, smelling like herbs from a lagoon, whose name was Miss Ho. Missy, as he called her, worked in 'The Fishy Fisherman' food outlet: and her parents had died in a car crash in Nebraska, three years before. A fine part-time student, workin' through college, which was one of da business-institutions;—she was a flowerlike girl, with fine skin and a tip-tilted nose. Besides Helen Rolland, she was the greatest knockout, Humphrey had ever in his life saw! The impression she had formed upon him right from the very start was first-rate and astounding, he told me; and he even remembered the Hawaiian fruit punch she used to make. 'Twas a drink that made her sweet on the Chinese lass; and it was so soothing to his palate. Missy had an engaging personality though it grieved Humphrey to the bone, she always was deliberately avoiding to smile back at him. Was it something about him, which betrayed the fact that he was up to no good? Was it the HURT TRAP, opening its gaping mouth, to swallow him up again? The savant, Doctor Humphrey Humperdinck, could not bring himself to admit:— knowing he loved Helen—he wanted something more than to be merely friendly with Miss Ho. And every time he bought food, she could get some other server to serve him and she would give him the cold shoulder; although Humphrey defended his ego by telling himself he just wanted her to treat him just like everybaddy else. After all, it's an equal opportunity wurl . . . He wanted a chance, just one, to show her he wasn't such a bad guy; but he was short on antics and he could sense in a chaotic way, she was afraid he might be coming on to her . . . !! They would be whispering when he kept on coming back at da same late hour, 'He is here again; your lover boy, Missy—is he loco?'—but this did not deter him at all. In fact, it made him even more determined to see her. For, anyway, to have Humphrey at his usual table 17, eyeing her doggedly and harmlessly, meant one more customer fer Missy; and therefore, good fer business.

Humphrey would oft begin to feel his heart opening up, with her at the shop, and more enlivened, he could almost forget his recent past. True, they had hardly exchanged more than two dozen words, but he began to think of her as his Mystery love-interest. Even, in the best of times, he did not know how to approach the girl, and so, how was he to approach Miss Ho, now? Certainly, he merited a friendly word or a friendly smile; but was the debbil putting da thumbscrews on him as usual? Why was everybaddy not only giving him flake, but also trying to shoot down his mangled ego as well . . . ?

Well, he was a famous scientist, wasn't he? And didn't he have more science at his fingertips than fifty thousand matriculating students? Wasn't he a very handsome albino? (Being an albino is the next best thing failing to be born a farouche like Rudolf Valetino.) Here he was getting hard knocks and hard knocks from her, too; just as he had been receiving hard knocks ever since he was born;—born into the Humperdinck Family. His Mother, a feisty nagger o' a woman, had ever since become the counterpoint of his spiritual growth, especially since his breakdown. Thus, he was carrying on in this way; though, of course, he knew it was ridiculous to lambaste his fate this way; for, it made da malaise of his heart only worse. So,—he thought to himself, Humphrey, poor luckless worm, you are not only mind sick: you are heartsick too!—and this left a bitter taste in his mouth— despite the pudding he was eating. His supervisor at work (they all worked without praise or pudding, either, ha, ha!)—must have defective parents like him, and all the while, the speakers of the stereo was blaring these romantic songs; and Humphrey curled up his lips like a Cayman Islander through his dripping sweat, and smiled like a culverin, bec'os, it was nearly the end of his work day, which ended all the same way: with the thought that he had been making some minor culinary history fer his Vietnamese bosses! And, when he was leaving through the gates he thought to himself now, to continue to get his mood upbeat and his blood flowing,—'That's right, jack it up! Jack it up! Doan let yer thoughts get bubbly awful all o' a sudden; also, doan git the softness ye feel inside yer head git worse, yer numbskull! Tonight, I won't give the factory rats another look and straight I will go to the eatery where the lights are bright and there is a pretty, delectable and sweet Chinese girl theer . . . If only I could snap out of it, fer tonight,' he said, begging God but to retain only the residue of his strange and mighty dread. Negative fumes seemed, however, to be rising from his guts, minusing out the clarity of the ordinary world by substituting this with suggestive shapes, shapes that clouded over his consciousness like deep shadows.

'Get on wi' 'ee; move out,' the supervisor had bawled aloud through the megaphone, and they all huddled in their jackets. It was two-thirty AM.

Today was a good day, however, at the eatery where Missy worked. It was one of the wonderful moments. Missy served him herself today, and just as she put down his order, he groaned. She said, lynx-eyed, 'You've got to unburden yourself, ya know? I have been watching you since you started comin' here . . . and . . . well . . . I thought . . .'

'What?'

'Nothing; oh, just nothing. I thought—'

'You look like a reel Sultana and I can picture you sippin' Persian shebert from the Sultan's golden bowl, and afterwards goin' breakdancin' wi' da boys in da clubs.'

'Geez, I'm Chinese, guy.'

'Don't be uppity, Missy. I was merely commenting—'

'Schizo, get real!'

It was her informed opinion she gave to him on one occasion: that what one in his shoes must do, was to, in Hokkien dialect, what is termed, "kua pua"—that was, to disburden yourself o' what whatsoever that holds you and letting go of da past; and comin' to terms with people in your life, especially with those deceased o' yours! Making every effort, to detach yerself from all negative spiritual encumbrances . . . !!! She had given it as her wise opinion, telling him how otherwise, she herself would still be mopping o'er her parents' sudden demise: her Pa and Ma whom she had loved exceedingly; about all da unfairness of life in general and feelin' da hurt inside, that would've gotten her down. She was very good in doing this, Humphrey thought.

'I tink I will bring da Pink Ghoast wi' me, when I come round 'ere da next time. I would like to show da cute ghoast to her,' Egon whispered muddledly into his tofu-and-salted-fish soup, 'at least, it would be half as amusing to me; and I hope it would be to her, also. Ah, Missy, your egg salad is exceptional, do you know that? I think I'll start next wi'—'

More than a week later, no thanks to da gunk-splatterin' Pink Ghoast, Humphrey got all the attention he'd been craving for. Humphrey had hidden the critter inside his backpack until he deemed it was the right moment fer it to come out; and, that was, when there was no other patron else in da shop . . .

'Yuck, what's dis? Salad ears or veggies on da cob,' Missy had laughed, maudlinly, with a certain cold directness when she saw the blob trying to come out, and from being entangled in Humphrey's big hands. 'Wot noise a-comin' from—? What's it a-doin'?'

'Oh, niver mind it: it's jus a sorry liddle, hairy ghoast,' said Humphrey tartly, all over his egg-tarts.

'If that's true, on your honor as a proper Western gentleman, what kinda ghoast is it?'

'Ah,' intoned Humphrey mysteriously and smiling happily; 'The Labrador—Tory kind! Ye see, I made 'im mysel' in the lab. And now he is my pet, my pet ghaist, you know? although he can be sorta destructive at times!'

'He looks skittish, at the same time, shy . . .'

'Doan git me wrong, he has got good Ectoplasm heart and pluck inside o' him and he's tender as a freshly braised or fricasseed spring chicken, Missy!'

'I am sure I am glad to meet him,' said the Chinese girl wi' da wonderful hazel eyes, 'as I'm alive: but what are you? Do you make— are you makin' ghosts fer a livin'?

'Have you heard o' da Ghaistsweepers; that's our professional line, we sweep up places clean of ghosts! This one is merely an experimental prototype . . . !'

'Why is he still hiding in yer bag, unsure to come out?'

'That? Oh, ahem, yes! That's bec'os a gam of whale-ghosts are arter 'im and bec'os he tinks 'ee is ole Capt. Ahab,—with the wooden stumpy leg! I had been just readin' da book. 'Ee has a fear of ectoplasmic parmacetti; you know Captainne Ahab,—Missy?'

'I have read Melville. But why does it wanna to come out, now? Does it think 'ee could hide under my skirts?'

'Dem skurts are rather skimpy, you must admit!'

For this, Miss Ho favored Humphrey Humperdinck with a long, withering look. The caprice of her nature being not attuned to the romantic weather of that night, she warned him, suddenly, just as his heart skipped a beat,—'Keep your fingers to yourself, Mister

Salamander!' She just snapped like him like that, thought Humphrey, for no justified reason at all . . .

'Howsabout a look at 'im, reel close? Do ye wanna?' proffered our savant, lamely, nodding towards da Pink Ghoast, which self-assurance, was of modest quality and quantity. He gave his smiling pet a sad wink, but the pink ghoastly creetur was now grinnin' from ear to ear. It was then pretending to be humming and singing to itself: it, the Pink Ghoast was, at the wrung wurl where everybaddy else was a juror. There was an indefinite long pause in which fer Missy to made up her mind.

'With its pink gums and liddle pink teeth and whey-colored eyes it was not too much unlike the 'spitting' image of Humphrey, if you are inclined to take that view: a bloated image of Humphrey like his head blown up like a balloon,' she thought to herself.

'Sure,' said the black-eyed girl, breathin' through her ivories, 'yuck, and double yuck!'

The Pink Ghoast, assured at last, began to rant or mew like a Eyetie bambino, sallying forth, and ducking its head again, with its ears ever cocked, ranting, just like I said, in mispronounced English, or perfect GOBBLEDYGOOK:—and Miss Ho, very amused and half-listening, said:—'I tink it can talk very well! Perfectly, I tink!'

At last, there was the sound of motor wheels, and the door slamming, and the Pink Ghoast hastily turned around and began to jabber when a fellow come in wi' a leisurely gait. It was a suitor of Missy's, and the Pink Ghoast turned a shade livider and screamed out of jealous rage on Humphrey's behalf. The fellow sat at a table in the furthest corner and began to knot his scarf.

'It's saying, "Won't 'ee let Humphrey try a hand at getting a date wi' you—"' said Humphrey helpfully, 'only bec'os you are very pretty, you know'd, an' also getting' on you, a . . . a . . .'

'Getting a—on me, WOT?' screamed the girl and lashed him with her lacerating eyes. 'On me what, buster?'

'Oh, da Chinese Water Torture (CWT), to be sure, lass!' said the savant sweetly, 'ho, ha, you know, puttin' 'ee in a darkened room an' drippin' water on yer 'ead every fifteen minutes or so; or I wonder, should I give da Sixty-four or da Thirty-two Steps Seduction Technique a try . . . ?'

'Bah! Humbug! You're makin' this up; the Pink Ghoast niver suggested this!'

'So that . . . ahem . . . !!' Humphrey went on, ignoring her remarks.

'So that what . . . ? Ahem, what?'

'You may fall head o'er heels in love wi' me! (Boy, I'm beginnin' to sound like Darius Mortimer!)'

In the midst of their exchanges, da Pink Ghoast was gibbering at a rapid rate, and it paused for breath . . . 'Poo! Fall in love wi' you! Get real!' Missy laughed, tossing her head haughtily. 'Doan lit the fellah a-sitting over theer overhear 'ee, that's all. He's my date, tonight.'

'Look, my ghaist wears out his heart on his sleeve, so, you gotta be careful! You might 'urt its feelings, Miss!'

The Pink Ghoast was still all excited and deeply flustered, as though it was trying to explain something to both Humphrey and Miss Ho; its enunciations, coming and coming faster; and it was less hesitant about gluing a lot of b's and g's and d's, in its speech; as if, its insides were about to burst out in a deluge . . .

'I don't have time to talk with you anymore. Other customers have come in,' said Missy, alarmed.

'Are 'ee hungry Ghoste?'

'Can't talk anymore. No fraternizing wi' da customers fer too long: boss's orders!'

The Pink Ghoast said something to Humphrey who said to it, 'You like her pendant earrings? Can't eat that you know, Pink! Explore? better not, my pet! You said you like the laid-back ambiance and the décor? Wait, don't go anywhere, you might upset—'

But Humphrey's pet ghost had dashed off, and it was makin' a squealing noise as though it was a maniac, laughing and crying, at da same time . . . And the savant thought to himself, 'I shouldn't have brought him here. Some tragic mishap is going to happen: I just know it!' There was a loud howl and a terrified yelp, like that of a dog being bitten by another dog, and the blob was having a hair-raising experience of its own, at one corner of the room, where the ancestral altar was. The blob had sniffed da air and didna like the smell of da rice wine and da joss sticks and he was queasy an' afraid, all of a sudden. The Pink Ghoast intimated that it detested da fact that it was about to be pinched black and blue, and it made a face and dragged up the corners of its eyelids! His actions said: 'Chinaman ghoasts! And then he shook his head, as if he had da ague, stuck out his tongue, to be examined by da doctor; and gargled and gargled. 'Twas as if, he was being hemmed in from all quarters, and he was resigned to his fate.

'Calm yerself down, Pink,' said Humphrey soothingly, 'Doan like da immigrants an' da past Chinese cooks? Yes, they are dead: jus like 'ee! Maybee not? We better go now, let's skip the washroom visit.'

And the Pink Ghoast answered, 'Ga, ga, ga . . . bratwurst, i wanna bratwurst, sukiyaki . . . Kikkoman sauce . . .'

'Oh, you silly pink bambino! Let's git outta here!'

But it was too late; as the Pink Ghost, feeling hungry and incensed by the smell all around him, began to leap out o' his fingers in an instant, like a scalded cat being ironed. It began tearing off hap-hazard inside the eatery and then, it got inside the kitchen (which marked Restricted Entrance: no admittance: staff only): and,—what a mess it made there! What shambles! And, then, when it was passing the bewhiskered suitor who'd viewed the commotion with great askance, the Pink Ghoast wiped its forehead with deft horizontal strokes, and upset his soup bowl into the astonished man's face, scoured the bowl with its green tongue; and stomped back to Humphrey, with a triumphant leer and huff. In a towering humor, Missy began scolding the dumbfounded and apologetic savant in her own singeing dialect; while the owner made Humphrey pay for the damage by writing a big check, looking very acrimoniously at him all the time, and he was thrown out by his heels, and was threatened with a lawsuit if he ever made any disturbance there again. Meantime, the suitor had fled into the night. Feeling Missy bristling as he walked past her, he said, 'Sorry! Sorrry! I shoulda know'd better! I was a fool! Sich a bluddy, biddy fool! Sorrry!'

'Idiot, cheese brain!' said the owner, still livid with fiery ire. 'Go! Get your head examined for bringing dat thing in here!'

'Sorry doesn't help,' scolded Miss Ho still pouting, surveying da damaged plates and things.

'Mayn't I see you . . . ?' hinted our savant, hopefully.

'Not in your life!'

'We can still be friends . . . can't we . . . ?'

'Men! What idiots they are! Idiots! Simple fools!' Missy screamed.

'Sorry!'

'Sorry—sorry!,' sneered the owner. 'You are not in the good lady's good books anymore. Don't come back here again.'

'All right!' muttered Humphrey Humperdinck; feeling small as though his guts had folded up inside him; and his vital organs were chucked inside a freezer.

Chapter Five

HUMPHREY HUMPERDINCK'S BUYANIAN NIGHTMARE

The solitary fresh hard-boiled egg was standing in its egg-cup, all alone in da half-dark, trying to prove to the pasty-looking omelet—what a tough, unbreakable exterior it had; as Humphrey Humperdinck looked on, nervously,—balancing his egg-spoon on one knee, wondering whether or when he should pounce. Then, he jumped up from his seat and fumbled for da kitchen's main lights, and continued to stare at his egg longer; for, earlier—at four o'clock in the morning, he had woken up suddenly—and started writing a billet-doux to Missy, but now the unfinished letter lay in the shoe-box, and he had shoved this into the store-room, which was at the bottom of the stairs. Troubled sleep as usual, of course; yielding a cold and lonely dawn, in which he had remained wide awake. He downed his white coffee. The smell of the distant misty stars washed the breeze, and he scratched his bald pate noisily, and trying to preserve a semblance of calm. Closing his eyes, he was hoping the feeling that has given him the heat had cooled off. Was that the end of his love for her? Humphrey buttoned up his heart, tucked underneath his jacket. He decided to eat the egg and spare the omelet. He bit into a peanut brittle which made a crunching sound in his mouth, and finished all the leftover cookies in its packet, to round out his early breakfast. He thought, it was impossible to ask love from Missy Ho, even beg for it; and 'tis like somewhere in the country where because of the wood, the sunlight is seven feet too short and it never reaches the ground, and naturally, there the light bounces off the goldfinch's wing like it niver touches the bird. Missy is now all a fuzzy impression, after the intensity of last night—and I can't bring my love to a sharp focus. Even our conversation seems blurry.—My heart has been inclined, I'm afraid, to too much loud throbbings at the sight o' her, nay doot.'

Humphrey Humperdinck was thinking, why he had taken it on the kisser just like that: bec'os it was not totally his fault: bec'os da Pink Ghoast had delinquent tendencies, at times—it was its mysterious natur'—and anyways, Miss Ho should've "kua pua" herself.—"Kua pua", rather than abuse his ear and, well, had not he paid 'em theer a hefty compensation? As one cartoon character said of another cartoon character in one of da syndicated newspapers, he was "a bee-bee brain'd knucklehead . . ." that's what he was! That 'bout covers it . . . !!!

Nevertheless, that early morning, when Humphrey slept, things concerning the late Bobby Bunyan was not nailed as shut as he thought it to be. In delving deeper into his distress and ocular oddity, he had often touted the darkness that surrounded his soul was like a hand fitting into a glove, and which was very neatly, dovetailed; especially, immediately after the occurrence at Canterville Chase, England. This, he told me, in our next session together, as he ran his fingers along his skull and scratching his eyebrows, as though, da skin of his scalp was tingling.—He was unusually nervous and jumpy and,—as soon as he had settled down in his usual place, he squinted at me, and said: 'I dreamt Bobby Bunyan early yesterday morning.'

However, the expression I read in his face was that he was again making bad eye contact (being in a high state of sympathetic arousal)—for he was re-experiencing his breach of mind. Precisely, he was keen to tell me about it, and yet, I might say, hesitant, to lay it all before me, his psychologist . . .

'Bobby Bunyan fared poorer than you, my friend . . .' I said waggishly, 'But he deserved what he got in his life, and arter he was dead: bec'os he was a worthless dude; that plain and simple! Nevertheless,—what? dreamt of him? Please disclose it, my dear Humphrey . . .'

'The dream, Professor?' he looked at me wanly.

'Yes, well—that is what I mean: of course!' said I, Professor John Wyndham Tanischi.

'I dreamt . . . I was takin' a ride on the subway, going where I doan know, and, suddenly, a tall man with a trench in his arm and fedora came and sat beside me . . . at first, I wasn't paying him no attention, and it seemed somewhere below da darty streets o' Haarlem; towards da UNKNOWN an' DANGER! Everywhere I looked I saw ferret-like faces, and pockmarked skin, and smelled the smell of gunk, stale beer, and cheap cologne, and eyes that glinted like steely cables, with eye-movements, deliberate and incurious . . . an old man was trimming his sourish cuticle, and then, da first man that just came in at the last stop asked someone for a match to light up . . . He turned his face up in my direction—and I saw it was Bobby! Well, not exactly, but his face was a close resemblance to Bobby's—as near as near could be! There were many fly-spots on that beat-up face; and it looked like a cockroach-nibbled muddy, unpeeled potato! Bobby said, 'Man, you have no soul . . . I might have hied wi' me tail between me legs to da debbil, but, man, 'ee have no soul!' This gave me a great shock . . . To add to my consternation, he jabbed one finger at my nose, his perfidious laugh, ringing out, from dat same ugly mouth that I'd hear, even when I had awoken up . . . and Bobby Bunyan, or his double, continued, 'I wager you will niver figure it out; what's wrong with you! From now on, you'll niver amount to anything, you'll become a filthy hobo and keep nuffin' but a filthy tee-shirt on yer back, unlucky fer you, ho, ho, har—!'

'What happens after that?'

'The few moments after I woke up, I reminded myself that this is again supreme and conclusive proof that I am a good guy; bec'os the bad 'uns out in da universe keep on houndin' me relentlessly; and, niver let me git by, in peace! My brains felt like a pincushion; and, I thought again of the day the bottom o' my life fell out and left me prostrated!' But, I told myself, I was not going to stay down, bec'os God is wi' me . . . ! I thought:—ever since that fateful evening:—I had been unsure who Doctor Humphrey Humperdinck is. Something inside my head is not quite right somehow and it doesn't get better. My childhood was niver secure, you know, Professor John, and after that, things are a lot of bleaker in my relationships wi' my dearest and nearest, Mom and Dad . . .'

'How about your colleagues and partners?' I wanted to know.

'To them, their investment in me just went bust, and I could hardly recognize myself as Doctor Humphrey Humperdinck! Tell me, Professor, how did thing come to fall out this way! Tell me!'

'Going back to the moment of possession, were there any physical sensations?'

'I fell that my Adam's apple was being squeezed outta shape, and a warm, sweat drenched blanket thrown or cast over muh mind or brains! Sumptin smothering had gone in inside and was doubtless stirrin'.

'Anything else?'

'My thoughts were bewildered, as if something was trying to access the rolodex of my experiences to use 'em against me; at the same time, each time, to up the ante, and tryin' to gauge my reaction to the effects o' it or they were producin', against me . . . Also, a cloggy sensation as though a swarm o' bees were buzzin' about my temples, ready to plunge their syringes in, and there were blood and foam in a mix from my mouth. I was scared to death as you might think, and I thought it was too much, I couldn't stand anymore, when Mrs. Umney, my housekeeper, discovered me. She said, 'Oh, oh, oh, da eldritch hae git da Maister!' just as I was feeling many malevolent presences were havin' a rumpus above my head. I was in a state, paralyzed, and I couldn't snap outta it; and I couldn't snap outta it, ever since. It started with a heavy sensation at the back of my parched throat, as if sumptin' coiled had settled down theer; an extremely unpleasant feelin'; but at first, being somehow detached from da bad experience, it felt like it belonged to somebody else . . .'

'Tell me, what do they look like?'

'What?'

'Those very things you see.'

'They look like—a bit like trolls, really,—all eyes, and mouth and nose, in fact they're ugly as sin, that is, very ugly; and they'd be staring at me witheringly, as if there is nothing 'soever wrong with them, and everything is wrong with me.'

'Indeed.'

'That is the truth.'

'Are they real or not? What do you think?'

'I know they are shapes just as before, but they are inside my head; something's happened to my brain I'm afraid, and the o'erwhelmin' nausea is projected outwards.'

'Pseudo-hallucination, I believe,' I quipped, thoughtfully; bringing the tips of my fingers together.

I looked at Humphrey squarely and enunciated carefully: 'You have received a great, jarring shock, Humphrey! But you are not Humpty Dumpty, which all the king's horses and all the king's men couldn't put together again. You have da King of kings on yer side, I mean; and HE WILL HELP YOU.'

'But I am feelin' like Humpty Dumpty, now . . . . an' out of curiosity I seem to tink, dat . . .'

'Cut it out!' I ordered sharply. 'Such a confession lends an air of spineless, insidious and scurrilous comfort, albeit a false one, of depressing resignation. Hist, I will not allow it . . . !'

'But,' Humphrey protested, 'Bobby Bunyan said I have no soul.'

'Pooh! Bobby Bunyan! You seem to be besotted with Bobby Bunyan! Fiddlesticks, 'twas only a dream although it might be a slightly singular one! Your subconscious seems to see what is buried deep and to hint to you something by putting this enigmatic sentence in the mouth of a very dead man . . . You might think you are out of your depths concerning Bobby, but you are in the midst of life you are in, yet you are doing things for the sake of going through the motions, and you feel a vague urgency to move on, but can't . . . You are very worn down!'

'Yes, like a hand-me-down, I do feel, and jaded, of course, as you know! A poisonous inevitability eats at everthin', and there seems nuffin' theer but death and decay and apathy!'

'What are you mostly thinking about now? What doth preoccupy your thoughts most recently, Humphrey?'

'Sometimes, I think it was worth it; that, because of what I did, some great evil that was about to befall the wurl had been averted for a time. At other times, I think I was but a demmed fool! But when I am in my excited state, then—it's like flyin' a bit high, isna, it—?' he hinted.

I did not say anything—not a single word—and looked thoughtfully out the window,

'Then I mustn't—I shouldn't???' he started, on da same vein again, more eagerly, this time.

'I didn't say that, either, Humphrey. Not yet, and I need to know more; I must delve deeper. As a Catholic Psychologist, I shall say, a person is supposed to be responsible for his soul and keep his conscience in proper order. Examine you and your own motivations, Humphrey, and me, as your psychologist, am here to help you understand what happened, and why it happened, yea, happened to no one else, but to Doctor Humphrey Humperdinck. But do you still have these terrible visions?'

'Most o' 'em has sloughed off but at da fringe of my conscious mind, there is sumptin' theer still waiting to impinge on my mind. Due to da regiment o' drugs, my level of anxiety has tapered off, a little though . . .' said he.

'Are these things unpredictable and may surface at any time?'

'Yes. My relationship with da wurl had changed dramatically to the bad, and when I bit the dust, something died inside me, so that something might be reborn, perhaps, eh? And I had been trying to find mysel' in tryin' to shake off this demmable psychic enchantment.'

'What do you think it occurred to you? Why do you think you ought to be Christ-like or God-like? And how do you feel about it?'

'I dunno; I guess it's because I needed to be important.'

'Okay, Doctor Humperdinck . . . okay! The hour is up. Your next appointment will be Thursday, the 3rd April . . .' I was staring down at him kindly now, and said, 'You are on the mend. Good man. We will pick up where we've left off next time.' In addition, I was thinking, he had lost the close-knit unity of his personhood and what he needed was to re-experience life in abundance once again,—with the graced help of God;—the which, God and Humphrey, are not the same being. As he was the last appointee that evening, I switched off my desk-lamp, sat for a few moments to recollect my thoughts, reflecting, 'I should look for a roomier office space when I built a bigger practice next time. But right now, I think I'll order a new couch and a few other choice things and smart fittings; some little refurbishment may be just what my rococo office requires right now— in terms of sprucin' up its interiors.'

Chapter Six

WAS THE GUMSHOE, BOBBY, RIGHT?

'Yes, mastic-shoe, gumshoe, you know, P.I.?' said Humphrey, helpfully, during one of our sessions.

'Yes, gumshoe, detective, Bobby B., of course,' said I, 'an', what was he right about?'

'Only, without a soul to myself, I am really, really lost, really.'

'That's a lot of "reallys",' said I. 'You have been thinkin' about your ocular oddity, your special declension, which up till now is dogging you, really, eh?'

'Now! That's, another "really", Professor Tanischi,' said Humphrey, who could not help smiling (feebly). 'And as you had been always getting me to understand, if you tackle the real reasons, you tackle the causes!'

'Yes, at the bottom of da symptoms are da root-causes . . .'

'Then, you have told me also, the symptoms are indications o' sumptin' wrong within my subconscious . . . yes, I have lost my self-confidence! However, I need to get the tings inside me out! Git 'em outta o' me in little pieces, or chock-a-block, it does not matter which! In a word, you gotta find out, what makes me tick, but, maybee, leave the little things unmolested! I see a LIFE out theer I can't git at, and—'

'Now, does it translate badly; to be without a soul at all, Humphrey? Since you had liked that idea . . .'

'I hate it like the GHOULS I purge for other people: uncomfortable, detached, feelin' almost nuffin'—numb, alone, defenseless, dead . . .'

'Why does it make you uncomfortable: explain dat first and everythin' else you enumerated.'

'I often catch my mind wondering, lost for a space; and then, detached: I lack coherence and unity (I know, you said, I looked okay, but . . .)—numb means being in a fainéant state of mind or mood, or mode. Alone, means I feel burningly lonely; defenseless: I can't cope well (as I used to with life) and finally, dead, and that is like being sucked into a twilight world where the unredeemed dead ends up.'

'Yes, go on . . .'

'Although I do not want to be somebaddy else, sometimes I just hate my life: vehemently! I doan believe I deserve anything from life most bad days; and at the mercy of muh own self-doubt and acute torment,—which medicines do little to alleviate: my psychic symptoms are jus awful right now. I know I am being morbidly self-absorbed . . . but could I sink lower n' that? You must tell me, 'cos I have to know; else everything would make me more wary 'n more afraid. I have a right to know!'

'D' you think it's the product of some kind of hallucination, Humphrey?'

'It's unlike any hallucination I ever read about; it certainly is odd.'

'Isn't that what most people would term morbid?'

'I suppose they would,' said Humphrey; 'Especially, if it's fuelled by fear and maintained at a high level of anxiety, which is still trapped inside that person. What must I do, Professor Tanischi?'

'In some cases Schizophrenics are known to have suchlike and bizarre symptoms, an' there are distortions or accentuations in their vision; and you have been diagnosed to have such. A certain percentage, though, not high, do eventually recover to live relatively normal lives or recover completely, and I shall help you—though without guarantees—to tackle the root causes of your problem. Perhaps, we can firstly, help you, to address your symptoms. Yet, it might not be schizophrenia at all; for, I wonder if it couldn't be . . . couldn't be . . .'

'Can you tell me the . . . your prognosis.'

'For the time being, forget about the prognosis. You are already making great progress, an' leagues ahead of many of my other clients.

Keep your chin up, though it must be very frustrating . . . is there anywhere you'd like to do, friends you would like to see? Spend some time with people who are close to you . . . Be good to yourself, love yourself. How about going to your Uncle's in a place outside Philly? I see you nod your head, enthusiastically. Good, go and visit 'em! Like I said, Humphrey, keep your chin up. They are discreet people, aren't they; an' stay there for a fortnight and then, enlivened by da fresh change of sight an' air, come back and see me on the 15th.

'Yeah!' said Humphrey slowly, sucking in his breath and expelling it. 'Yes, I was just thinkin' to see them. Rather!'

'Good, good. That's da spirit! May I wish you, Godspeed, and all the best be yours! Time spent with people you are emotionally close to, letting 'em befriend you in your pain, an' deep loss, you will find your wounds will heal of themselves, of themselves . . . ! God and time does the real healin' but it's the physicians and the psychiatrists who get the credit and da checks (by the way, doan forget to crossed mine, eh?)—you know? Give yourself time, don't get worked up; and then, find, you will not find yourself in tatters an' ready to fall into pieces all o'er again. You'll take my advice, won't you?'

'Yes, certainly, doctor, I mean, Professor John. Definitely! I can't wait to sink my teeth into my Aunt's Baked Alaska, spare ribs, smashin' Cajun recipes with gumbos and oysters and sirloin steaks with peas and black pepper sauce again! Seeing Abel again would be such a wonderful treat, and better n' all the food theer! Muh reel roots are there; to be back theer again will allow my Psyche to solder back da unhing'd part o' muh Ego.'

'The choice is, of course, when to bide your time, as you have chosen the place! The time to heal . . . healing will come when you are ready for it . . . grace is not inimical but conducive to it. I have no doubt about it; and so be hospitable to yourself; forgive yourself and others! Do not hate Bobby Bunyan! Lean on a greater power, trust in a good God, and don't chide against the bit! We are mortals with narrow margins and limits! Learn about takin' some spiritual direction; but don't be one-sidedly religious! Admit, you need to change something in you by deciding to make the change! Pray even, if it helps! Nevertheless, keep in perspective your problems. As I have said before, though you have been more than a bit audacious,—and have to pay da price, I suppose: like yourself, love your neighbor as yourself! Remember these exhortations and keep a positive mindset. You are already on the rebound; more than you can ever suspect, but remember your medications . . . yes, you can get up now. Your session is over today, my assistant will jot down the next date, and good-bye . . . take care! If while, in Philly, you need to call me, you know my number. Don't hesitate to call me anytime, night or day, both at my office, and at home. Cheerio, then, Humphrey! Bon voyage!'

The savant left my office, full of muh thoughtful advice, all slowly permeating his mind; two days later, all the travel arrangements had been made . . . and when he came back again more than two weeks later for the next appointment, the first thing he said was, 'Having implicit faith in your words, Professor I was really glad I had gone down to see my delectable cousins again!'

'Listening to the happy talk of a happy family, which really lifts up your spirits, eh?'

'I enjoyed myself very much during this trip,' he said . . . 'I had send my luggage ahead, deciding in advance, to get Abel and Sally and Little Jim a couple of silver-black Angelfishes.' These fishes, you see, was his special delight when he was a little boy, and getting Abel and his sister a couple offered an excellent excuse to return to his old haunts which still loomed large in his memory, after all these years. Yet, there was some disconnectedness in these memories too, which always seem'd to be so seamless. He thought of going to Bradenberg Hills to see the sights, and to see if a shop called The Bearded Carp was still open for business, after thirty long years . . . Its owner was Ballymoney Georg, who told stories of mining towns in Quebec and about bootleggers in Chicago, he, whose shop, was a regular hangout for Humphrey and his schoolfellows. They would save on their lunch money, and buy fishes from Mister Ballymoney. In addition, Humphrey reminisced about some of his old "friends". And, he thought whether he could put back his brain's axle, which had dropped off. The memory he conjured up was mostly pleasant, despite his Old Man, and that one-time savage an' needless canning, which was most humiliating, and the two or three occasions he was scared clear outta his mind, which, even his Mother, not in the least, a touchy-feely person, knew nuffin' about: she, being the person he cared most for in the wurl but, which he didna care to let her know. He knew, as a scientist, that babe mice ignored by their mother would display abnormal and disturbed behavior due to the deficit, and their thought patterns would be different from normal an' healthy mice: How he wished he was a healthy and normal mouse! Was he always turned off an' rather reclusive an' lacking self-confidence in social situations bec'os of some personality problem? Did what occurred in Canterville Chase, the inevitable result, thereof: a rubbing o' salt in his wounds, which had been festerin' since childhood? Was he nurtured da wrong way? So that—the dissatisfaction, the fear and anxieties, secret wishes and irrational hopeful dreams a part of him now that cannot be changed for the better? Of course, being a quiet person, he seldom shared his private thoughts with other people. With Ronnie, Stanislaus and Darius what he did was to unlock their technical expertise just as he let them into his sheerly scientific and innovative mind;—yes, they were his fine buddies. It was all steely, hard work, which calls for a strong pump, but, as he said, that was part o' da fun:—but they knew nothing of the emptiness deep inside that was haunting him.

When he was gazing up at the sign of The Bearded Carp it was not the sign of the "bearded carp" any longer but The Sign of the Bearded Gentleman. The paintwork was peeling, and there were a heap o' rusty pots and pans out in front, bestrewed like some brewer's yard; waiting to be wheel-barrowed away. All the auld brass was gone; no friendly mouser or two, nor rocking chairs, in the corner; and the air of the people living an' working here was definitely different. No homely smell of peppermint and sawdust. He thought again: 'His parents did protect him when he was young. But, they had not consoled him when he needed consolation. His Mother always had a bad mouth, and he had suffered many a rebuff and rejection from her, although she never called him sissy. His Father never saw him as separate from his brothers and sisters; never acknowledged he had his own emotional needs. As he was going through Philly, he thought he might see his Mother also and be in her slipstream for a while. Why

did his Father neglect him all these years? It was a cipher to him . . .
When he was still a little child, when his Father was a little late from
work, he would get all worked up; and he thought, God, because his
Father was bad, He was going to involve him in a car accident . . . and
he would pray that his Father be spared . . . the workings of a fervid
child's imagination, and if his father did die, it would, no doubt, be
his fault, bec'os he didn't pray hard enough fer him . . . He was now
inside the shop, which felt, cool and agreeable. He bought his fishes
for Abel and for Sally, biggish ones! Something stirred vaguely in
built-up anticipation as he sat at the taxi's backseat, and journeyed
across the city . . . He was always conscious of da other (anxiety-
riddled) part o' him, but, well, he would forget that! How could Mr.
Humperdinck Senior and his Mother be God's gift to him?—he
thought. He could never understand that. Wasn't it better, if he had
never been born or wish, like Job—that? Perhaps, his story might still
have a happy ending, who knows? Doctor Humphrey Humperdinck
had always had a facility: the ability to use words: and, as words were
oft tools for a rigorous self-examination, he was keeping a diary of
sorts. It was a jubilant and festive welcome at his Uncle's door—for
Humphrey! His Auntie May's face, all shining, bid him with bright
eyes and laughing voice to come in, and they saluted him with tears
in their eyes and a warm, hearty handshake. A little Springbok was
little Abel, capering about, when he saw those fishes, and he hugged
him and both grinned like delirious apes. 'Let's have some ice-cream!
Fetch out da Haagen-Dazs for da children and Humphrey,' said his
Aunt May.

'Yes, yes,' shouted half a dozen voices: spirited, pleasurable outcries
of, 'Yes, oh, yes!'

'All right,' said Uncle Ben. 'Humphrey, keep your sweets and
basket for the children for the morrow.'

Afterwards, when they were all eating ice-cream, his Aunt May
said, 'How are you now, Humphrey? Being da best person to judge,
if you wish to keep to yourself what's bothering' you, that's fine, also.
You know, Ben and I only want what is best fer 'ee! You know that . . .
you did say, about two weeks? Well, room an' board you shall have an'

da very best o' your Aunt May's cookin' and that's a solemn promise, my dear.'

'Looky, Cousin Humphrey's eyes are big wi' tears!'

And, he began, chasing the younger girls, three, four and six year olds, pretending to be a roaring lion wantin' to eat their Haagen. 'Those are MINE HAAGEN-DAZS!' their richly-fraught-with-delight voices exclaimed, 'No, no, no: BIGG slobberin' LYONESS, no!'

'But I want to eat yours,' the mischievous Humphrey persisted, 'but I shall give you fair advantage first, liddle ladies . . . !'

'Else, what?'

'Else . . . I'm gonna eat you!' and so, they played and romped and he pampered them with kindness. For a while, Humphrey seemed to have charmed himself with da delight and happiness that surrounded him, and he was almost his old self again. They played again, until it was time for the older children's studies, and Humphrey helped them with Add Math, Economics and American History. The children's bedtime saw the household settle down for a bit, after da earlier excitement of the late afternoon, and he borrowed his uncle's Apple computer and began to type up his personal reflections into it and recompressing his experiences, and read over his notes; busily engaged upon cerebral activity. His Aunt May bought him cookies and nuts, and then, casually, his Aunt May gave him a kiss on the head—the first time she ever did so, for a long time—before she left. She said, 'It's a shame, but don't worry dear. Ben and I, will take care of you here. You shall find an Indian lobster in your plate tomorrow. I thought you would just like to know.'

'Hurray. Good night, sleep tight, Auntie Maylie.'

'God bless; and see you in the morning. Have a good night's rest. Don't overstrain your nerves.'

'Yes, dear Auntie.'

Then come Sunday, and Humphrey and the family went to Uncle Ben's local Baptist church. They heard the preacher preached his text from the pulpit and then Humphrey walked all by himself to another church, a Catholic one. He put his hand on his breast and sauntered in, but not afraid, to be noticed. He was remembering that Helen

Rolland was a Catholic, and since he had only once been inside a Catholic church, he was shy. 'I wonder if He knows about Spaghetti: not Doctor Humphrey Humperdinck, but the little boy! Hi, Jesus, it's little Spaghetti have come here and sit with you!' And he thought, about his oddity, how much of it is self-induced and self-inflicted? 'For if I anticipate a breach, it's bound to occur sooner or later, without fail!' From experience, he knew, the repugnant thing would be the result of a little physic upset, a little increased tension or worry, of being discomfited: even a lull regarding his more or less even mood. He knew seeing da faces were easy, being triggered somehow by his anxious mind, but, to deny them, to forget them, was hard. 'I am Spaghettii, I am Spaghettii, little Spaghettii,' he would say, hoping for an infilling o' himself, and he stayed for Mass and day-dreamt of Miss Helen; until a quaint, kindly peace stole o'er him, coming forth, from some great ranging distance until his heart was stirred up a little to the wonder of—

Chapter Seven

MY RECORD-KEEPING OF EGON'S CASE, WHICH IS THEN EXPANDED

I had a long talk with Darius and Stanislaus, and it was on the second occasion I observed to them what I suspected for some time already;—that Humphrey might have been misdiagnosed. It was clearly a thought, emotion and perception disorder, but I do not think it was schizophrenia. What it might be some mental ailment akin to Charles Bonnett Syndrome, and Humphrey was seeing things because of a trauma in his pre gyrus and due to high levels of fearful excitation:—but I did not break the news to my client yet—and he had not asked me about it, also. Charles Bonnett Syndrome it was said, was quite common in the elderly whose faculties were defective or impaired; but it was seldom properly diagnosed, and even rarer reported. We had decided to break the news to Humphrey when I was surer, but first, I wanted to know more about his condition and how he wound up with the Syndrome at his age, if it were that—

These entries are based on clinical observation, which is paramount. They are recorded down in shorthand and later written out, also, from memory (as I had a keen interest in his case):

Oct 21. Complained of acute disorientation, lack of appetites and insomnia, which he found hard to articulate, but nevertheless very real to him. Suddenly, he threw his eye out my window and told me briefly he was ready to get back on his feet. Said he wished he could only say what was on his mind. Instruct him before his next appointment, to go for a general check-up.

Nov 2. I believed I have projected enough candor and professionalism and there was enough trust and sincerity on both sides to go on. Mentioned having trouble sleeping. Said he was already on tranquilizers. Physically healthy, had not contracted any serious disease.

Nov 16. Not very forthcoming. Asked to see me in the evening session: the reason he gave, not a morning person.

Dec 1. Thought that the cause of his oddity pathological, and he mentioned God.

Dec 15. Was angry, because he thought I was wasting his time and not being sympathetic enough.

Jan 5. Progress not very forthcoming. I sensed deep grief and shame inside him, very evasive . . . he said he was a little disappointed in me since I came so highly recommended, but I told him, if he chose to be disappointed, that was his prerogative an' his responsibility.

Jan 19. He said, "He is a hard taskmaster!' And he meant God. He'd like to settle accounts with Him, too.

Feb 5. Mood better. His former nurse, a Miss Rolland, called him up over the phone and they talked about old times for five minutes. Out of the blue, he said he loved his Old Man; I see the developmental tasks ahead for him. Something seemed to be emerging from the psychosocial situation.

Feb 12. I had to be very empathetic. We just talked (about meditation, aromatherapy and alternative medicine) and books that might help. Said he was actively shopping for the right cure for himself. Said he liked T.S. Eliot's poetry, and some of Graham Greene's thematic propositions . . . went down to Martha's Vineyard with his ghostsweeping meter with the others just da other day, to check out a sunken submarine . . . His dry heaviness was watered down by sporadic and sudden thoughts that consoled his nettled soul sometimes.

Mar 2. Deeply resented Mr. Mortimer's attempt at preventing him from seeing Miss Helen Rolland. Darius later apologized to him, saying, with sentimentality like weak tea, 'I'm sorry Humphrey, but I still want us to work together.' I talked with Miss Rolland over the phone and she confided in me certain things only both of us know about and which she felt foolish to mention. I said nothing about this to Humphrey or Darius. Except, 'Development does not grow as a necessity or inevitably, but via an inner decision to grow, or else it might never occur.'

Mar 15. Missed appointment. Having refused to comply taking his medication, he was drinking. He was back home and avoided people during services. He was strange and wild-eyed. As though, living in a fantasy world. Was he, at that time looking for mature independence and spiritual autonomy, for the sake of an exclusive and deeper relationship; to wit, Helen Rolland? The same woman had told me: Humphrey told her, 'He needed her to want him: he cathects her . . .'

That is some of my record-keeping. In addition, I must admit, when we are vis-à-vis, I thought it was going to be a prolonged state of mental prostration. But neither I nor the clinical specialist can have the absolute last word. God alone judges a person's heart, and my attitude is, to let Him speak. All we have to do is to hear: HEAR WHAT HE SAYS! I had seen the savant in England, in Allenby Psychiatric Hospital, and at first, my interest was that of a mere consultant psychologist. But when I moved to America, and we crossed path again, I was finally glad to take his case on. During that while before I saw him again after a lapse of nine and a half months, I had gotten married as a man of fifty-two who was beginning life anew. I had noted his body language then, with his still very workman-like habits being evident; which bespoke qualities of a first rate operate! However, all throughout our initial work together, I could not give him a clean bill of health, that he was perfectly stable, but, not completely cured, until some four years later. On June 12, the first year I worked with him, I joined them for a little informal chat downstairs in a little place called Gustavo's Liquor and Coffee. 'I think I'll cool my heels here,' said Humphrey, as he sidled into a chair by my elbow, and began flipping through a Life of Soren Kierkegaard. He smiled testily at us. I purposely allowed for da rudeness, because it would afford him da opportunity to reflect, we wanted to be kind to him. 'You should read Tillich,' Stanislaus said, but Humphrey only shook his head. Then Stanislaus said, 'Well, Professor, Humphrey— how is our Humphrey' 'Oh, that was it, was it?' our savant glared at us both. 'Have your bottle of flavored mineral water,' said Roper.

'Come, come, we are only trying to be friendly,' said Darius Mortimer. 'Coffee—black—two sugars!' 'What are you doing, Humphrey? You seem to be catching at your thoughts,' I said. 'You shall need pen and paper fer that, silly! But, may I know Professor Tanischi, are people constantly whispering about me?—I feel like an open-book and they all know my insides and capitalize on my deepest shame an' fear!— Sore an' sick an' discontented is muh own heart!'

'We are only trying to cheer you up a bit,' said Ronnie, rubbing his broad jaw.

'Persecutory voices, eh, bah humbug!' snorted Darius Mortimer, bring down his fist.

'My old man—he—niver showed his love to me, you know? He always turned me down.'

'But you are grown into an adult a long time agone, isn't that so, and how do you feel, now, anyway?'

'The same #@%! Meantime, I just have to grin and bear it, eh, Professor John Tanischi, maybe, till somebody will stand by me to da end of muh days . . . But, I still have my usual bunch o' friends: you all! We don't click as we used to, that's all, and, we have been far, far apart.'

'Do you want to borrow some o' my books?' I asked him, helpfully.

'What have you got? Freud and Jung, perhaps, and maybe, Winnicott?' Humphrey had sounded rather bored.

'Yes, and people like Kohut, Chessick, Schafter, MacIntyre, Spence, Browning and Messiner. And, oh, incidentally, Paul Tillich . . .'

'No! Another time, Professor Tanischi. Thank you.'

We downed our drinks and let Humphrey read while the light began to fade outside. Meantime, I will sketch for you the other members of the team; first, Ronnie;—Ronnie Roper had an abundance of confidence in Humphrey's ability to bounce back, thinking his leader as the most tenacious of men. Very romantic turn! Second, Darius.—His primum modium as a team-player was its potential to turn a fast buck; a promulgator of the American Dream concept, he was infuriated by what happened by Humphrey's own hand. Agnostic, irreverent, infantile; a product of da modern culture. Stanislaus, the third member, was also another smooth-talker. He had an easy and careless charm but is at least as intellectual as Humphrey. Niver been to church except for marriages, christenings and funerals! Prefers not to drag up awkward questions or face 'em; these being what he preferred to ignore. Mortgages, bills, the children's education is what spurred him; and if the others will back him, he isn't afraid to take on the most dangerous of jobs, like fumigating an entire building o' ghoasts. Best hand the agency ever had, they all say . . . 'I would offer you, Professor Tanischi a glass of moselle if Egon is not on medication,' he says with a wink. 'Humphrey can have a cup of hot chocolate to help him sleep well—you don't mind that, do you, Doctor Humperdinck?'

'Well,' said I, 'he is getting along fine and coping better n' ever. I'm sure he doesn't mind.'

And then Darius butted in: 'The only thing he doesn't sleep properly and sometimes wakes up drenched in cold sweat, which is a token of evil, but—'

'I would like moselle, too,' the savant suddenly replied, bec'os I'm not on medication anymore since three days ago.'

'When did you take yourself off your medication? What da hell d' ye think 'ee are doin'?' screamed Darius. 'Professor, tell him to have his kiwi fruit juice, lotsa ices in fact, or iced lemon tea and tell him to git on his medication back fast!'

'In that case: we shan't have any drinks,' I chirruped,—diplomatically.

'Oh, yes, we are,' grumbled Humphrey, stubbornly.

'No, we are not. Waiter, make it, iced lemon teas, all round,' said Stanislaus smoothly.

'Why did you take them off, Humphrey?' I ventured . . .

As he was sipping his drink, he glanced around him at the other patrons, and the grilled windows and a flash of anger registered in his face. 'Ah, why?' They're not working! Doctor Humphrey Humperdinck suddenly cried, and thumped his knee. 'My beastly psychic solecism, doncha see? I needs must face that awful demmed mob that molested my soul, and violated my mind! Face 'em without the aid of chemicals, if I can!! That is da way, I'd rather face them!'

'Why is that? Tell us?' I said.

'To find out how far I could control 'em and drive 'em far back.'

'Sounds like crap and bravado to me,' said Darius Mortimer. 'Looky, Humphrey, you'd better do what your doctors ask you to do and strictly follow their instructions.'

'I will, Mortimer, if you are able to convince me! Come to think of it, all these psychotherapy stuff and doctor's orders are a rip-off on someone else's misery.'

'Hold on, theer, Humphrey, I tink you are being insultin' to da Professor, here,' said Ronnie, a liddle browbeat.

'I doan care!'

'Don't you think, chemicals are legitimate ways to fight against sickness, and pain in a person's soul. Medicines, if prescribed conscientiously, are a great help . . . there is no shame, Humphrey, in taking medicines for your psychic ills. You don't have to be squeamish or afraid; you should consider the etiology of the illness and find a cure for it, you,—being an eminent professional scientist, yourself.— You know that yourself!' Stanislaus roundly told him.

'I doan care!'

'Git all da helps you can git, methodology aside, suh!' proffered the black man, Roper, crestfallenly.

'Just as I don't want to be in that dark place you are in, don't you think that, without the medicines, things are goin' to be darker? You need some little alleviation, to mollify the harshness of your condition . . . and without those medication, you simply aren't going to get better wi' time! Don't I make sense? We, all of us, are trying to open doors for you, help you exercise your options and you've got to work with whatever you've got! Do you understand, Humphrey? You said your medication is not working; come, come, calm down, have a little water. Give it another chance or two, won't you? Medications are not magic; over time medication with psychotherapy, it has been consistently proven, or at least, there is consensus among us professionals—work best.'

'Though, I think I have a better chance my own way, very well; I will do it; resume my medication!'

'Promise me, you will not try that stunt again. When the time comes, I will ask 'em to reduce the dosage. Tired?' I said.

'Drowned tired, to tell the truth. Weary. Exhausted. Round and round, a blackish rigmarole!'

'What, Humphrey, suh, you are always remindin' us: no follow-through?'

'From what I can see it's nuffin' but a raw case of nerves . . . !!'

'No! It's the knitting of my soul has come loose and I'm now at sea. Whatever might happen, I am not the same sane person I was . . . and though I wish I can undo my past, I cannot.'

'You see, Ronnie, some horrible darkness had invaded his soul, and he has to come to terms with himself, bec'os, Doctor Kelly and Doctor Quentin Sparstow, the clinician I recommended, told me—' I began.

'A pretty pickle I am in now! He's a pious hypocrite! Now, a great parietal darkness had sucked in my eyeballs, a horrid shadow had fallen over my great albino dolichocephalic skull, and—'

'Enough! But what did the clinician say?' I muttered, wiping my glasses, for it was a hot an' sultry night.

'He said, "A person's actions speaks louder than his words, and his character an' core personality speaks louder than his actions".'

'Nothing the matter with that.'

Suddenly, he turned to Darius and addressing him in his deep bass voice, he said, 'Did you get the readings of the Vainly Apartments?—Sixteen clicks in the Zent-van Buren Numeric Scale, is it?'

Tossing him a crumpled notepaper, his colleague said, 'Yup, I double checked! Righto!'

'Yes, I forgot to tell you, Professor. We have to git back to work. We have to sanitize the whole o' da basement floor, too!' said Humphrey.

'Thanks fer seein' us. But we have to go, and make up for our lost time. As they say, you know, in for a penny, in for a pound . . .' muttered Stanislaus Mortimer; and they all rose to go.

June 25. Humphrey started to open up, to the tune of Engelbert Humperdinck's Three Little Words, as tentatively, he confided in me, his disappointment in not being able to pull his own weight as he has always done. Said the impression of the memory of his breakdown was still fresh in his mind, and started telling me in some detail . . . I told him, 'That is what hinders your normal functioning and mental processes. Your faculties are paralyzed and the fear of the inability to cope successfully with your psychic situation, of course, renders it worse . . . You must not feel you have been victimized by fate! You must own what you did and on your own level of understanding, your own freely willed decision, that night, in Canterville Chase, even if your reasons are too good or too dubious!' Seeing he seemed to concur, I added, 'If you suffer much—you must love much; and therein you shall find the healing you crave for.'

July 7. He related to me of another dream of Bobby Bunyan.

August 4. He had an episode at the office. His features were pinched and his jaw drooped when I spoke gently to him. He was slightly catatonic. Having responded positively to my gentle assurances and the suasion of my caresses he was able to drive back the faces, which were crowding him in he said; and, after a while, I noted his eyeballs were not rolled up. Martha, my assistant, brought him some Perrier. He said, he caught a whiff of her sympathy . . .

August 28. We talked about the nature of evil, how intimate it is to each of us. Both of us talked about sin and its effect. Loss of innocence, grace, stagnation, restoring love, safe relationships and Christ's Redemptive Love. Humphrey observed, we all know what unadulterated evil feels like, but not all of us can recognize its many guises, per se. And I said, 'but we trust in "the good" which truth is sometimes "experiential", but the possessor of it, at least, most of the time, cannot say to himself, he has it; do you concur, Humphrey? Those who say they have goodness by an act of divine election, more than often, do not!'

September 12. Could Humphrey work with parental figures in his life? I asked him. I emphasized the notion of choice . . . the radio was on and this time it was playing, 'When a hero comes along . . .'

September 26. Today, I was all the more unprepared, because I didn't expect after such an accretion of positive built-up of successive waves of healing, he should suffer from such a severe setback. I was on leave, at that time. My wife, Sandy, and I were having a conversation and sitting on high back chairs, and we just had been having pears, mangoes and pomegranates; a beautiful sunny day, that was ending— and it seemed after almost a year and half of blissful marriage, our hearts were still beating as one. Suddenly, the phone rang, Sandy answered it, and she said, 'Yes, he has been pressed a little of late.' I gathered, she meant me, and she frowned, 'Are 'ee sure you want for him to take the call? It's for you, dearest. It's about Humphrey!'

'Who's it?'

'Joanni Selkirk from da Ghaistsweepers Agency!'

'Oh, Joanni, what are ye jabbering about? What's wrong muh dear wooman?'

When the poor woman poured out her heart to me what had happened, in replying to my questioning her as unobtrusively as possible, I understood Doctor Humphrey Humperdinck had lost control of himself; and, for two days, he had been behaving in a very strange way. Fearing the worst, they had been afraid to let me know: and he had stormed off the old library building in a huff; but he had called her from a paid phone booth, possibly, from Kings a few minutes ago . . . I asked her did she think he was capable of doing sumptin dangerous to himself, and Mrs. Selkirk said—no! Make as many phone calls to as many people as possible who knows him, and I'll do the same, I said. She answered, she'll do that. And, she rang off, saying Doctor Humperdinck might call her again. Then, Mrs Selkirk suddenly called again, said, he might be coming to see me at my home. So, I put my entire household on the alert in case he showed up. I told the servants to watch the white shore road, and we waited and waited . . . I was haunted by the vision of a broken man, straitened, and beyond our help, comin' to our gates, and, as the hours crept by; still, however, no Humphrey! 'Yes, it's strange: he hasn't come!' my wife observed fearfully. We have taken to lookin' at anything that moved down the white road and I ordered the lamps quickly lit. Soon a smattering of rain had fallen, and then the evening turned wet, grimy, thunderous, and suddenly, very cold. 'By good Heaven, John, I think it's the presentiment of some impending tragedy,' said my wife, but I shook my head morosely. The night lengthened.—It was near upon midnight. Where could he be? A black rook-like chidden billow was snapping about the gables and I thought of ghoasts a-walkin' again, in the world of living men; but the wurl was a-topsy-turvy now . . . Poor Sandy, seated by the parlor heater, in a brown study, had uttered not a single word, for some time. The storm continued unabated until nearly 3 AM but by then, I must have fallen asleep, for I was gently shaken awake by an Indian servant, saying, 'Someone has come from the road: he is standin' at the gate now.'

'I hope it is our Humphrey,' I said, and went out to the gate, in the crowded dark; for I, too, had been snoring a few minutes in my couch, and had dreamt of zombies—and it seemed, in this particular nightmare—I was both da ghoul and da victim.

Chapter Eight

DOCTOR HUMPHREY
HUMPERDINCK'S TROUBLED PAST

Now, when Doctor Humphrey Humperdinck left in anger out of the old library cum the Ghaistsweepers' Residence, he wished he knew what was being worked out then (sumptin' WAS—but what? The day, being a very windy one, before going a few blocks, he was aware of his acute physical sensations;—for his primal instincts were up. He could taste the asphalt's dust and the ubiquitous smells that hung like a corpse out in da streets. He registered the sky had turned suddenly o'ercast.—Tinsel caught his eyes, and, folding his brash arms tightly across his chest, he hurried on. It was darker now, and out of the sky, leapt a capillary o' lightning, grooving the flaky purple above both sides o' the mass of buildings, and in his present upset and determined mood, his blood pounded.—As Humphrey crossed many a busy street, the pedestrians and the drivers of vehicles seemed to be oddly exaggerated wi' their incurious, almost formal, gestures! As he passed along Black Sambo Street, beside the wells of St. Cyprian, he lamented in this most downcast and excited manner: 'This wurl, what a savage place to be in! Not every eye contact I make is evil, however, and, outside Yuen-Yuen's Little Mermaid, there was a little young girl eating chips and she reminded me of my Sally. It's a head-and-scarf-bobbin' and feet-trampin', well-dressed, fashionable crowd, and my, are the New York cabbies riled and impatient! There is an old lady with sich a face as warms da cockles o' muh heart! But these people are few and far between. Luckless man, it will be your funeral, or otherwise it will be a wedding, in which last case, Humphrey,—you shall be a lucky man.' Humphrey had been mentally alert, but in a haphazard

way, silencing his customary thoughts. The perambulatory motion o'
his arms was fluid and leisurely, niver having once, stubbing his toes,
as if, actin' out a script which blueprint seem'd to have existed before
time:—he was towards da mendin' or da dissolution of his center. He
felt, he was out on a limb and acting out before SOMEBODY WITH
DIVINE ATTRIBUTES—who notes all that you do, and WHOM
you can feel it is HE who JUSTIFIES MAN!—Yet, that is not the
whole picture. (At this, Humphrey, who was telling the story, stopped;
and I asked Sandy to take shorthand notes, and bring her writing
materials . . . Sandy Wilkinson sashayed in and sat down beside us.
'My, my, you are demure, my dear!' said Humphrey, without looking
at her.) After that (Humphrey said), 'I had the singular experience of
not being able to tell which street I was on, and the landmarks, well,
they were like water, sluicing out of my memory. I became more n'
more confused, and dared not approach anybody fer help. Is that what
da script calls for? What grounds was theer for it—sudden amnesia?!!
What did I do then, eh? Grounding my teeth, I was determined
to go on, to wherever da journey will lead me; the sun, being now
hot, and I felt now baking like in a clambake. Next, I heard a bus
screeching as the brakes were being applied. I suddenly just realized
there was a bus stop behind me.—Were the people and the things
and vehicles part of the moveable mise en scene that was revolvin'
around me? However, the best way to make sure or find out, was to
git on the bus, and that was what I did! It seemed that a feelin' o'
unwonted superiority and untrammelled power, surged in my veins at
that moment. I was feelin' in control in my wurl o' strangely unclear
boundaries; but now, the other passengers were formin' my immediate
milieu: hence, from my random choice of action, a pattern was being
formed. Sich queer thoughts! Moreover, the strong blue sunlight seen
were bright through the half-drawn curtains, and, every significant
action I did was accorded with an appropriate reaction, I thought,
and I was in fer da ride . . . ! After he'd punched my ticket, I just
stood near the front of the rectangular-box-shaped bus, as it hauled
off to whither I didna rightly know (its number and its city route, I
couldn't remember); and didn't care, so long as it was somewhere. The
driver who wore a blue cap looked like some kind of ferocious catfish,

and he had oily yellowish-brown skin. He wasn't actually perpetually sneering at anybaddy, but it was a kinda facile simperin', dodderin' smile. He wasn't helpin' it, as, I was drowning in a sea of contradictory impulses and urges. I was lost. Though I had no opportunity for reflection, at da bottommost bottom o' it all there was a rejection of SOMEONE who sees and who cares, a deliberate distortion of da true state of affairs, or a deliberate betrayal, you see? The bus was getting forward at a spanking pace and I could see the sparrows fluttering on the copestones and pavements. I remembered my college days: I felt saddened, because I was seeing familiar and personal things through a stranger's bewildered eyes. Everybaddy's face looks like a conundrum. Something had contaminated my thoughts and after that, they canna be hermetically seal'd up again, I thought! Scrooge and Marley, doth these dread names ring a bell? Marley and Scrooge! That is what I saw, with Scrooge's eyes: Marley's face in da doorknocker! Then, again, there's that other tale by Montague Rhodes James, called Whistle, and I will come over to you my lad!—Read that part about the crumpled linen that affrighted the narrator too much, now, an' you may understand my devastating experience!! My mistake was, if they didn't move, it had sumptin' to do with my visual nerves, or call it, what?—sensory overload . . . !! But, no! But that was not it! I can only tell you da sheer punishment of it, da staggerin' punishment! and what misery! Never forcing myself to see it, but whenever I vaguely sensed it, it's there staring at me in da raw with callous, incurious animosity! Were my brains like Touchstone's or da fool in Lear, or as Shakespeare described a lunatical condition, da fellow's brains—'Half-cooked and all roasted on one side?'

Yes, I had to desensitize certain parts of my noodle by not succumbing to the impulse to panic by those panic-inducing eyes . . . I had missed my regiment for a few days, and I can't give you any reason why I was in a vicious, moribund mood: except some kinda rebellion!! In the bus I was seeing 'em as I do every day, but with a conscious effort and an unsuccessful one, I tried to slide 'em off my duck's back with deliberate nonchalance. It was unsuccessful!—Still, it was a mangled, heightened awareness! In addition, it looked like a severe, high-grade angst. I got myself off the bus, at the end of a very long route, over da other side, beyond Williamsburg Bridge, and it was three o'clock bec'os I happened to look at my wristwatch. With the stretch of water nearby, I could smell the tang of the salt with my keen nostrils. I felt half-alive, after stretching my limbs; but it was suffocating and warm, inside my overcoat. I ambled here and there and bought a ticket for a matinee and sat down, a good show, in da sense, it made me cry like an ape—trice o'er!! The shabby-out-of-da-way movie-house was next-door to a second-hand bookseller's and an Armenian Restaurant. I really believed that the heroine did not, like me, understand or know the value of her life, until it was too late . . . ! She died, of course . . . !! A person is never more herself than at the moment of impending destruction, I thought to myself, sardonically. After that, I was feelin' less sorry fer myself, and less sore with my life. The sun was shining down, like all da jewels of the King of Spain's royal regalia: and I said,—yon Sun, good, honest big sun you set my white skin burning: and suddenly something made me think to look at da sun! But mine eyes! These weren't cauterized—no! For five minutes, I stared but nobaddy came or accosted me. Yes, and I did pray wordlessly. Then floating in the air came Neil Diamond's Sweet Caroline and as I knew some o' da snatches o' it especially "Touching me, touchin' you", I got da goose bumps bec'os o' it! For me, Mr. Diamond has always being a class act and his talented singing swelled my chest. A heady intoxication wafted o'er me! The need to draw closer to someone, to touch somebody's life drew me onwards . . . and how full o' a heavenly sweetness! As I walked down another gray-hued street, I suddenly felt sore hungry. I went to an ATM and withdrew some cash. I got my dinner at a foreign restaurant and tipped da Mexican waiter more generously, I think, than he had ever been tipped in his life. He thanked and saluted to me as his amigo,— profusely. Then, I thought of da poor derelicts o' New York. I shall give until my pockets hurt when I see any o' 'em! A bottled beer, I remembered, tasted niver so fine as that evening; washing down da delicious mussels, lamb chops and followed up by sweet brown tea. In fact, after that, I was in mood for a casual stroll. It was then the gong sounded and Mrs. Wyndham Tanischi said, lunch is ready, Doctor Humphrey, I hope you can resume our informal telling of your experiences at past one . . . Is that okay? Oh, by the way, we are very old-fashioned here . . .' 'Fine,' murmured the savant, Doctor Humphrey, acquiescing gladly and he following her nimble-footed and went into the dining chamber, where the repast was being laid out . . .

Chapter Nine

The Savant's troubled past: (Part 2)

We regrouped at the said rendezvous a while later, wherewith from without, he could hear the decanters and mugs; and foremost Humphrey sauntered in, being invited; picked an' found his spot and without further ado, without da least shiver went through some o' da foregoing narrative; and then he continued:

I was at the scene outside the restaurant, and arrived at last, at little interconnecting streets, on one side of which were some kinda colonnades. That was the margin of some inner city, and there I was, then! Suddenly, out of some office doorway, came a Mother and her child; what seemed like some kinda shabby-lookin' solicitor's office in da corner. Though I was rarely able to feel anythin' fer a stranger's children, as I felt for that child, with it clutchin' at its Mother's bowed shoulder, the pitiful sight wounded me, then. For, both of these people were deformed! It was five-thirty PM: da witchin' hour . . . ! I did not see or notice their deformity until they walked obliquely towards a parking lot. Nevertheless, from first sight I sensed the great tenderness of da Mother for da Child; and da Child was lookin' up intently at her withered an' blighted face. One of the child's legs was only a tiny, limping stump. Feeling an imperative to do so, I followed 'em, half ashamed; but doing so meekly so that I shouldn't be imputed with bad motives. They were about to board a greyhound coach when I accosted them and said how-do-you-do and emptied my entire pockets of bills into her hands. She took my money with gaunt unseeing eyes; but da child cooed or seemingly gurgled! After that I lost sight o' 'em. That was da evening of a very eventful day; but it was gettin' on to five by now, and never duskier that evening had look'd of aspect! I called Joanni, got her all excited and squeaky-voiced; Mrs. Selkirk roundly berated me; however, I just told her I was going to take a trip to look you up at home, Professor Tanischi . . . Something just gelled inside; and to finish that, I had to see it through. I wasn't too uptight, or too uneasy, though I was that, to be sure! Yet, I feel I must forge ahead, go deeper into myself; and deeper, despite outward portents, into da heart, da very heart o' da cosmos, if needs be! These be two interlocking realities, and dynamic, vibrant, realities, at that; which symmetries exist! I was somewhere in New York City, in Brooklyn, and I had left my blond-headed employee confused and slightly hysterical . . . I was standing near a taxi station, I recalled, looking at da maps on display, in their glass cases, but memory blurs again!—loike waves rollicking up some forgotten and broken up beachhead many, many an eon ago! I looked at my reflection and my eyes were melancholy, wi' unforgiveness in 'em: a film seem'd to have risen o'er 'em! Ay, a momentary weakness stole over my resolute mind, my mood changed! Does He still care? Was he, Doctor Humphrey Humperdinck, going to hell, in a handcart? However, by slow degrees a nauseous free floatin' sensation seized me, in da pit o' his stomach.'

('Wait a minute, Humphrey, my dear,' said my wife, Sandy, again, 'a little tea is in order an' biscuits and puffs, so as not to overburden you too much, as it's about tea-time! A very early teatime, to be sure! You, I see, have been using up no little expenditure o' your energy to tell us your story, and ungrudgingly, too. Tell him, dearest John, after that, to rest an' get some shut-eye in our rest room; a siesta, a little siesta: he has been so super good-humored.' As Humphrey concurred,—there we must leave him, but meantime, I will also give myself a moment to catch my breath . . .)

Chapter Ten

THE SAVANT'S TROUBLED PAST: (PART 3)

At six o'clock, Humphrey came down and delivered the full statement that he was well-rested like a new creetur, fully-alive, who had tasted sleep's sweetness & languor! It did not take him but a moment to realize that my luxurious house, my study and I, was open, at his service to command—as da moon hover'd palely over Long Island Sound—that evening. Also, becoming very wakeful myself: I was anticipating a hot dinner of pot-roast and cold ham and salad with mayonnaise and watercress, and very little French dressing—very delectable anticipation indeed, together wi' what many side dishes, else; and, as he, Humphrey Humperdinck, closed the door of my sanctum sanctorum after him, the savant addressed us affectionately, 'I have asked Cook to prepare a jug o' sumptin: my own recipe: Science-squash if I may! It's delicious: fabulously delicious—very!'

'Yes, fabuloso,' I made reply, helping myself to a large glass which he poured for me: 'Your own concoction: eh—Doctor Humperdinck?'

'Yes,' said he, grinning; ''tis juice, all right, but not without a difference.'

'Viva la difference, then,' said my pretty wife, smiling at both of us . . .

Humphrey drank up also, and, as he wiped his wet lips, he tittered joyfully, 'Ah, I needed that!'

'And now, we would like to hear what happened next . . . won't you oblige?'

'You know my Father died unexpectedly about three months ago, and though I held his hand in the hospital, I niver prayed fer him properly. Groping that night, amongst the shady people in da streets in New York, I was reminded o' da Garden of Death. Somehow, struck me, jus then . . . My Father was in da Garden of Death, and, like in muh many dreams of him, he was sleeping there (although I haven't told you this). Even in death, I was prejudiced against his ever enterin' heaven's kingdom; but thank God, that I had been thoroughly aired o' that. I had been very angry still, and judgmental o' him: however I must have gone off to sleep somewhere or other, sometime, my eyelids were very heavy! I could sense something cold and gelid: but now, having emptied my glass's contents, I will resume my tale, which needed singular telling. I was having quaint ideas sich as if 'tis Hamlet's mother dat was murthered; the King would've gotten a new hussy, and where would Hamlet also be? Queen Gertrude a-walking da ramparts! haunting Hamlet's weak mind! If you have not guessed it, by now, I was accosted and assaulted, by a band of skeletal-lookin' gargantuans, with grimy fingers that bent backwards, an' bloodied an' shoeless!—Dimwit, pick-pocketing, gaunt, cigarette-butt picking, daemon-lowlifes, I tink! These were a couple of shoulder-to-shoulder comradely—Tashtego, Daggoo and Queequeq tryin' to give me da hearty salute an' halloo; but how the likes o' 'em came to be in New York City after chasing all those monstrous whales, I don't reetly know! The ghouls looked like they were prey to some topping disenchantment, and having not a single apparatus, I fled 'em, like from deadly poisons or da plague; and they, raising a hue-and-rattle, with their fingers bending backwards and forwards, yes—like reeds in a moving body of water—pursued me to a church. Doubling-up, I ran in. Fortunately, I was not followed.—Suddenly, on a seat, I caught sight o' a folded Times newspaper and it was carelessly crumpled so that the only words that appeared to incurious eyes were BE STILL—BELIEVE . . . this was a startling fact, and some kind of handsome joy flooded o'er me an' was reinstated in the castle o' muh heart! My uncertainty quelled. However neither verger nor anybody came; I was left all alone inside da Metropolitan Christian Church. 'Twas then I felt overwhelmingly sleepy . . . Yes, as sleep came over me, almost immediately, I was huddled as best I could. I was haunted by a queer feeling that I was going to meet my Dad in da Garden! It was now very quiet and very still and almost totally dark. I peered at the dark entrance, which was shut and from elsewhere a mist was enveloping the entire vicinage, in thick white, swellin' veils.—Was the Angel of death out traipsing on his rounds armed with firebrand?—Something like Latin that smacked of something vague and authoritative, which I had seen a long time agone, flashed across my sometimes-lucid brain. It was very cold. I shuddered. I thought my faculty under the dregs of a disturbed sleep had an unreal quality about it: sometimes, I was having a converse with Him, sometimes with Humperdinck Senior, my Old Man. I will stay by you Father, I said. And he told me, 'Sometimes it's very difficult to sort oneself out; and what we want to do do not lie to our hands.' 'Yes, Father,' I made reply; the first time I talked to him, like that. And he said, 'Pray me the Catholic prayer, "Eternal rest grant to him, Lord, and let perpetual light shine upon him," every day.' 'Yes Father, I don't blame you Dad.' I replied again. 'May you have the peace you have been searching for all your life, which, obviously, you hadn't found in us. I shall not cast the first stane, and shall put it all down all to the sin of our first parents: Original Sin.'

'Yes, yes,' I, John Wyndham Tanischi mumbled, 'that's right, Humphrey. Let me just read the Sunday Missal, randomly flipped through. Psalm 79: Responsorial Psalm, "May your hand be on the man you have chosen, the man you have given your strength. And we shall never forsake you again; give us life that we may call upon your name": taken from, First Sunday, Advent, Cycle B.'

'I started praying, for my late Father, with a will, in great good sincerity and earnestness! "Please give him the peace that he longed for, O Lord . . . ! In addition I felt immediately the better for it, and remained in that attitude; until morning was come and doors were flung open. By this time people outside were moving about. I got my lunch wrapped up in a piece of newspaper, and some cooling drinks. Then I went back inside da church. I stayed on until evening when lights were again about to come on. Then I walked casually to my dinner, more than anything pleased, thinking happily of my Father, this time. Then, it was nighttime again . . . A balmy night. I decided to move on. There was a car parked outside and the window next to the driver's seat was rolled down. There was no key anywhere, I noticed as I got in the front. Began drumming my fingers restlessly on da dashboard . . . Suddenly the engine started to life just like that and they all came out to see, but was painfully much too polite . . . someone had telephoned NYPD which came with guns and badges and with flashin' blue siren, and took down muh name and address; da usual stuff. Asked me, to git in their backseat were I to behave myself and make no sudden movements,—wi' broad grins: da officers in blue did, for, they would fetch me to wherever I wanted to go, they said. Replied, Glen Cove, Long Island, and gave 'em your address . . . They said, sure, okay, sure man . . . ! As if I manufactured it for the set purpose, they started complimentin' me on da relatively fine weather, and I took a look at my wristwatch. It read, 10.07 PM, SAT.

Idly, I began to turn the dial, fiddled wi' it until it said 12.32 AM, SUN. I called out in a strange, absentminded voice, to the two NYPD officers, "12.32 AM, SUN."

The one next to the driver grinned as he look'd at the dashboard clock below the plastic geraniums and said, 'Heigho, that's right!'

Licking muh lips, I again tried this trick, and repeated da experiment! Again I got the same response, seeing the chronometer resynchronizing itself every time I called out a different time and date; sometimes running it backwards, sometimes forwards. 'Where are we now?' I asked da NYPD officer, at da wheel . . ."There will be a bridge's ramp comin' just up ahead." he said after a minute, peering in front o' da road, "We're close upon Nassau now: See that over there? New York is on your left side . . ."

'Doctor Humperdinck, Professor Tanischi—well, John and I, are very glad you have come to our home safe and sound. How do you feel now?' said my wife, in her usually voluble manner, her lips like fluttering rosebuds.

'I myself can't account for the lapses of time, but crazier things have been known to have happened, you know? We got no news of you for . . . about thirty-four hours Humphrey . . . !!! What time does your wristwatch, say now? Eight-thirty? Sunday, the 28th September, yes? However, more than anything, do sit beside those dimity curtains, I shall pour into your ear da best exhortation and fine, touching words that could ever have come from a friend's generous lips . . . But later, we shall make our late dinner a splendid supper: and a festive one, to boot: sumptin to remember. Something mildly sweet and refreshing, again for you, Humphrey, I should think? Ask Cook for something fer him and Mrs. Tanischi, Daisy, dear . . .' I said. 'And, some passion fruit juice fer myself.'

His long story, here, therefore, was half told. Humphrey got back to New York, with a good deal more zest an' some enthusiasm . . . He had found a modicum of peace by willing peace upon another, having known greater realities than those mapped out by our Modern Age. Like da hardest o' flints, those experiences struck, with a brilliancy, which had remained undimmed inside o' his spirit, as something piquant and extraordinary.—So, voila!

Chapter Eleven

IN THE BLINK OF AN EYE INTO DA FATHOMLESS LIMIT HE PLUNGES

Into the middle of July the year following, he was for a time wrapped in a mood of self-sacrificial fervor, continuing in this vein for months, almost equal to his interesting inner drama: facing it with tranquility an' equanimity. At that time he acted mostly, and did not think about da implications of his visual disturbance, nor did shirk from getting up to face da day. He was almost brilliant at times but he still felt a little trapped, despite his psychological respite, and then another blow came. He was still praying for his Father that God might grant him the rest he craved for all his life, the peace and the understanding fer himself. As he was returning home rapidly after his stint at the noodle factory, he suddenly felt that, maybe, the solution he had tried upon himself was untenable . . . even though the pain, a prolonged one, was getting lesser and lesser; but he was afraid a golden healthier tomorrow he desired might niver come! But God's pursuit of him had an extremely absorbing quality and it taxed all his faculties of understanding an' intuition to read the signs. Was some unholy power also mocking him; and makin' him see those faces at especially inopportune moments to make him feel especially down, venting its anger at him: wanting to drive him—like a lemming—to death? For an answer, a clear answer, Humphrey waited in vain. A sadistic force seemed to pummel him with a dose of fear that was bent on wreckin' him, annihilate him, until he could not cope anymore:—Was this his reward? Would he have plunged the needlepoint if he had known the price he had to pay, mayhap, until the end of his days? Sure, judgmentally speaking, he would not! He felt as though left in the large; and the words of Act 4, Scene 12 of Antony and Cleopatra, when Anthony, was about to die and fey (his high school teacher taught Humphrey that) beginning' wi' da words, 'Sometime we see a cloud that's dragonish; /A vapor sometime like a bear or lion . . .' and which ended with 'The rock dislimns and makes it indistinct, /As water is in water' rose naturally, to mind. Then, he recalled somberly Antony is wondering in the brain and this is followed by a bitter laugh on Humphrey's part which faded away like lightning, 'So the great Shakespeare knows of this uncommon condition, also.' His, Antony's, seizure of warped impressions, with which the fallen hero was imprisoned by.

'That also is a dissertation, an analytical display, of da powers of his mind, a vision . . . Once the great man's mind was shaken loose, Doctor Humphrey, you understand, Antony could not control its haywire state anymore; he is now existing' on a different plane. Well, about your case you must continue to make the right choice; because those who are under the influence of the bad 'Uns o' da universe will be on devolutionary paths sooner or later,' I said . . .

Well, though I had lowered the drawbridge of my soul's citadel, I can slowly and albeit painfully expunge da undesirables that had come inside, and as my earthworks are being reinforced, I think I might still be able to do it,' he replied.

I, Professor John Tanischi, had mustered all my resources to talk eruditely with him in our consultations, to git his derailed life back on track. Kudos, John Wyndham Tanischi, you might say! The salvaging of Humphrey is not without its problems and obstacles, issuing from myself and him, but, as the Professor, being the incarnation of great avuncular benevolence, he found himself surprised by my tact, kindness, and unfailing wisdom, spurring him towards greater wholeness. Being the realist, I told him his disturbed vision might possibly be a lifelong affliction; but nobody can predict the course of a disease like that however wise he might be!

Chapter Twelve

IS LIFE REALLY BAD OR IS IT GOOD?

When—in summarizing, to continue with Egon's story, the two salient points that was needed to be absorbed are these: first, Humphrey must not allow anything to jar or jot his already invaded mind, to stop if he could, himself from being disturbed, discomfited, harassed, and injured, by anything that penetrates into him from da outer sensory world. Second, not to be unduly worried if such suggestive faces are seen, and the breaches continue to occur; but take comfort that the attainable is within his grasp, and will be won one day. Thus, would his breast and soul surged with manly joy. It was real! These are the fundamental principles, I sought to inculcate in him, as the whole crux of da matter, is that this is a working solution, outta his predicament, 'Even if he thinks God has not given him da permission, he must act and believe as if He has!' I had pointedly told him . . .

Furthermore, I was aware that Miss Rolland had said to him, 'Humphrey, are you waiting for somebody to love you so that you can get out of that responsibility, of loving' yourself, isn't it?'

That question Humphrey told me, startled him.

'You mean relinquishing my own responsibility in favor of somebody else doin' it?' he asked, shamefacedly.

'Yes,' intoned Helen, looking up at his blushing face.

'I guess so—if I am that downright honest wi' myself—if you choose to put it that way.'

'You fear, you are not good enough, even for you to love yourself, and a do-gooder ye must be?'

'It's my childhood,' Humphrey rejoined, with sad tears springing into his eyes, like watermelon pips being squeezed outta 'em.

'That's no reason for supposing, for thinking you are unlovable,' she went on and she exclaimed, 'Knowing you, Humphrey, if you were given a cold choice, would you still allow God to let you be you? Would you bless his handiwork, which is you?'

'No!' cried the savant presumptively, 'you ask me questions that I am totally defenseless to answer,' hearing the hollow clicking of her spoon in a cup of hot cream-laden coffee which the waiter had just brought for her.

'No, eh?' said a severe Miss Rolland sententiously, 'That's it? Silly, don't you know that you are not given a choice whether or not, but you must like and love yourself; else, what else do you have? Don't you know? You are His GREATEST gift to yourself, no more no less!'

'You are a brilliant mind, Miss Rolland. Yes, I suppose that must be true,' he lamely admitted.

'Do ye suppose you can love anyone properly and deeply in any meaningful way if you first don't lavish love on yourself?' she challenged; 'I presume you know what I am talking about?'

'I suppose that would be illogical,' I made answer, not fully understanding her hint.

'Yes: illogical, dumb, foolish, presumptuous and mad. Really, all these things.'

'What must I do then, love and like, myself?'

'Your double-mindedness and the clamor inside o' you might try to dissuade you from considering this and putting it into practice. Our thoughts and our feelings are sometimes not in our best interest to give in to 'em! Dangers are fraught and couched in thoughts, improperly conceived, and in actions in executing 'em thoughtlessly.'

'Are there such potent powers in our own beings?'

'I don't know, but you can try to refocus and use repetitive words or names, to break the spell of the feelings and voices that tries to unhinge you, and bring you tottering to da brink; you can silence 'em with great efforts of concentration, so that these fetters do not bind you. Be their master, Humphrey!'

They had been, one afternoon, sitting at table in a bistro, drinking lemonade and having a buffet dinner; it was Humphrey's idea and treat.

'You shouldn't compare how your life was and how it is now; how other people's is like and how fortunate this or that person is, was and will ever be—'

'Why?' Humphrey ventured: 'Tell me, Miss Rolland . . .'

'Bec'os, then, you'd be discontented and you'll feel down,' she made answer, touching his finger.

'It's da demmed hypocrisy, that's what it is!' cried the savant. 'The Professor also said as much, but I'd rather take your word for it.'

'You are uniquely yourself, and you are beautiful, and that's fine by me,' she said rather gallantly.

You are beautiful yourself . . .' he replied, equally gallantly as, well.

In the eccentricity of a pair of lovers, or would-be ones, they avoided the other's eyes, bec'os for a moment, Humphrey's voice had sounded slurred an' thick as if there were thongs in his throat, and each knew the veracity of each other's true statement or comment. 'Yes, Miss Rolland, I tink I won't be barkin' up da wrong tree from now on . . .' he added, significantly.

'Do you care about me, Humphrey?' she inquired.

'Yes, Miss Rolland, oh deeply!'

'Then for your sake you must get well. Read St. Ignatius's method to test da spirits . . .'

'You have me made me distrust and shun my own propensity towards over-generosity to my own inconvenience and detriment, even. I have come to put away all riddles, signs and heavenly or hellish or suchlike morphologies; but I think, that is not saying there is only the present, and after that there is nuffin' worthwhile to consider. Death comes to man, woman and child, the very old, the very young, often, without warning. After that, a blank state that is the subject of much philosophical consideration an' speculation, apart from—'

'I have come, Humphrey, to infuse true godliness in your life, by not . . . what, 'this' coming from a ghaistsweeper?'

'Puttin' all my eggs in one basket, yea?'

'Er, something like . . . ! The hens won't be able to lay 'em fast enough if you do,' rejoined Helen sipping on her straw and looking about her. 'You are very pure and innocent, Humphrey. Let's dance. The jukebox is playing Melody d'amour, you know it . . . ?'

Whilst they were holding hands, she whispered into his ear quite flatly, 'You 'ave to think of which direction you are goin' in your present life . . .'

'It can't be nowhere! It can't be nowhere! I have be going round in circles as my past still haunts me. Ech, a wonderful crooner this . . .'

'Give yourself a head start. Say to yourself, it isn't vital, and now it's behind you. Look ahead, since your life is ahead, don't look back like Orpheus, and be trapped in da underworld. Even, as you go along, some of your more formative experiences must be let drop like yesteryear's snaw. That kinda life isna worth it, for 'ee cheat yourself if you do not listen like da wurl's greatest cheats . . . da wurl has ever known.'

'Some of life's dreams are like that, perhaps, and, I must shift my perspective.'

'What dream?'

'Not important now, I tink. I shall get a new dream.'

'What new dream will that be, eh, Humphrey?'

'Oh, you, Miss Rolland.'

'Oh.' It was one of the softest, salubrious "oh" he had ever heard.

'And, well, that DREAM is very HEALTHY, FINE and SWEET, I can say! I feel like smiling and go on an' on dancin' wi' you,' added Helen.

'Dance, then, I will not shrink from such friendliness as yours, Miss Rolland, my dear friend.'

'If only things are different an' we had met and gotten acquainted under different circumstances.'

'I was thinking also—'

'Yes?' said Humphrey, 'and what are you thinking about Miss Helen Rolland?' trying to fathom her woman's mind.

'If wisdom has dictated otherwise, oh, nothing, Humphrey . . . I was having one of my reveries . . .'

'And what are these reveries of yours about, Helen?'

'Oh about a certain wonderful man that I have found, my kind of a fellow, but whom I cannot deem as a suitable match to—to—'

'You mean—?'

'Yes, you know what I mean,' she answered his questioning looks frankly, not avoiding his eyes this time, knowing that it was small blame to him. 'He would suit her to a "T" had things been different,' she said coolly. 'That's Perhaps, perhaps, perhaps now that's playing . . . but I have to go now, though I love to dance one more dance wi' you. Ciao, Doctor Humperdinck. You have fewer faults than most men have, but I can't be yours.' And she pulled away her hand shyly, and shot a long and regretful look and shook her golden head. 'Not now: not today, anyway.—Be seein' you.'

Humphrey finished his iced drink and ordered another long one; when he had paid his bill, he strolled out, whistling thoughtfully, down the sunlit avenues, thinking and thinking, what if it had been another time in another place . . .

Chapter Thirteen

LADY KATE AGAIN BECKONS
IN ANOTHER DREAM

'The watchmen shall lift up their voices:
With the voice together shall they sing.'
(When the Lord shall bring again Zion)

Doctor Humphrey Humperdinck greatly admired Miss Helen Rolland, his former nurse, and promptly obeyed her injunctions which the reader got to be hearing about in the last chapter preceding. Sometimes, for a couple of hours altogether he would daydream, and sit thinking of her, and when he couldn't stand it, he would call her over the telephone and added he liked to see her, if he might. 'Whenever you are free,' he often added tacitly; 'and I assure you, Miss Helen, everything would be on da up and up an' havin' no nonsense about it . . .'

On one such occasion of their casual meetings he disclosed to her about his Father, Humphrey Humperdinck Senior: How 'twas a sudden stroke that took his life, and how he had niver prayed for the repose of his soul; how, in addition, to his inclement problems, he was having palpitations o' da heart now an' again an' how in his nighttime dreams, he continually saw his Old Man, who seemed to be sleeping in a dark garden or room: da Garden of Death! It was not very pleasant to be about his Father, when the old man was still around bec'os da man would almost squirm at the thought of touching him or brushin' against his skin; as though da Junior Humperdinck was havin' a contagious or incurable disease like leprosy or sumptin'! It was very heartbreaking upon reflectin' this when he was growing up.

Someone has swept the decks o' his Old Man's soul, and now he was holding da Old Man's hand as he lay sleeping, theer in his death-sleep, lying on da gray ground. And he recounted to her, in due course, all his unmundane experiences, told some pages earlier, about how he ran into a church, pursued by da ghouls and had his dream. Also, about his filial decision to pray for his Father and simply wishing that da Old Man had da peace he had been longing for all his life, which, he didn't suppose, he got from his own Family at all, somehow . . . Like what Missy Ho said, to use the Hokkien parlance, he must "kua pua" and make a clean break with da bad and disharmonious feelings of da past and find real signatories of freshness and of life in da present! Once da heart and da mind are yoked together, I told him, working in efficient harmony and salutary unison, the troubled past can be slowly put behind him. However, these two had to be yoked together, and their combined force, acknowledged, and their mutual interdependence, understood, and then the man grow towards unity and greater wholeness . . . One night, back in his familial home and under his old Mother's roof after long being absent, there had been some liddle merry-making during a bank holiday, and it was also potluck night, with da old folks an' neighbor's children coming around . . . Humphrey had turned in and fallen asleep afterwards, which came almost immediately; an unusual thing for him. He had been thinkin' da usual gaunt an' circuitous thoughts about evil, which took the turn now of having 'coming from the outside.' It was the many permutations of his thoughts on da subject; yet he had a peaceful, sound night's rest after praying for his Father, and he heard a man's strong voice which sounded like his Father's saying, 'When they came to a place near Caesarea Philippi . . . and then Peter's confession to Jesus, 'You are the Christ, the Son of the Living God, then that part about the Savior healin' da demoniac boy . . . Then, the dream-vista changed, and after Jesus's voice faded, havin' remembered it vaguely how it sounded like, suddenly he saw Lady Catherine Howard sitting beside his bed. The loving ambassadress was much the same, but this bed became nondescript, and he was now every sick man lying on his sick pallet. The apparition or dream-visitant smiled down at him and radiance poured out from her to him, her beauty being sich an indescribable beatific one. Her mere presence was potent medicine; irresistible, an invisible magnet, which drew da bad humors outta him instigating health an' restoration. Salubrious, potent medicine— Katie! He couldn't think of her as somebody from da past but of da heavenly PRESENT. She did elicit a smile from the poor sufferer and it was evident from her contented gaze, he had, after all, done her proud! A single fleeting look assured him that the heavenly visitor's thoughts were reflected in his, as well as from her lustrous smile. She held up her soothingly generous palms and placed 'em on his. 'That is all I ask,' he said, with a heaving, trembling voice, 'your Ladyship multiplies an' multiplies that glowin' happiness that I can feel inside when I see you. What have you to say, that, later, when I am wide awake, my spirit might imbibe?'

'For Pete's sake . . .' she began, and a puff of air seemed to escape from her parted lips.

'Whose sake . . . Mortimer's or Roper's?'

'No . . . no . . . no! Just listen, don't be afraid. The time will soon come when you shall return to the world of living men, put your dreadful past behind you, and bury it forever. For particular reasons, which I think, you know justice demands it! You are indeed feeling a premonitory awareness, how it would feel like to be unburdened off your psychic disturbances.' Taking a look at him for a moment she added, 'Humphrey, life is an ecstatic experience, but it hasn't been like that for you for a long time, has it? Are 'ee still looking down a deep an' dark TUNNEL, without an ending? And tears and gnashing your cuppa, for forever an' a day? Change your key, and put on His armor and withstand the worst of da enemy's artillery if you have to. But FETCH joys and the pomp of life's celebratory richness, the reward o' a justified and righteous heart and begin it at once! God does not demand too high a price of anyone, or place anybody a burden too heavy to bear, but will see that you are paid just wages for your woes, that IS your due. But I haven't asked: So, how are you, Humphrey?'

'I am now mending, Kate, thank you very much fer asking . . . dear Katie,' he said, letting her toy playfully with his collar. He choked back the sobs; and succeeded.

'But life is troublous and not ecstatic for me, for too long, it seems. Mightn't I think God is not good all the time, and HE can be savage; and HE can wound like he did, to Job, and then—'

'He doesn't mince anything wi' anybody; but the wonder is our consciousness, and our being ourselves: focus on that, Humphrey! When you are alive to the wonder of consciousness, yours and mine, you begin to realize that God has done well for us; and that releases us from thinking that God is not good. We begin to be glad we are alive, and we begin to thank Him for it.'

'I haven't tried that yet,' said Humphrey.

She said, 'Go an' find yourself a mate. Marriage becomes you.'

'But has the situation altered? Has she changed her mind: Helen doesn't want me, I think.'

'It may not be so, if you are quickly well again or vastly improved. In your woman's spirit, you are espoused to Him already, and now touch your head, and feel the bridal veil; be more sociable, and trust in God still.'

'Is that a sign, dear Kate, a significant one?'

'You will find out soon enough. But say again, "love and trust in love", bec'os, 'love is stronger than declension or death; be a sweet and most willing spirit, unto HIS OWN. Yet, patience, a while! Say no to sin; and yes to God, and unto Jesus Christ, a most unequivocal yes! and stand firmly convicted of your sins that you might also repent.'

'Repent of what?'

'Don't you sometimes think, even for a second or so, you are a Christ or even God? I know you are not after worship, but that is wrong, and it is sinful.'

'Yes, I care about my brethren but wot a dirty mind I have.'

'You have fallen prey to a temptation, and you have inadvertently succumbed.'

'Yes, I am after all an ordinary human being and I am Humphrey Humperdinck.

'What I want to tell you is to eye those faces you see . . .'

'Yes, what about?'

'Don't you see one, when you have a strange feeling . . . and don't you shut your eyes hoping it will have disappeared when you open your eyes?'

'Yes, but they usually don't but I can't help myself shutting my eyes. You are right, Kathy!'

'My husband, Harry, used to summon his courtiers to his court and he would eye them for anything unusual or suspicious; and Harry was most afraid of traitors who might rebel against his authority. I have watched his expression as they filed past. Often, if a potential trouble-maker was spotted, Harry would shut his eyes and then reopen them; and often on reopening them, he would catch sight of another trouble-maker as well; and then another, possibly. So that, he would think that his court was full of traitors. Sometimes, the first person he suspected would smile at him disarmingly by the time Harry opened his eyes a short while later, and the threat did vanished and he did not suspect anyone else, although he still has his eyes on that earlier likely person. Sometimes, if that person, realizing the dread personages eyes were scanning him for any betraying sign, behaved even more suspiciously, the King's blood would be stirred, and if, likewise, other suspicious persons seemed to Harry to behave suspiciously too; the King in a royal fury would have all of them arrested and send off to the Tower; and a beheading arranged if he could find the slightest shred of evidence against them. I think your seeing faces follows the same pattern as well.'

'It's the sympathetic nervous system being aroused.'

'Yes, that's it,' said the acknowledging spirit of Lady Howard.

'Ah, how great a comfort you have been tonight . . .'

'I can give you something that will speed your recovery, some metaphysical morsel. Here, chew on it, Humphrey, a pellet. Ope your mouth, but do not doubt or feel afraid.'

After she had given it to him her smiles became wet smiles, all flowing out wi' tender alluring words of endearment, mingled with her fading accents.

So it had been important, this dream, in Humphrey's continuing personal journey towards the One, an inward exercise of refining and purifying himself; because, often in life, a good man is hit long before he was aware he had make a mistake; but the evil consequences were often a saving grace. Lady Catherine Howard now called out, 'Consciousness is a mystery—be conscious of the mystery of consciousness and be conscious of your pleasure and your pain, Humphrey. I think this you know. I will say goodnight to you now, because this, my last minute to linger with you.'

Humphrey told Miss Helen Rolland this dream of his afterwards, and they put their heads together oftentimes to discuss it at some length. He, however, also disclosed to her about Miss Ho of his own freewill, and as was her wont, she calmly heard him out as he said his piece. Nevertheless, she made no reply as to what she thought when he finished speaking . . .

Chapter Fourteen

THE LAST DEW IN DA MORNING

When Doctor Humphrey Humperdinck had his dream (which description had featured in da last chapter) after a while something struck him like a lump inside his Adam's apple made him call out, in his agony of his manly spirit, as to some heart-rending tear o' his insides. 'Oh, you innocent! Oh: you innocent! You are an innocent! You do not know about the wicked ways o' the wurl nor much about its sins; and yet, you are called upon to bear its worst peens! Oh, you are still a child! God has knit you finely and upright from your own Mither's womb! Humphrey—Humphrey, I weep fer you! You don't know whether you are reet or not, all my earlier assumptions about myself are cast off—but are they bad anyway? Woe, woe is me! I doan wanna cry, I doan wanna cry, I must not cry!' And a strange and unaccustomed waterworks began spouting down, unrestrainedly, from his heavy-lidded eyes; and it continued, for some few minutes. His pent-up thoughts seemed to strike together as if they were gathering up a new view of Humphrey Humperdinck, that was altogether too novel. It was as the song says, all grief and summer rain. He knew there was an old Vietnamese saying (learnt from someone at the S'anyone Specialist Noodles) that, if anyone shed tears like that, Heaven had noticed at last, and was sending its compensation; paying him back for all the bad things he had ever experienced in his life . . . He just sat there leaning his head upon his hands, pouring his heart out, and babbling, long after the last sniffles had died away . . .

Now, this is the tale Doctor Humphrey Humperdinck told about Missy Ho; about how the Chinese lass rejected him and made it abundantly clear to him, once for all, during her birthday party, her twenty-forth one, which somehow, he had been invited and ended up going to.

The scene in Miss Ho's apartment, he told Miss Helen Rolland, his former nurse at Poole's, was, at first, wrought up in wonderful colors to his inward-eye, which had lost its appeal, by the time he got home . . . ! He had been desperate to go because she, Miss Rolland, was holidaying in the Bahamas; and so, he sought Missy fer comfort and companionship. But having returned to his flat he sat awake after the troubled hours of that long night, da wind blowing raw and wild—as raw as his emotions were in turmoil. He was still wearin' his party clothes, having fled from Missy's apartment and he remembered with a blush of rage, shame and morose frustration, colt-like, how it all went theer as he had poured himself a double-scotch and sat down on his wicker chair and then, pour'd himself another. He had kept on tossing drinks one after another, until his head was pounding; as he pondered the extent of the catastrophe and the rending of his fond hopes concerning Missy reciprocation of his affections; which was beginning to affect him badly. He had been too wise a customer even to ask why this thing happened to him (why fate was always trying to sock it to him). A deep sense of sorrow now permeated his fuddled perception of reality and inwardly he staggered back. So here he was to pick up da fine pieces, confoundedly, of a halting limping romance that niver was, and niver would be! Four hours later, he had slept fitfully, though it seemed longer; already, he had blocked off some memory of last night's event, bec'os, it was too painful to reconnect with 'em . . . ! He felt he was almost the same man he was before he started out to da party, and in da gamblin' parlance he broke even: but not entirely! It was just too painful to face another day; and as it was nine-thirty AM he decided to stay in bed the whole day, especially bec'os da prospect of having to deal with his problem of Eyes made him feel he did not have enough strength, just then. Therefore, daunted he just trembled, an' groaned a long drawn-out groan; to let the air out between his teeth; and, for his distress to subside, casting himself back on da mattress. His mind was black for a while, then it became a choking realization, which was too terribly poignant to bear. He expelled his lungs again havin' banged his head on the headboard; and sobbing spasmodically, he called out to da vacant air, 'Why, Missy? Why?—she'd let me down!'

After hastily taking his medication, he shut the curtains and fell back asleep; and when he woke up dusk was coming on. He felt better with da uninterrupted and dreamless sleep and he went to the fridge to get sumptin' to eat. His mind being clear he seemed able to husband his own impressions and everything had a miasma of normalcy, an accustomed air, of the ordinary in an ordinary rented flat, on an ordinary uneventful day. An earthquake, which he had hardly been able to understand yet, (as Miss Ho had seemed so friendly of late;) had flattened him, when he thought she was at that point she would acknowledge she was ready fer him. How could he be such an idiot? How could he have misread all the signs, as if when he was sure the magnetic love-needle was pointing due north it was all the time, unbeknownst to him, pointing due south! Sirrah, whip thyself! Your binnacle is all crack'd, an' your compass, mangled! How could she have had invited him knowing this and played with his affections all da time like that? She was a no-good customer, selfish, and self-centered, but then again, Humphrey thought, with chagrin, to be fair to her, and to every woman ever born, so she has a right to be! He just wasn't suited to her she must have thought; and if she had really liked him it was less passion than a pitying kinda o' love which nobaddy (especially a man worth his salt) really wants . . . !!! He had thought he had really loved her with a deep, innocent and enduring love but on a proviso his only condition to be imposed, (and therefore not negotiable,) that she must help him, and accept him wholeheartedly first (before her givin' pay dividends)! But unfortunately, it was not to be . . . He could see her, even now, in his mind's eye—she, of the dark, soulful eyes an' wearing white shorts, loving to ride her sports bicycle everywhere and a Walkman at her hips: her blindingly cheerful smile, had always been a knockout to everyone; and, at times caught up by the warmth of his feelings, he, Humphrey, had said to himself, 'This is the girl I want to marry.' He liked to see her in her white shorts, and like a reagent, these had made him weak in the pit of his stomach. That was how she had affected him . . .

Still, it was unfortunate! Her feminine form was flawless, was Missy's, and he had often fantasied how on their nuptial night, the opposite role he would play with his beloved; how, with a fierce, manly joy, he would sit her and love her; till the red cap fell off her tremulous head letting it slide off her raven-black, silky and bouncing ponytail unto the floor: then the passionate love that started between 'em would last a lifetime . . . ! That was how he had always visualized it; how it would be between 'em and the debit in the account of his unrequited love brought to the good. It was Missy's cheeks that made his eyes smart again, and turning sardonic of a sudden, he thought bitter things about her, and so stubborn was he, he was determined to have nuffin' to do with her ever again. Always at a disadvantage in wooing a woman especially, at this period of his life, fer him 'twas not open season to chase after anything on two legs that wears a skirt but he had always to prepare his heart first. It needed a lot of careful consideration soul searching and discernment. It wasn't open season on every Friday night. But, havin' very conservative inflexible ideas, he would never ask a woman twice if he felt she was being insincere, bec'os he couldn't stomach rejection twice. That was him all over. Once he was ready it was her call whether there was going to be relationship or otherwise. And if she answered in the affirmative he was already committed fer live—an irrevocable decision, and stance as far as he could help it—bec'os once he had decided on the right girl he niver permitted him to second-guess him again! It was a DONE THING! It was as if his Whole Universe was waiting for a woman to affirm his choice by a mutuality of feeling.

The night we were concerned about in a tale he told Miss Rolland it had begun promisingly enough. He drove all the way in his newly purchased used BMW to Missy Ho's apartment in Oakland Drive Road after firmly deciding he must let her know he wanted to have a permanent romantic relationship with her (thus, by-passing a temporary one)! He thought he had a notion of how she would take it: about their first real touch, their first real smile; for the only truth he cared about then was that he really liked her—adored her—and felt or seem to feel she was somewhat attracted to him too (despite da strange unfeminine illogicality o' da notion)! What if when they shook hands he let her know by innocently caressing her fingers?

The words he wanted to say to her had always got stuck in transit between his brains and his vocal cords; hence the unavoidable impasse that arose between them, because each knew the other's feelings were too real . . . ! As he thought about her going up the elevator, he fumed, because it might be for this reason he found it impossible to it hit off in an easygoing way, with her. There were always petty annoyances havin' to be curbed all the time; and he always found himself vacillating between the extremes of joy and despair. Even before he rang the doorbell, a sense of a despairing familiarity, a futility of da exercise (you see, 'twas as if Humphrey Humperdinck already KNEW . . .) crept over his consciousness, and when she answered the door and smiled in a less than convincing way, (that she was less than very glad to see him!) and spoke half-heartedly, his feeling, rather than being ameliorated, grew more pronounced. So, he thought, he was not dat somebody special to her heart in any big regard! He was just another one of her nondescript male friends or acquaintances; she just thought it was the more the merrier at her silly party, and just liked another person dropping in. At first, however, his heart refused to accept this fully. He thought she was being coy, and was saving the best for da last moment: she was going to attend to him, and give him her fullest attention, when, somehow, he could get her alone with him, since there would be plenty of opportunity. Then, the notion that he was right all along would prove itself, and they would be huggin' each other, at least, he would get a kiss, at least from her, to seal their compact . . . He remembered clearly someone's words to Missy about him when he got in, 'Who is that, my dear sweetie pie?—A gawky bear, you have invited up all these floors, Abigail?'

'Oh, this is Doctor Humperdinck, glad you could come. Doctor Humphrey Humperdinck is da most famous member of da famous Ghaistsweepers Group,' said our birthday girl. 'Doctor Humperdinck, meet Miss Shepparton St. Bride: Ginger Shepparton, meet Humphrey Humperdinck. Josefina Sanchez—Humphrey Humperdinck. Humphrey Humperdinck—Josefina Sanchez. Milano Rybnik— Humphrey Humperdinck. Humphrey Humperdinck—Milano

Rybnik.' And she introduced more and more people, quickly and efficiently as well; and they all said to him 'How d' you do,' in a singsong chorus.

'Pleased to meet you all,' he answered mechanically, having eyes only for Missy's flashing ones; made brighter by her mascara; as she handed him his favorite Australian cooler (no doubt, to placate him fer sumptin') he thought . . .

'Si, senor Humphrey, amigo, did you bring your own date, pour favor?' someone called out to him from behind da hangings or curtain; whose bearded face he had entirely forgotten, in the dimly lighted and whirling room.

'How come you knew Miss Abigail Ho? Are you two—er—and so, where did you pick up her, Humphrey?' gurgled da brilliant an' clever Ginger Shepparton St. Bride . . .

'Why do you ask?' Humphrey replied; angling his clean-shaven chin away from da crowd theer.

'Bec'os, ha, ha! You two couldn't have been more different in every way.' Then, turning to Miss Ho, another voice laughed heartily in da same fashion, 'Not that he is not rather handsome, Abigail—no! But, he looks kinda brokenhearted, eh, muh dear . . . ?'

'Shut up, Nikki,' you aren't what I would call a kind influence . . .' but Nikki had already turned up the raucous pop music to almost full volume, some 80's disco beat, and he could not hear whatever reply she might have given, but, the above exchanges, not only, doing nuffin' to sooth his nerves, it undid his earlier steely resolve, also. Each time he could not keep Missy in his line of sight, he felt he could not breathe, and his mouth was parched. He could not stand the suits and ties there, or the leather or denim jacketed, sandy-haired, handsome grinches in belted tights, but, struck as if by some enchantment, he just couldn't leave yet (so empty-handed eh, you say?); although his heart was all squelchy; irate by this time, that she didn't dance with him but only with some special boy of hers, or some another, whoever he was, he didn't know about but could only guess. Grabbing a glass of cheap champagne, he downed the drink, looked for an opportune moment, went over to her, got her attention by tapping her on her shoulder and saying (amorously, he was afraid), 'I wanna to have a word wi' you, Missy Ho, if you please, as it's kinda private. Let's go to the temporary cloak-room and we can talk in theer.'

'What is it?' she said, nodding her dark head, half swathed with da party lights, the other half in blue shadow . . . 'What is it?' she called out distantly.

'Just come with me . . .' he replied curtly, but softer this time. 'Nice party . . .'

'What is it about?' she said, automatically lowerin' her voice, too.

'You will know . . . when you find out,' he smiled, with his Humphreyian hangdog look.

For the first time, she smiled at him—I mean, at da party— and he felt a surge of salubrious feelings: this was it, he thought, from here on in, everything would be all right: Right, Humphrey Humperdinck, no pains, no gains, ha! But once, in the cloakroom he faltered nervously; and he stared at his shiny, pointy-toed shoes; when he found his voice again all he could only mumble was, 'You look very nice tonight, Missy . . .'

'What's that again? Come again?' she said, looking straight at him, 'Speak up, can't hear you . . .'

He began timorously and said, like one in a hypnotic trance, 'I said, you looked very pretty tonight . . .'

'And . . . ?' she murmured, trying to be somewhat helpful . . .

'Well,' said he, blushing, and putting his hands in his pockets, 'Well . . . I . . . er . . .'

'Go on, what is it you would like to tell me . . . ? Humphrey . . . ?'

At the mention of his name from her lips, he was emboldened again, and he declared softly, 'I love to kiss . . . your . . . I—I—I— er—like you!' he wetted his lips a little; his eyes, getting perhaps, a little bilious . . .

She seemed to scrutinize him intently; then before turning on her heels, she gave him a cold, cutting look (which he knew so well from a while back already), and it seemed she had imputed on him bad motives!! 'Look, Mister Humperdinck, you can treat me to a drink now and then but don't—don't! Gee, can I reelly help 'ee? That's all!' She scrutinized him again, reaffirmed her decision, her mind firmly made up; but as she was about to go, Celine Eng, a Chinese girlfriend of Missy's burst in on them, and the way the thin birdlike girl's eyebrows contracted wi' amusement, just then, made Humphrey suspect she must have been listenin' in on their private conversation. 'I was looking for my spectacle case,' said da sly Miss Eng with her head lowered, and began to fumble about the piles of heavy perfumed female clothing. She was still cocking her eyes sideways at him and this had been the girl who had been trying to flirt with him earlier by tellin' him about all her rich uncles and their families' factories in Omaha and other Midwestern cities and she, he had coldly ignored da whole time, although this might not be apparent to Missy Ho!

He fled without getting his coat and leered at himself inside his heart as he left the apartment, hearing laughter behind him, 'Oh, what a catastrophe!' A stab of self-pity shook his frame and he felt like doubling up in the lift with intense pain. Was this once again, the HURT TRAP, that the Furies would be always a-pursuing him? Perversely, because he was wounded he found himself wishing for a world o' pain—more and more and more pain—until the whole earth is swallowed up in it! Then the world can be Stoical as he can be! That would be just and fair! Nevertheless, he checked da slide and repressed this bitter feelin'. Still, he thought, she was as finicky as they come, and so it had come out: she had not really liked him at all; or else she had fancied someone better, which amounted to da same thing: and so, it registered automatically: 'Girls! They're so typical! But it felt so bad! So bad! She's so COMMON! There's no symmetry between our hearts and minds! This is da end! The end of my fondest hopes an' dreams!' He didna wanna go back, yet he didn't want a night at Missy Ho's to end abruptly as that. He really wanted to pay her back for da slight, not to spare her feelings; but also not to carry it too far: he wanted to give da impression that he was still highly upset. When he had been driving his car for five or ten minutes, it occurred to him suddenly, was he da one that was being unreasonable and not Missy? Weren't they, tonight, like two proverbial ships passin' in da night . . . ? So, perhaps, it was better that it was niver meant to be, but he couldn't unshackle a deep sense of some kinda bereavement, from his mind.

He now got up from his rocking chair and went over to the window-side. It was a large oriel window and he looked out into the park, where the tough, rough necked neighborhood children played every day when they were not otherwise playing in da streets. He couldn't see very much and could only make out where the park-fences were, and the streetlamps, lighting some corner o' da park grounds beyond the near trees (for it was now dark). He ordered food from the hamburger-shop, cooked himself a light sparing meal, ate quickly without relish, and showered. Then he was off to work at S'anyone Specialist, not lingering when he walked along the vicinity of the eatery where Miss Ho was still being employed; but his heart faltered inside o' him as if it was being overran by a big black dog. He wanted to forget about his completely unpleasant experience, which he felt deeply ashamed about: as if he had deserved his pain because he was being punished for doing something bad. How horrid. He could no more show his face honorably anywhere near the place anymore or even did he care to get back his coat (which he had paid five-hundred bucks), and, from thence, he would avoid all places associated with Missy Ho! He had been simply an idiot! He was somebaddy's fool . . . !!!

It was now two-thirty when he came back to his apartment from da Vietnamese's' restaurant. He felt da tough physical workout whereby he strained his clustered muscles had made him feel slightly better. The night was enwrapped in a muted gray, a silver sheen covered his car parked outside, and the surprising sight of dew caused his heart to leap bec'os it was a novelty: he hadn't seen a sight like this for some time in da scorching summer this early . . . He unlocked his car, got in and sat down. He looked at the discernible shapes that were now not so familiar, through da windows. In four or five hours it would be daylight, and he saw the lamplight being caught in the droplets of dew on this windshield, there was dew everywhere—the first dew o' da morning. It will be all gone when the daylight came and the sun was high in the big blue sky, but now, how pretty it was, like da beads of perspiration on a bottle of his favorite cooler, and, wasn't that like my infatuation as regards Missy Ho? Not infatuation! My feelings and desires have deeper roots! I thought! but there was no point pursuing da matter further . . . There, you are, Miss Helen Rolland, a true story about this Missy Ho, who taught me about a profound Chinese concept called . . . er . . . Well, sitting here with you an' having confessed to you the truth, I shall let bygones be bygones, insofar as Miss Ho is concerned, and let you judge fer yoursel' the rest. But be kind.

Yet was it that Missy saw through his intentions; that, he was not informed of his own motivation? So that, it was bound to be a fiasco? Did she sensed he was holding sumptin' back; withholding some vital information: that he might also be interested in someone else that he didn't care to mention to her? Was it His will for him that He wishes him to know it was all an illusion, all summer madness in its entirety . . . ? Yet, Doctor Humphrey Humperdinck was not one, also, who would pursue memories, by willingly makin' mistakes if there is any helpin' it; his was about permanence and stability in relationships: responsibility and giving generously to a fault!

Chapter Fifteen

TOWARDS THE END OF HUMPHREY HUMPERDINCK'S PSYCHOTHERAPY

'At twenty years of age, the will reigns; at thirty, the wit; and at forty, the judgment.'

Benjamin Franklin (Poor Richard's Almanac)

My analysis was falling at last into shape. Every mental illness has its unique trigger or detonator when pressed will shatter the nerves of the patient with an inner World War Three, and the victim's inner peace would be blown to bits thus incapacitating him, and so every mental patient must be advised and earnestly urged to locate and remove this unique trigger or detonator so that he can pull another trigger, a reverse trigger: which is the key to health, strength and wellbeing, for these two triggers function in opposite ways to each other. The key to each of these triggers are always psychological, physic and emotional. So, he must engage these same resources available to him—physical, psychic and emotional to regain his health again, and he must tete-a-tete with himself to marshal these energies. The circuitry of Humphrey Humperdinck's brain had been badly taxed, because he kept on pulling the trigger that induced fear—and this fear must be killed, be'cos it had caused him malaise and discomfort for ever so long.

During one of our latter sessions, I asked him:

'I suppose those faces will appear when you are self-consciously aware of yourself which is quite often? This sinewless shape that suddenly appears; like what . . . ?'

'When I feel a weakening of my psychic powers, a dull ache seizing the sides of my skull, i.e., my temples,' he said, invariably a trifle breathless:—when I asked Humphrey, the same question in our sessions together:—'then, I see it.'

'A jarring of your faculties, a clammy feeling—'

'That is what I always said,' Humphrey Humperdinck would reply, 'these are not secrets nor new to you . . .' and he continued this time: 'I had told you I often have dreams of Lady Catherine Howard. It is as she says also about King Henry the Eighth. Looking keenly over his courtiers his majesty might suddenly realize with a kind of jarring shock that there was one among them a hostile or threatening visage staring coldly back at him, and then on a roll, he was likely to see more hostile and threatening faces among their numbers, and then it would seem to him the crowd is peopled by his majesty's enemies. Enemies, seeking to rebel against their sovereign liege! I readily understand this, because something like this very often happens inside my head, too. Sometimes, if the King fixed his eyes on the crowd and did not discern anything untoward or when, fixing his eye on a potentially hostile lord, whose dubiety did not increase within thirty seconds, his majesty's suspicions would cool, and likewise, if I did not notice it the first time around, a full-blown attack would often be starved off. Then, in such a scenario, the other faces the King rested his eyes on are unlikely to became hostile unilaterally, and it seemed, that the first face had a softening influence on the others, and there was no greater evil intent in them: in the second face or third face he saw or scrutinized; his majesty then thought or the thought registered that he had been able to check his subjects from rising up against him in discontent. But, as it might possibly happen—and this is what Henry the Eighth feared—the second or the third face he noticed might spread the evil charm, despite the ameliorating influence of the first, and once the poison spread in the King's mind, the King would try to find ways to bring these nobles down, if these reactions had gelled inside him. So the King, in losing control of his rationality, would put a stop to these shenanigans his mind had discerned by arresting the greatest of these lords, so to set an example, and bring the 'perfidious traitors' nasty notions or hostility to rout.'

'Yes, yes,' I said, bringing my fingertips together. 'They are part of the fleur-de-lys and other suchlike stylized patterns, or "the figure in the carpet" (to cull Henry James's phrase) dat you see.'

'Yes, that's correct, Professor Tanischi.'

'The effect is the same as before?'

'Right, yes, it's an ingenuous yet raptorial stare, I'm afraid. But it is less intense—always less intense.'

'They are ugly? Hideous and repugnant? I think it's the natural nervous system, trying to discern enmity.'

'Right, again, sir.'

'And, you are being violated in your mind, eh?'

'That's precisely the state of mind I often find myself to be in.'

'Well, violation can also be a matter of allowing it to happen; a matter of choice; how far do anti-psychotic drugs help, you think?'

'A little; but not by much.'

'Do you think the cause is chemical imbalances?'

'No.'

'Are you positive?'

'Maybe. Not sure.'

'So, why are you having it? You must have allowed your own key to the trigger to be pressed, isn't that why, Humphrey?'

'Hmm, yes, sometimes I wish I was not seeing things and I caught myself saying, "Not yet. I will allow it for the time being."'

'Did these faces ever talked to you?'

'Never. But they induced such a feeling, or I felt they could talk or it felt sometimes they are talking.'

'Tell you what, continue to take your medication, since you had been taking it for some time, please do. Do not stop, try to live a balanced life, and, I see your face has for some time now accommodated a smile that is slowing becoming glowingly engagin'. Live gracefully, and keep your feet firmly on the ground. Do you know your eyes have quite lost their glint and you can be quite charming, do you know? Continue to keep your journals or diary, write down your own thoughts and feelings bec'os that's therapeutic; do not stare wherever your eyes happen to rest!'

'Yes, Professor Tanischi.'

'What do you think spiritually happened at Canterville Chase?'

'I basically don't want to rack up old embers, because that is not, I think, very productive.'

'Yes, maybe, you are right there.'

Suddenly, Humphrey said on impulse, 'After all I have share with you, what do you yourself think about what happened to me, sir?'

'God alone see clearly into the human soul; for my part, it's not for me to judge you at all. However, I know, for a fact, you are an upright and good person; now-a-days there are few people like you! You are noble, kind, and such sincerity an' honesty, your disclosures, your obedience, your love of God—your making peace, wi' your Father at last . . . you are really an inspiration, Humphrey, an' I am bursting with joy to see you twice every month, I can tell you; literally bursting with joy. The part of your mind under the sway o' trauma has reduced day by day. I feel that the day is dawning when you will be fully restored or to a great degree restored; that, you might live a very normal life again.'

'I know,' rejoined Humphrey, 'what you are saying, Professor Tanischi. Nevertheless, sometimes, unfortunately, I caught myself off guard and made the same old mistake; and in a split-second, the old aberrations came back . . . but, as you have heard me tell, they are rarer and rarer now; or at least, I feel they are. In odd moments, when a calm has settled on my nerves and I got my self-confidence myself back and feel I am my old self, then, I feel I am completely well. I only wish such lingering moments would stay on forever inside me; and then, I would be assured I am completely well. I might be concerned about my neighbors' wellbeing as few people are; and Isaiah had said suchlike, that my healing of my wounds will come eventually, if I do away with the yoke and selfishness, did he not? But isn't it my over-generosity that has gotten me into this mess? I might have a good and upright heart, but I think my mind is very dirty because I have many a times caught myself thinking I am God and that's my thought and emotion disorder. And this has left me skewered inside and my success at healing myself, as much as I can, then becomes truncated.'

'Give yourself and God some time, Humphrey,' I said, 'What you said makes me very glad anyway. That's brilliantly and honestly said. I think God has good things in store for you; but he is postponing his Blessings; because thinking oneself as God Himself is blasphemous, sinful, therefore He has to put a stop and warn you of the dire consequences which is everlasting hellfire. I know, you do it innocently and out of distress and fear; but that's no excuse.'

'Thank you.'

Loss of self-confidence and fear breeds something—something that seems to have a life of its own inside one, and it's the chemicals that sticks to certain patterned cells or connected or clustered cells like fly sticking to fly-paper, and it is difficult to shake them off if this lack of self-confidence, coupled with fear is habitual. And so, you've been living wi' 'em.'

'Yes, sir.'

'But what about your relationships with the opposite sex, if I might ask.'

And he told me what was mentioned and set before the reader in the preceding pages; describing his falling out with Missy Ho, and looking to his prospects with Miss Helen Rolland, and I said, there and then, there was not a finer woman in the length and breadth of America than Miss Rolland (as I had remembered what she said to me in our few confidential telephone conversations I was privileged to have wi' her).

'I think I will go and see her and buy a dozen of lovely red roses,' said Humphrey, brightening up, with some spirit; and his white teeth flashed.

'Ha-ha, do that,' I replied. 'It seems your feelings were given to be of no account and your feelings were always and ever ignored in your family; that's your family dynamics. You said your Father was unfeeling and so is your Mother. Find a girl who respect your feelings and cares a lot about them. That is the kind of girl you ought to marry. Do you know the kind of girl you really want? What is a girl you love, but who disregards and considers unimportant your very important feelings? Love would sooner or later turn into a pain.'

He, likewise gave a quick laugh, and added, 'And perh'ps a big bottle of sumptin' to take along.'

I gave his hand a hearty shake or pump, and patted him on his straight shoulder (which was not more than a light, gentlemanly brush) and I said, like Wentworth did, in Henry James's The European (a much loved-book I had read ov'r and ov'r), "I think that if you marry, it will conduce to your happiness . . ."! You know, I've said that before, Doctor Humphrey Humperdinck, and so I'm saying it again, now.'

Chapter Sixteen

PERHAPS IT WAS DESIGNATED THAT IT SHOULD HAPPEN TO HIM AFTER ALL

For half an hour, Doctor Humphrey Humperdinck opened up his heart to me, so that I might probe further into the cause of his declension and, why it had persisted, at the same time why his illness had developed—or rather had ebbed away in such a way it did; unlike so many others: Was it due to the force of his personality, his faith in God, his implicit faith, too, in himself; or certain traits of soul or character that had not as yet come to light? I sat in my chair facing him and listened attentively, while, he told me he the most frightful nightmare of them all. He had been sleeping the whole afternoon, and had not showered or eaten anything for twelve hours and when he opened his eyes it was already late in the evening again (his usual sleepin' pattern!) but this time an unaccountable drowsiness stole over him. He ate some leftover cantaloupe, raisins and cake, and went to sleep immediately. It was then, that a dream, he was being locked up in a mental institution of the criminally insane, came to him. The place was predominantly gray, an unknown God-forsaken place, where grace was fugitive, a place of people with souls of some Ethiopian hue, where evil is most palpable; an impression, retained, even after he had awoken up. Everything, especially the light had a painted quality, a dripping resinous shine; as though they were shapes in a dark canvas, where, here and there, sumptin' catches at the highlights. Nevertheless, where was this place located, he did not know. There was depth, or a kind of depth in the canvas and black eldritch figures, with gaunt an' withered shapes disport and disappeared to reappear again, in a kind of sequence as though a story was being enacted. To him, it seemed a very real world, which struck a deep chord inside his psyche. 'I was inside this world but not a part of it, more like a temporary resident or some kind of casual visitor. I was lying on a white bed and I was tied with restraining straps, both my wrists and my ankles. I heard someone gave sharp orders, and two hospital orderlies came; or were they doctors, but anyway, they were people with brute-like faces! In my dream, with an exceedingly evil laugh, someone, a man dress in a white uniform, gave me two jabs, one in each arm, and broke a needle, which reminded me most unpleasantly of the injection I gave myself in the cellar of my residence, in Canterville Chase, England . . . I could hear the crackle of walkie-talkies, and uniformed police officers slinking about, and when they turned back, they were no more the police officers but lizard-like creatures with bulging eyes. I got into a police car and I again took the long ride to your home beside Long Island Sound, but suddenly, I was back, at the hospital. I seem to sleep most of the time. They couldn't wake me up, even if they dragged me by the tail. I thought I was a lizard-like creature as well. Then, I thought I was their King. I saw the mother an' child again coming out of the solicitor's office; and this time it seemed like da Mother and the Child, a little white lamb, in her arms and she was an ewe. All the time, about the frames of the windows of the gray rooms or cells, was the resinous light, which seemed to be dripping all the time. I do not remember having my meals or doing anything except lying in bed—and fearing they are plotting to murder me: and so, I had to watch 'em all the time. I watched 'em all the time, in fact. Everybody seemed to have a brown snout here. There was no concept of time, and I was in this place as long as my dream lasted. I thought, 'Will I see my friends ever again? Will I ever see my beloved Abel and Helen again? Will I ever be released from this institution? Everybody seemed to have a favorite snatch of a popular song, and the inmates would bawl out this or that tuneless melody from time to time; as their prodigal hearts prompted them, without warning. I was suspended in the days—months—years that passed; but despite being in a crisis, it seemed terribly important to me that I did not become frustrated, but maintain, still, a patient mind!

'I was not afraid, no spasms of fear riddled me; but, contrariwise, I was very calm and resigned. I was in for the ride, and will go where the boat took me. At the back of my mind, was this, one, fearful, and nagging thought: had I committed some fearful and momentous or monstrous crime? If I was here, I must be a criminal, and a dangerous felon, at that. I feel some kind of divine justice was being meted out to me, if I had the temerity to hurt someone; someone had the right to hurt me back. Yet, I did not think it would last forever, that I was immured in this place for all eternity. Most times, I was very well aware that part of my mind or brains were not functional or functioning properly, and there was gaps in my sense of selfhood, just as one would describe a book as having missing pages, or an old mackintosh, where the moths had got at, as having holes. Sometimes, I was being transported in a black van to some other building to undergo Gestapo-like interrogation. Yet, through my trials and tribulations, He was not absent from it all, He was there; and He shone on like a kindly light. I held on tight to his Hands metaphorically, with a steady tranquility so that, at last, I was sure my faith was unshakable. After that, I was able to feel I had won the battle against the dark forces that surrounded me, and with me, victorious, and knowing myself, to be so, the darkness loosened its hold on me, and the chains that bind my soul began to fall away. Do you know, my Old Man, did figure, as an unseen but very potent force, fighting on my side, although, I had long since childhood, to think of him as not much of a lovin' Father. However, he was witnessing what was happening inside me, from another place, a better world. I blessed him, and prayed for his Father, my Grandfathers, and also, my Grandmothers, as well, like I said I would: I will not the first to cast a stone when less than ideal families conditions exist, and there is family disharmony and disunity. You know, I chalk it off as da effect of Original Sin, from which contagion no one is spared. I have learnt not to take a hurt, not to plunge headlong, into the HURT TRAP but to make a clean break with other people's past and present sins against me. I tell myself it will be all right; it will soon be all right. In addition, it was then I thought of Helen, after briefly making an excursion around the aura of Missy, and it was at this point, that I woke up. By then, of course, most of the most frightening aspect of the dream had faded away; but the nightmarish part was long and took up most of da long hours, while the sugary part was like skimming the topmost part of it, like takin' da cream in the milk, which might not have lasted not more than a few seconds.

Thus, I prayed, 'Eternal rest grant unto him, Lord, and let perpetual light shine upon him; may he rest in peace, amen.' And repeated it with unaccustomed fervor a few times more. Since that time, I was convinced that praying for the deceased members of my Family makes the bitterness to go away, gives him peace, which my Father longed for all his life, which he never found in us; from which blame we are not totally exonerated, and helps my declension, to lessen, at a much faster rate. Thus, the dead are always watching o'er us.' (Although Humphrey's Father had been a hard an' an unfeelin' man, with many unresolved childhood issues o' his own until the day he breathed his final breath, Humphrey said he cried out aloud now, 'Pray fer me, Papa, also! Papa! I love thee Papa! Thou art loved, Papa!')

'Perhaps, it was because, knowing I should pray for my Grandparents' souls, but failing to do so that resulted, in my punishment, which took the strange shape as it did in Somerset, England. Perhaps, it was meant to be, it was my own doing on two counts, and a means, and a way, for God to provide a way out for me. That must be it . . . ! I also got Abel, my sweet cousin, to pray silently for his forebears and his dead relations, and when he had finally done it and stood up in the pew in church, I saw his cheeks were streamin' wet, and big tears had rolled down each side o' 'em.'

My own assessment was there was a number of baggage from the past Doctor Humphrey Humperdinck needed to unload (and my new trusty couch is an ideal place to do this), things, like his bad childhood experiences; and latterly, the incident in Somerset, England. (What I disapprove of is people who are afraid to understand a situation or who don't want to understand themselves; preferring themselves to be as amorphous as a paramecium.) As a young boy and while he was growing up, he was badly burdened by secret guilts, and sad, traumatic experiences, involving both parents, and maybe his siblings too, which shaped his perception of the unity called selfhood, and that poorly constructed unity, was shattered by an illusion of grandeur, of purported self-mastery (when the opposite was most clearly manifested by him, although he wasn't aware of it at the time); by a temptation, a despair, a masochistic delight, by a blasphemy, by a corruption and a desire to wallow in the forbidden or what is evil, by uncontrollable rage, by unmitigated frustration; and most certainly, by great, walloping despair. There was a mixture of ambition, of sinful pride, the putting of all his eggs in one basket; and foolishly risking all his fortunes at a jump. It was presumptive sinning! When there was no one to comfort him, he tried to gatecrash unto the divine, and I was always reminded of poor Pip's case, swimming along helplessly in the vastness of the open ocean, totally and terribly alone, this same Pip, the black boy, of nervous temperament; in Herman Melville's Moby Dick, who lost his mind because Stubb had threatened to leave him a castaway and da thing came to pass when he most feared it. Poor Pip! When they eventually picked him up, he was never the same sane Pip again, and was seen to babble incoherently, when his periods of lucidity forsake him temporarily. Humphrey, for a time, was much the same as this black boy's declension in Melville's novel, but Humphrey, with chemical aid and counseling and psychotherapy managed to claw his way back to shore on the far side of da ocean. In the meantime, as his house was put in order, he made room within himself for personal growth. Bittersweet memories might mellow a person, but to be continually buffeted by the omissions of the past is always a bitter pill to swallow. To be caught up in the unchanging landscape, a nocturnal scene, of a diseased mind—that is, the bane of being unable, utterly—to forget! That is, like being under a permanent curse, like one being damned! For a long time the pain he felt had remained more or less poignant and fresh, as though his psychic wounds were raw. He also needed to forgive himself for what happened. Perhaps, that was da most important thing of all. When it came to romance, he thought he was every bit boorish and clumsy, especially, with Miss Ho. He felt as interesting as a two by four. He sought to impress people by his technical wizardry and by inventing sophisticated and masterly gizmos, and things without blood and guts, interested him, more than those that have. There was still some distance between him and his Mother, although he was never closer now to his relations, especially, Abel's Family. He always complained that whenever he called at his familial home, his Mom would be always raucous and would always browbeat him, niver letting him have a moment's peace, and scolded him incessantly. They differed in the kind of food they liked, each had different tastes in many things, and they were growing more and more apart. His Mother was eighty-five, but she was still quite strong. She was always straining towards the garden, moving and removing things and the patter of her tiny feet would sound familiarly in his ears, as was that of the garden hose, being turned on and off. Sometimes, as if she remembered some distant fault of his, she would clack and belittle him, making him feel inadequate, as though, he and not she, was the one who omitted to love—or show love, to the other when he was a young boy, and a man. When she looked at him that way, it was with thoughtful fascination that he frankly, returned her gaze: the fascination of a cony staring at a striking cobra. It was the denseness of her ignorance and the apex of a woman's foolishness; for she never understood, much less appreciated his work and contribution to science; and in this, she had a woman's very prosaic heart! But, he says to himself, she is old, and so, I must not grieve her, because that is not good for my soul, I must unburden myself of all negative spiritual encumbrances that has to do with the living, too, and let her live out her life as contentedly as possible. One day, I will make her proud of me, if I still can. From here on in, I will cry to God for help, to mend and build up relationships, not built up fences, or indulge in internecine struggles of totally worthless or dubious value, which in the last analysis, leads to self-destruction, or even worse.

ABEL'S LITTLE PRAYER

'From a great distance, from the deep of my heart
I call to you, My God! In my despair and sorrow,
O, hear me and answer me! Let your ears pay attention
To my cry. If you keep in mind our sins, Lord, who
Shall survive? Or, tend to our heartfelt prayers? Should you that

We should give an account of ourselves, Lord, can anybody
Really be saved? But, you are a God of FORGIVENESS; therefore,
I wait and long for YOU; more than the night watchmen for dawn!
Our God is MERCIFUL and his LOVINGKINDNESS lasts forever:
In Him I place my hopes that my Father's relatives and
Uncles and Aunts and Granduncles and Grandaunts shall
Not be left sleeping FOREVER in the garden of the shadows.
Grant eternal REST to them, O Lord, and shine your light
Upon them; may they may live with you, in the happiness,
And joy of your Kingdom, Forever and ever:
O People of the Lord, I urge, trust, that HE shall do all he says;
For his love is UNFAILING even if the moon fails,
With him there is complete exoneration from the guilt
Of a lifetime! Praise the Living God forever. Amen!'

(Psalm 130, paraphrased)

Chapter Seventeen

DOCTOR HUMPHREY HUMPERDINCK'S PLACE IN THE PROPHETOLOGY MAP

'When you find your Blessings are piling up, it is a psychic sign that you are gradually and slowly being released from the vicious cycle because you are releasing yourself from it. It is a sign that God is forgiving you. Are there people you should forgive?' I asked.

'There are people I thought I could never forgive, there was a Humperdinck, for instance. I think my troubles mainly all began at school, and in school in Junior High few people wanted to be friends with me. I was mostly ignored and very lonely; and I wonder how many adults led stunted lives because of what happened in school. At school and in childhood because my feelings were not considered, I traced it was from there where I got my wanton thoughts from, which as you say, I must cease the vagaries of, my demented thoughts and perceptions, because the brain is deluded by what it sees! It is because of my fear that I think I am God so that I could protect myself and feel important.'

'Protect you from what—those faces?'

'Even before seeing faces, although I am a Ghoastsweeper, I am morbidly afraid of the DEVIL. How I hate him.'

'God never told us to hate the Devil. We are supposed to hate sin and not the sinner, also. Isn't it more prosperous to be a sinner, like the good thief, and enter paradise when death comes to him at last, rather than be more righteous and deny God?'

'Yes, I judge people, and I am working on this. Now I know, I am the greatest sinner! And, this in whatever milieu I happened to be.'

'Do you realize Humphrey that being a human being is better, and then one rest content and happy being one and not try to be a saint, angel, God or the Devil, for God can help us better, which otherwise, He might not be so happily willing to do, because of our pride, vanity, or whatnot, isn't it?'

'My mind had kept on caving in, my emotions and perceptions had kept on collapsing on itself, but you have given me an important insight, Professor!'

'You said you are always seeing faces? You are saying those faces you see?'

'Yes!'

'Pooh!'

'What?'

'I think it's your feelings that is the matter! You have a feelings disorder, like you said, your morbid fear of the Devil or dread! No wonder you see these faces wherever you go! No! You are not actually seeing them, but you feel you are seeing them! The shapes still remain the same, there is almost nothing neurologically very wrong with your act of seeing, but it's your feelings of dread that you can't shake yet that "caused" you to see these things. It's all dread, dread, dread! And dread paints everything you see in its own colors! It may be, that certain cells in your brain laced with certain chemicals mimic something in these excited cells . . .'

'Black vesper's pageant—of William Shakespeare:—the Bard's coinage!'

'Yes, you see a patterned set of faces, set out in a tapestry, or filing past you on da roads—like the visages King Henry the Eight saw. These patterned set follows you wherever you go, am I right?'

'Yes, you are right. Now, how do I beat it?'

'Try very earnestly to locate these patterns in time and space which had been haunting you time out of mind. You take the venom and bite out of these patterns you find specially suggestive, by using your ears to listen intently to the sounds surrounding where you are; and, where these "faces" habitually happens to be: sounds like birdsong, the chirping of a cricket; or, white noises; the sound of a dog barking in the neighborhood; the squeak of a perambulator and suchlike. So that the auditory part of your brain takes over the perception: listen intently and flood your brain with calm and joyful familiarness of the ordinary, you will find the threatening visual perceptions will have slowly switched off. At the same time, try to look at those customary threatening faces with wonder and amazed surprise, and develop this into a yawn—don't underestimate the power of a yawn!—and you will feel the better quickly for it. That is how you beat it! I am talking about reorientating and re-educating your feelings, and once you know the reason why you are seeing faces, that is, be'cos of your feelings of dread, morbid dread, you can take steps to change it! That is what is called centering . . . though it might take some time.'

'I see those faces because I am morbid?'

'Precisely!'

'Yes . . . I have kept these feelings for ever so long.'

What was Doctor Humphrey Humperdinck's mind or core personality really like? What notes of what whistle made him come calling, and, given the thin line that divides the divinely inspired from the incurably insane, pleasure from pain, there stands not a great deal; it must be said, although, strange as this may sound. We are all finely made by the fingers of God, molded from clay, and invested with his breath; it is this vest we call our body that holds the precious ointment of God's SPIRIT; but like a sensitive and finely calibrated machine, anything, a slight jarring, would tend to throw our nervous system into disarray: the mind is like a place in the map of the universe, a place ever expanding and without boundaries in God's viewpoint and in the case of Humphrey, it was with what skill I could muster that I chose consciously to lead him along the path towards greater reintegration and towards life, by giving him confidence in dealing with the still extant issues that held him back from making progress. The concept of life is not stagnant: and to see his own more as a blessing rather than a curse to himself: until he reached a point of wellbeing whereby he no longer needed fostering. He was ready to revisit Canterville Chase in his mind, a place that was a short holler away; but of his horrible experience there this had always been suppressed . . . But, 'twas only, because he saw it as essential, to get rid of the question mark that had been hanging over him for so long. He also said he might want to go back there to the old place to try to understand completely what happened to him.

'In any case, you do not have to go to England, physically. All you need is to think about the place, where you are. Are you ready, Humphrey? Picture to yourself exactly at the place, put in as many visceral details as you think significant. How do you feel? What can you see?' I said to him in one of our last sessions together.

'I see myself in my living room leafing over the Borges book. I feel my ennui and my lassitude. I feel my insignificance as my human being, a mere cog in the scheme of things! I feel, also a sinking feeling as I considered the state of the world, suffering, genocides, hunger, poverty, unhappiness, loneliness: I thought of the fecklessness of human beings, the smallness o' da human heart with its petty meanness, the fickleness, the faithlessness, o' the disbelieving world, and wantin' to change the world! I feel the audacity in me rising, as I thought of some hazy cockamamie, and bizarre, and ridiculous scheme, to save the world! It was then, I read Borges's The Three Versions of Judas. Though I tried, and my own intuition unsuccessfully, warning me, I was emboldened by a maniacal delight that quickened my blood: I felt fear, and elation, both mixed in a double portion. I checked the fear, so I do not experience it physically; but I could not starve off the excitement a-growing in my mind. I don't remember going down the staircase very much, for my heart seemed to be sleeping; and my mind was praying to God to forgive me. After that, I remembered my trembling fingers and hand, and the weakness in my legs, as I prepared the equipment for the most dangerous of experiments, which fatal result, I had to face with every day, and which you know too well. My thoughts might have tried to warn me, but I ignored these premonitions. I knew I was contending with spirits, and bad 'uns at that but in my headstrong mindset I was not afraid. After I stabbed myself and a most horrible change was going on inside me I did not pass out immediately; though I wished I did. My mind just rolled on and on like the waves combing a beach, but something was floating on it, something that spread gradually all over me, which had come from the furthest reaches of total blackness. A whole universe without light! My mind, in its high state of excitation, could not shut down, and I was left prostrated, dazed, and in a drunken stupor. I realized that Humpty Dumpty had fallen down and cracked; and instead of a perfectly wholesome egg, I was a runny mess, and broken eggshells; estranged from myself and everything else.'

'What happened next?'

'As the minutes passed, it dawned on me that I was kicked out of the paradise of the ecstatic experience, and from now on, all I will get is a kind of low, motoring or humming bad feeling, I shall evermore sit with the destroyer in his house of pain, and eat da bread of the mentally ill, suffering the lot of humanity: suffering with da orphan, da bankrupt, da disenfranchised . . . I shall never more take my place amongst my fellows of da vital an' healthy spirits in the land of the living, but must hobble, kept apart from others (which made me feel lonelier and sadder), and go to bed weeping and rise up again to weep an' gnash' my teeth: In short, I was in hell.'

'We have been taught that things have to be NAMED: called by their PROPER NAMES! If you name these properly, including yourself; if you call and know your proper name in GOD'S EYES, you can have a measure of control; and in da spirit world (and this is important!), that also means, you shall have ascendency over 'em,' I went on: eyeing him tranquilly as he pursed up his eyebrows and lips; and continued:

'I think my ocular problem is caused by my mind bearing the brunt of the psychic assault. I was too much of a coward to face 'em in any big way in the flesh, and so they reverted, and changed tactics, and assaulted my mind, by a displacement of that o'er da body. But I now thanks to you, called these A PROBLEM OF MY FEELINGS and I call it DREAD!'

'Are you still having such bad sensations and experiences now?'

'Not at the moment; I have it mostly at night when I am alone, and time hangs heavy on my hands. And then, muh mind, er, feelings plays its little tricks on my eyes. But, I'm okay now . . . really okay. The mind was so deluded and so delirious that it thought it saw faces because I dread, but now I have changed it through conscious willing and practice!'

'I'm glad to hear of it,' I said, 'Breathe! And an oft-repeated, mantra-type prayer, often will get the mind back to focus on itself again; and remove the disturbances . . . You can try Ayurvedic Medicine as alternative cures and you can try Ashwagandha. Ashwagandha or Winter Cherry is what is called an adaptagen and can be used to fix what is wrong—here, psychically—inside you. It might prove effective, really effective for you, at this late stage! You can just repeat, "Ashwagandha is helping my mind and brains and pre gyrus to recover; ayruvedic medicine is helping me to cope and sleep better" bec'os such positive affirmations can help to speed up your body and mind's recovery process, because of their cooperation wi' da efficacious elements in these compounds; but don't mindlessly repeat these statements, however, and too-oft repetition might suggest a rising inward tension and 'tis not working. Be judicious.'

'Yes, I think you are right, Professor John Tanischi! I have often tried repeating to myself, as you have so often recommended. But now I can do it better, thanks to your directions! That usually does the trick, and I feel and sense I am myself again. There is nothing left in my psychological bureau that is left unattended, but to help myself get completely well again, I think, but askin' for His help to speed things along, but at His own pace; to touch my mind, to touch my body, to touch my innermost being, to touch my body's chemistry, sinews, nerve, bones and every tissue, the vestment that He clothed his spirit with. The psychic shock had made ruts in my spirit, no doubt, like the cuts made by a cats-o-nine-tail, my psyche had been seared, and lacerated, by excruciating pain, but time, His HELP, and other kindly human beings, have helped me from being a resident of Hades, with an interminable season in hell to a . . . a . . . Hmm, did you say Ayruvedic Medicine and Ashwagandha? Well, with this I will keep guard over my feelings and not let the shapes dictate my feelings, but my positive feelings of wellbeing dictate the shapes that I see; I will resist the urge to keep on checking on these shapes, and I will promise to change my bad feelings into healthy ones.'

'Yes, yes, there are others Ayruvedic herbals, too, and they might help to strengthen your mind, too. Be normal as any normal ego: yes, you have since learnt that saying yes! to blind impulses is a very dangerous thing! But don't be hurryin' things! You do not need to be in sich a great hurry! Take things slowly! Hurryin' things along— hadn't that not been one of the causes of your downfall? But, having come a long way indeed (and He has lifted you up!), don't rush blindingly into things—even into romance! Love is not a make-it-or-break-it proposition that could only be transacted today, and only today! Love is not a one-night stand I must say, firmly, also: So more haste, less speed.'

'What you are saying, that, in entanglements, unions, rather, "look before you leap", eh? I must not overlook that,' Egon said, giving a quick chuckle, as if something suddenly tickled his funny bone. 'I will make sure there is cohesion in my heart and in my mind and both are informed of the other. My heart shall be the Leader and my mind its Aide-de-camp. The heart is the seat of the emotion but not the emotions in itself. Yes, on my own accord I will not be flying so high from now on, and will acknowledge my humanity and I am sure God will help me and is helping me to get this far; and I will see myself in my lowly state, for I have been a humbug without knowing it! Then, and, I am doing it now, I am stopping my crazy head from rearing its ugly heads!'

'Excellently put. It has not been unproductive and insipid work trying to educate, counsel, and help you to get back on your feet, after that multi-leveled disaster in Canterville Chase. You, I think, are well enough now to get back and tackle life. I think that is a fair comment. Yes, though it has been hard and trying at times it has been rewarding: today we had touched base with the few last issues that I think is only appropriate that it is covered; because it needs to be covered before there is any real closure of the Case of Doctor Humphrey Humperdinck. The file is about to be closed. I have learnt many things from you, en passant, in the course of our work, together, and your sickness or debility has brought you in contact with genuinely caring persons, who are not only attractive but also good and wholesome of characters, gentle and loving persons, whom, you otherwise would have not met, and, whom you would have passed in the busy streets of this our great nation without so much of a second look. That goes to show, there are still people in the world that cares and works for the good of others unselfishly and disinterestedly. The melancholic and incessant drumbeat of "I must make a fast buck, and make it my entire raison d'être", is not the only drumbeat out theer! With people, you must not judge the book by its cover. You know that! Do not speak in whispers to shadows. Helen is sensible, and has noble feelings and if her fair, golden head, commands your high esteem especially when the gold on the ducktails o' her hair dances in the region o' her ears, be her real friend still. Do not heedlessly rush into things blindly! Conduct yourself proper with honor, like a gentleman should and do things with your eyes wide open. If you really care about her, body and soul, you will go slowly—'

'What is your suggestion, Professor?'

'Since that time of your extended season in hell: you have not really had the chance to know what you really like: get to know your own ways really well first; get to know yourself really well. Then get to know her ways and get to know her really well. Watch out for telling signs such as signs of compatibility as well as da degree of it, and signs o' otherwise or variations from it—'

'You have a point; you have a point,' said Humphrey. 'It's only that she might have liked me a little . . . I don't know . . . I—I seem to be blowin' things out o' proportion when I come to my tender memories of her! Well, very much, then, she likes me very much, then, and we seem to have hit it so well, then, am I to suppose—?'

'You remember you are not a well man that you are sick?'

'That's it and then it spoils it . . .'

Then, I applied some reverse psychology: 'Humph! Maybe! It's your self-preservatory instinct that draws you to her; and, her sweet womanly pity! A true woman might choose to behave that way towards a man when it appears he needs a little gentleness and tender, loving care. In a word, mere icy cold Professionalism!'

'No! no!' cried Humphrey with alarm in his eyes which made me smile, 'it's much more than that! I feel she cares—she loves me with warmth—but we shall see what she thinks of me . . . eventually . . . !!

Once, and this I shall always remember, her tears curled her sparkling eyelashes like sapphires dat one time she hugged what has remained of me while the rest o' me was wasted away by illness.'

'Yes, eventually,' I heartily agreed, and with a twinkle in my eye, but I couldn't resist to intone another flat, 'Humph!'

'Meanwhile, Professor, I will make so bold as to show her a little special attention. That sorta thing; nothing heavy-handed, o' course,' Humphrey said, tetchily, breathing a little heavier and quicker . . .

I couldn't resist a third, 'Humph!' and shrugged my shoulders, but eyeing him very carefully with the corner of my eye again, 'It's a free world, Doctor Humperdinck! You know that.' I shrugged my broad shoulders inside my tweed again, and continued, 'By all means, Humphrey, do! Pray about it, see how things develop, and all that might signify.'

'I will, I will!' he answered somewhat hastily, 'He shall sustain me as I grow in strength, as for my frailty, I shall follow Him in all my endeavors, and what this entails . . .'

'Good. Good. I say Amen to that.'

'Amen!' he responded, as we used to, in Church.

I clapped him by the hand, 'Thank Him that we have journeyed this far. Come and see me in three months' time and we can have another friendly and interesting chat. You have come to grips with what would really have literally petrified most people, I mean; turn them into stone, forever. Bravo, Doctor Humphrey Humperdinck! Like I said, see ya arter three months. Good Evening. My kind assistant will let you out.'

And with a kinesthetic movement, because I was very fit, and, da talk, an' da discussion, having put me in a very good frame of mind, I went towards the extended kitchen and mixed myself a daiquiri straightaway, and laughed out rather diffidently to myself. 'All for a good cause in a day's work, Doctor Humphrey Humperdinck, eh . . . ? Ho-hum!'

Chapter Eighteen

ASHWAGANDHA OR WINTER CHERRY AND HIS BLACK LINING

Ashwagandha or Winter Cherry, as it is also called, was able to overhaul his negative mental tendencies and proclivities with the advantage of my counseling added on top of it, and so Humphrey Humperdinck's mind got clearer and sharper. He was able to nip certain thoughts from forming in the bud (because his problem wasn't exclusively emotional ones), and from his continuing to make certain mistakes in his life and as he was willing to move forward and not be trapped in his past, his former madness and old feelings, due to the trauma he experienced, the loneliness, the rejection, and, his feelings not being considered, so that these became gradually a thing of the past! He learnt to speak for himself and aired his feelings around people who cared about him and for him, and he never turned his mind back to certain issues and thoughts much too overwhelming for da individual brain, bec'os that was where madness lies . . . Bathed in da emotional cleansing powers of da herb, he felt he had successfully addressed his problem:—that was, his feelings in the interiority of his inner space or sanctum.

As Humphrey Humperdinck's inner parts were mended and his feelings healed, that was the tail-end of his trauma because at the same time he gave up his old habitual dodges, secret morphologies and actions that had an element of morbidness about them; in short, he made the firm decision not to be crazy ever again. The bitter pill tree, that gave him the herb supplement he never let up taking, like his bitter tea; and it was an Indian tree called Withania somnifera in Latin.

There was a certain man, deceased now, and Humphrey Humperdinck told me, how he hoped he was rotting in hell for what he did to him, and how he hated him still. But lately, he realized he must make a clean break wi' da past, and he realized that hating a dead guy and wishing him in hell did not add to one iota of his own happiness, or was conducive to his very joy and wellbeing. For he knew he must forgive all his enemies and those he did not like; including sinners who parade their Christianity, Christian sinners, who outta've known better and yet sinned; for they hated the innocent along wi' da guilty; for if God was to forgive his arrogant presumption, must he not, Humphrey Humperdinck, also not forgive? Consigning the unfortunate dead man to hell in his mind, was the way madness lies, he realized at last. God never told us to hate the sinner. People have no business hating other people, he admitted today to me:—and he surrendered at last every particle of his unredeemed being to Him, to do as He pleases—

'Yes, Humphrey; Christians sinners should have known better; and you, Humphrey, should have known better than to perpetuate the feud inside your own soul and spirit,' I told him.

'That man I hated was a Humperdinck,' he confessed.

'Forgiveness is an act of will, and it is also grace, and when one is gifted with that grace, the heart which then opens up, knows,' he added, with a smile that becomes him, I thought.

'Yes; I see you have begun to forgive. Good, good!'

'Hating, bad as it is, it's even worse to encourage other people to hate similarly, or inciting them to do it.'

'You are right, again, my dear Humphrey Humperdinck.'

'—and I have a bad tendency, and I have a schoolboy's habit of judging people; and often it is brutal and cold. Like I have said, we are all what we in adult life is because of what happened at school. I had few friends because I judge them, and I continue to judge my school-mates and classmates in my mind at odd moments because of something they did or failed to do thirty years ago. Children's sense of justice and fairness and morality is totally black and white; but I have grown, Professor Tanischi, though I still judge people, I am working to fix that.'

'So, let me get this right: you have found it necessary to forgive every one of your enemies and people you disliked and put your past behind you, if you were to get well completely?'

'Yes.'

'And you have given up judging people?'

'At least, I am trying to, kinda.'

'What kinda people you judge and hate?'

'Fools; I can't abide stupid people, and I can't abide stupidity. And I dislike bimbos. I use to think stupidity as da Unforgivable Sin.'

'Why do you dislike bimbos? Be'cos they're stupid?'

'Yes, they are stupid and they belittle me.'

'And, you have given all these up?'

'Yes.'

'How did you do it?'

'I said, "Humphrey, you are a man. You must forgive the opposite sex."' Humphrey Humperdinck replied.

His had been embittered of heart, and they have wounded his heart because o' their stupidity, and he had always had this thing against stupidity. It was the sin he loathed the most, because stupid people have wounded his pride and had no tact, and it was not until now that he had decided to set aside his anger.

'What are your reasons for setting aside your anger, Humphrey?'

'I had no business making an enemy of every stupid man or woman, and I want to get well, of course.'

'Good reason. Do y' know stupid people whom you rejected so casually out of hand could be your potential friends as well? They might have been even good friends, don't you ever realize this?'

'I niver see it that way! Yes, that's true! Think of the friends I might have had, and I spurned all these people. A friend is an enemy turned around.'

'And forgiving is a spiritual satisfaction that is everlasting and indestructible,' I rejoined. 'How is your Charles Bonnett Syndrome of sorts?'

'Much better, thank you fer da askin'! At first, for a long time it has been like wearing a suit o' mosquitoes forever and a day, or living in a suite o' mosquitoes because I carry my declension wi' me wherever

I go, because o' muh feelings! But I have successfully re-educated muh feelings! They are clean and sharp, as if almost pristine now! There is a psychic trigger which turns people into friends, and friends into lovers, and I must learn to use the key to this trigger well; be it conscious or subconscious, and I'm still larnin'; a work-in-progress I am!'

'Yes, according to the Pink Panther, even a single mosquito can ruin a night's rest. Better to sleep out in the jungle, ha-ha. Are you still pathologically afraid o' da Devil?'

'No, I am happy to say I'm not; I don't consider whether his reputation precedes him or not; I call myself a Christian and believe in God.'

'Do you think that there is something that manifests itself between the subjective and the objective, something that is REAL between realities, that is at once a presence and an autonomous power?'

'You mean, those faces?'

'Yes.'

'It is as you say, they are the construct of muh feelings o' dread, my pathological feelings! Once those feelings clear up, I am normal, and no different from you or anybody else. Like the making o' da Frankenstein Monster, it was a crazy experiment I'd wrought on myself; and it was carried out fer an indeterminate period only.'

'And that period has expired.'

'Yes; it has expired.'

'It might be there is a cluster of cells, a strange cluster of cells that has now lost its excitation; a black lining in your brain, they have ceased their activity and have wilted away. The rationale for their existence, of course, had been to keep the declension in place and perpetuate it. These cells play the devil's advocate to test your self-resolve and trust in God, but after sich a long time of bearing their brunt, these unmitigated impacts, your thudding intellect tells you is time to get on wi' your life, for I know your crazy experiment was began wi' a protest against all the craziness in da unfeeling and cruel world, and deadness and isolation, even more so, ironically, is da result. You have now removed dat emotional trigger, and have regained confidence in yourself greatly, and your heart is now stable and full of healthy emotions. Are you now very confident, Doctor Humphrey Humperdinck?'

"Well, I can say, the severity of my loss of self-confidence has dropped off considerably. I now go out and about, and in my own apartment, I look at things and objects and people with a clean pair of eyes and clean emotions.'

Chapter Nineteen

HUMPHREY HUMPERDINCK AND THE BOY WHO WALKS THROUGH WALLS

After the end of the quarter year in late January when there was snow still on the ground that day, he came into my office, looking hale and very spruce, dressed better than usual, and he said, 'Hello, John, so glad to see you,' and he shook my hands heartily. We exchanged gladsome looks and after the words of greeting he whipped a thick sheaf or bundle of paper from his gentleman's briefcase and said, 'Oh, look professor!' and handed them over to me to see and passing along a page or two to my curious assistant to peruse.

'What is it, Humphrey?' I said, though for the life of me I could not make out or understand why he was so excited by just a bunch of papers.

'Your research writing, sir?' said my assistant politely,—equally, not comprehending at all.

'No! My writing writing! I have taken the liberty of writing down some of my experiences and these have been properly typed, edited and printed out! Here you are! This one here is called The boy who walks through walls, and it occurred four years before my breakdown. The place was a remote fishing village in Wales, and the boy's name is Stevie Applecross, or just plain, Applecross. Please read it, for, I will be greatly flattered if you do, and you can keep da copies because they're Xeroxed ones. Well, enjoy da stories, Professor.'

'During that visit, Humphrey and I, talked about many things, but not about his stories; which were the compilation of his most interesting experiences as Ghaistsweeper Number One. The things we talked about not being entirely relevant here, I will as soon, for the interest of brevity, skip 'em, at this juncture. That night, in the leisure, and comfort of my own home, in my bed, and lying horizontal with my legs propped up, by a bolster, and a cup of coffee, in my hand; I was at last prepared to give his productions some o' my attention, and did at least flip through it and this was what, in da main give and take a few words I had read:

'. . . firstly a few words about the Welsh Rector, as this was also partly about him. I shall begin by saying that unlike Hyde's deformity which was the spiritual translated into the physical in Stevenson's The strange case of Dr. Jekyll and Mr. Hyde, the rector's deformity was purely spiritual as he had a clear, red and clean-looking smooth face and hands. However his parishioners and people who had somehow got to know about his heretical views would often fling lip-curling glances and grimaced at him as if to say, "Look at him! Just look!" I should say, he had a Falstaffian fondness for all da intoxicating drinks; and he was chubby like an overgrown schoolboy, with round spectacles, and a curly forelock of indeterminate color, somewhere between chestnut, and pure white! People would sidle away from him with taciturn alacrity,—as though, each of 'em was afeared he would swallow 'em up with his bright, glinty eyes . . . He was an experienced and avid reader of obscure religious writings and theological tracts, and author, o' many quaint books and difficult papers. He kept odd hours when he was not lecturing on divinity, and his students on holiday to the seacoast, would sometimes say, they had seen him, with his soutane flapping in da breeze, up a steep hilly incline with a telescope, and his erudite and learned books in his arms. I heard about da man only after the good priest had passed on to the next life; but oh me! having never met this Welsh Rector, Doctor James D. Dumbarton,—was a thing I was glad to have been clean spared of. So much the better, niver to have met the man, than to find him dead in his car,—having taken a whole bottle-and-a-half of aspirin. What would a phrenologist say about his head; just as he might say sumptin' about muh 'ead?—And, talkin' about heads, he had a King Charles's Head, an idée fixe, being an intellectual man, who put his entire faith alone in da human intellect. Needless to say, his idea of God was sometimes strange,—the product, and perception, of a man who relied solely on da intellect; someone, like a heretical Voltaire or a ascetical Rousseau, perhaps? But, he wanted mastery over God's ruach, or spirit . . .

Doctor Dumbarton was both a dangerously sinister man and a reclusive spirit; dogging his betters' heels, grown accustomed in his preferred life of self-imposed isolation from long usage. He only spoke from the podium and the pulpit; and in church, specially, the music from da organ-loft would stir up in him sumptin' to a vapid pitch, as he indulged in a mood of one; as it were, cut off from his bemused congregations. One day, a large packet of old papers and tattered copies of books had come to him from Sweden, or Finland, and he was coming out of the Rectory to the next building or shed;—which was the Photostatting Room. The boy, who was da center of this story, was coming from down da cobbled road and bumped into him, and you, see, for some reason, not necessary to be disclosed here, they knew the other, except to say:—da boy was an orphan; and his parents had recently died of the consumptive disease. With a grunt, and a bad oath, he did not acknowledge Applecross's presence, and then, changing his mind about seeing about doing some Photostatting, he put it off for, until da latter part of the day. The boy's narrow shoulders had collided with his books and papers, but lately arrived from Northern Europe and scattered them, pell-mell, all over the patio, (therefore, the reason for da Rector's swearin')—and so the boy, very much frightened, tried to help him by tidying up, fast . . . But, his fierce gestures, and knitted brows, and incensed hot eyes warned Applecross away,—to all but cease and desist. 'I am having trouble at the Orphanage, sir, please, sir! Miss Stacy and Martha Roxburgh are very angry with me!'

The Rector gave him a look of puzzled annoyance without kindliness or reassurance, and growled, 'I will speak to 'em when next they are in church. Git behind, hist!—don't touch either vellum or book! Scamp!'

'Yessir, I mean your reverence, sir,' said Stevie Applecross, who shrank back, due to the cleric's acrimonious and hostile outbursts— and bec'os o' the fearfulness of his childish nature; for he had suffered too many great upheavals in his young life already. He huddled behind the Rector's greatcoat, and trembled: while da Rector Dumbarton busied himself, with clearing the terrazzo floor of every object that belonged to him. The boy piped up, cheerily, his farewell, sir, at last—and cut and ran—all the way back to the orphanage; it had been an unluckily kinda day; although from his young throat arose his accustomed hue and cry, hum and rattle! The meanderin' roads were dusty that day—and peeling off his outer garments that were threadbare something fell onto the floor. He placed it in his palm and he liked the way it shone or reflected da light o' that particular afternoon. Then he put it in his trousers pocket and sorta forgit about it. The rest of the day was spent helping plain Mary O' Callahan, the laundress,—and peeling potatoes and chopping carrots in da kitchen. Later after a meager dinner of thin watery potato soup, and some lean cuts he tried to recollect what happened that day that he ended up with a strange object in his pocket. The next day, therefore, he went to see the Rector,—having made up his mind the object must have belonged to him, but just as he was passing the Rectory he saw the door of the white shed next to it was opened and he caught sight of the Photostatting machines. That was how it began! The boy didn't say much 'bout it—but apparently, he had got a machine working and then a hush fell on him at four o' clock in the afternoon . . . It had been a wind-battered day with some rain threatenin' in da offing. And, Miss Stacy had vented her shill temper at him, but now, he felt like someone called Enoch in da Old Testament—who was taken up to the seventh heaven . . . . !!!

At that time, I was in Maine, having da famous fish chowder and baked mussels, roasted crabs and shrimp cocktails, in da best sense I was holidaying in that Northernmost State of East Coast USA. It was da table d'hôtel, which I was preferring, to da restaurant's a la carte. It seemed that, on this particular Tuesday, the 13th, when da said boy, Stevie Applecross, Photostatted his hand with his right palm pressing down on da strange object, like a medallion,—that same moment, I had fallen asleep after consumin' a quantity o' da sumptuous table d'hôte, but while I slept, I saw in my mind's eye a long jumble of meaningless letters, or words; which ran on and on like armies marching into the darkness o' da night. Nothing happened after that—and after a splendid hot soak, I forgot everything about it. Two days later,—I was in the same restaurant again; and as the table d'hôtel seemed too much in demand just then, I opted a la carte, and had a sizeable lobster flambeau and highly seasoned flounder. As I picked up da papers, I read a headline that says: Boy vanishes while using Photostatting machine!—The boy's name: Stevie Applecross, aged 12, birthplace, Ffestinioq, Wales, Great Britain . . .

Thus, it become the chief subject of meditation for my morning. I balanced the other overlapping news reports on my knee, hastily put away Corbett's famous essay on beer-brewing (I had been reading Hutchinson's Book of Essays), and read and reread da newspaper accounts, which, for some reason, enthralled me.—Was the machine that the boy used, which was now impounded, and subject to police investigation, haunted? How could a boy of such solidity an' palpability simply disappear just like that? I could make no head nor tail of it. It happened that I was reading some books on religion, also,—and a salient sentence that stuck in my mind was, 'Of course no human being can manipulate circumstance so as to set up the ineffability of God to undercut the reality of their own lives against the DIVINE WILL!' Another was, 'The mana or holiness of the Unconditioned One is something as terrible as can be experienced in whatever circumstances it touches a person's life . . .' Were these sentences—relevant?

There was also the other tragedy being reported in the same daily papers, and it seemed the two were tied together. Somehow, the disappearance of the boy had sumptin' to do with da other more serious one, the apparent or actual suicide of a Rector, the Reverend James. D. Dumbarton, D.D., who sought God's kavod (glory) and drew up nuffin' from da barrel's bottomless bottom!

(When the boy who walked through walls returned to tell his story, he said, there was a roar and a clatter, and the light of the Photostatting machine changed hue to blue and then to red and green, but no paper dropped into the chute (while da other Photostatting machine roared to life, also!); but he felt stabs of heartfelt joy and lightheadedness and it seemed that something fell from the Doctor's books,—and had found its way into the boy's hands;—and this something finally entering da boy, Applecross, through the exposure to da light of the Photostatting machines. It's seemed that, Stevie Applecross was elected to experience Him, as Mysterium terribile et fascinans! I returned to New York a day later, and booked a Trans-Atlantic flight to London. I checked out o' Heathrow, and went by rails to that particular Welsh village (the last leg o' da journey by rented car through mountainous and muddy terrain)—to see about da matter; that was, to gather da plain facts at first hand and see for myself what had happened there. This was the land of one of the earliest Cristonogyon in Britain, I think.—When I bought da latest English papers in a kiosk, I found the headlines read, that, sensationally, the boy had been found. Some of the headlines read, 'The New Enoch has reappeared', 'A trip to da heavens' and 'Stevie, the boy who walks through walls.' For, it was consistently reported that when they were saying their night prayers together in da prayer-room the boy suddenly came in amongst them, though the door was locked shut. And, he left, by literally walking through a wall da same way,—until he should grace 'em with his selfsame presence again. The boy was usually very quiet and never gave the people at the orphanage any clue to his whereabouts in between his disappearance and reappearance. Naturally, it was to the orphanage—my eager feet led me; I wanted to see little Stevie myself, and how he did it: taking my bulky scientific equipment and accoutrements wi' me all across the Atlantic to perform some experiments on da strange boy; to find out whether he was actually spirit or matter or partially both. The boy was said to have some kinda sheen, and his hair had become unusually soft, and had changed to a lighter hue of golden brown that turned slightly bluish sometimes. They received me well, right cordially, I should say, at da orphanage;—and they offered to put me up there; together with my heavy stuff and boxes, which I reluctantly agreed; mainly, for reasons of convenience, and, also, I could be on hand at a moment's notice. The meals were meager, and the food was poor and cheap,—and the children there were shabbily clothed in starched caps, overalls, and second-hand dresses;—and sometimes one child would say to the other, 'What darty legs o' mutton!' I was trying to test some of my workin' hypothesis on da fourth an' fifth dimensions; and da structures of certain spliced molecules, and how, they were being altered as one moves, as it were, per example, up one notch, from da third to da forth, and its effects of bombardin' certain very tiny particles, almost nonentities in actual fact, in a highly charged . . . well,—I need not you bother you too much with all these sophisticated language; about, suchlike things as quarks and photons and quasars and God—particles! I was suddenly summoned with cries that Stevie Applecross, the boy who walked through walls, had suddenly appeared with his body right through the mantelpiece, and then right through the dining table, and just one look at him, and,—simultaneously listening to the counters clicking I knew da reports were undeniable and wholly true. He was still a fresh and blood person to you and me; and well, as a matter of fact,—with his neck sticking through the mantelpiece (an old-fashioned one) and his nimble legs, standing on the ashes of the chimney and kicking at the fire-irons, and then, with one top half of his body—rising above the table and the bottom half, touching the table's leg.—'Twas was a strange sight: made me want to curl up under my bed; and forget I ever left Augusta, Maine, or ever heard about Applecross, aged 12 . . .

The first words his parted lips uttered was to me, 'It doesn't hurt! I have seen HIM, and he is GOOD, really good! But he—the Rector, Papa's friend, is dead! He's dead because he wanted to control Him and have his sinful ways over Him, d' ye see . . . ?'

'How did he die? Do you know? Did HE tell you?'

'He took a lot of pills! He was jealous that I was the one God chose to bless instead of him, he played a fool's game, despite his knowing a lot of wonderful an' beautiful, learned things . . . Though, I know it ain't right in some way,—yet he died by his own hand, and no one can blame anybody for it, least of all GOD!'

'Stevie, what's that place you sometimes go to like?'

'Beautiful—beautiful! I get to wear a tiny coronet o' light and play with other children up there an' we who have been washed by His blood—talk to Him. In that place we are all very happy as one big happy family, and there is no slip-sliding ways for anyone, and so, we doan end up hurtin' each other.'

'You love Him?

'Oh, yes! But there is much more than that in his love fer me, in loving me back. It's much more perfect and stronger! It's truly eternal. Our earthly life is but only a preparation for a more intimate relationship with HIM!'

'May I ask you a few questions?'

'No, go ahead, sir.'

'Stevie, how d' you feel now?'

'Okay I guess.'

'Do you sometimes feel not so good, like maybe, sad?'

'No, I think not. There is something inside that protects me now against all that bad stuff.'

'What bad stuff?'

'Getting frustrated, mad, angry, you know . . . ?'

'Yes, unfortunately, I do. But do you have wonderful powers, Applecross, my boy?'

'Yes—no! All powers proceeds from HIM: he is the Author of all that is GOOD!'

One of the children, a little girl of four, said, 'Stevie, it's my birthday tomorrow! Can you bring me a liddle present? I want to see me Mama again and I want you to get Snow White and Bambi to come to my birthday party.—There must be matches and candles and a cake, and me Mum can blow out me candles . . . !'

'I'll give you something, Felicia, my dearest sweet innocent lamb: a beauty almost juss as good!' murmured the boy with a mysterious grin, 'Juss you wait, muh girl!'

The next day, a parcel arrived from someone with a fashionable address in Cardiff, it was mailed through the post to FELICIA, age 4, at The Cambrian Mission House, and, inside was, the smartest suit of clothes: child's outfit or smock, complete with bonnets and petticoats and gloves, that ever a girl received from a wealthy Uncle, or distant relative as a birthday present. Not much more to be said!—There were other stories: like da two European ones entitled, 'The reversible castle of Viborg' and 'Prince Culp, or the Impaled Cavalier or the Mace-like Skull.' The last, an American story, has the really good and usual pungent Ghaistsweepers flavor, and it recounts Egon's own experience together with the other members o' da team in making a "test-tube" babe ghaist . . . It is called, jus as one might expect, 'Birth of a laboratory ghoast.'—Though his European experiences I took da trouble to skip recounting,—I shall now turn my attention to da other story, about da Pink Ghoast, that shall be told in da next chapter.

Chapter Twenty

HUMPHREY HUMPERDINCK AND THE BIRTH OF A LABORATORY GHOAST

Hoping the reader will bear with me for another digressing chapter, back in the Nineteenth century, it was, Jules Verne had put his idea this way in, Twenty Thousand Leagues Under the Sea, 'The human mind delights in grand conception of supernatural beings.' That is—tellin' stories that involve plot, a beginning, a middle, an ascending movement, a climax and its resolution, about fabulous creeters;—although this tale is not about supernatural beings grandly conceived, it is about ectoplasm:—created, under laboratory conditions and quite follows the ordinary rules of story-telling. It was Doctor Humphrey, who, being one of the most innovative minds o' his generation, conceived it first; but 'twas Doctor Stanislaus Owen and da others who made him to write this down, based on an account of it, as seen through Darius Mortimer's eyes:—especially, since 'twas he who'd kept da notes of how the laboratory ghoast came to being.

This took place in California, in the National Psychic Laboratory for Research into the Paranormal, in da great city of Pasadena. On a wet Thursday afternoon, the 4th August, of which there was a heavy downpour as it had been the livelong night (typical Southern East Coast weather, niver rains but it pouts!),—Doctor Mortimer had been doing some little promotional work, on behalf of our pest-control outfit; on the electronic media on da other side of da continent. Do you know what I am talking about? I think you do! Darius and I had been discussin' da ongoing project a day or two before, and it was five PM when I reached him o'er da phone, and told him what was going forward. He was in New York at that time, and I, in Pasadena;—and in our long distance call, I told him a few things about the intricacies involved, which was a top-secret project, him, as only havin' seen some of the apparatus in various stages of its construction. Needing his expertise, since he has got da brains fer some o' da intricate calculations and equipment handling, I told him, to get his ass over here, pronto.—I was annoyed that he did not pick up the telephone earlier; despite the many messages I'd relayed him, (telling him what was going on,) and to freight some of da lightweight equipment to da National Laboratory,—which I left on his answering machine. 'Hullo, Darius, drop an' chuck everything at once, an' come o'er here at once . . . !' I said, in my customary laconic an' dry voice. 'Loud and clear . . . loud and clear, Doctor Humperdinck, I hear, 'ee! Yessir, Number One!' said Darius. 'You know, Humphrey, gee, I had entertained sich high hopes in this project, and we worked perfectly well together as an awesome team! Humphrey, you have outdone yourself again. Hurray, Pasadena, here I come!' he suddenly added with an abrupt mannish giggle, and hoot . . .

'Stanislaus and Mr. Roper, da other two hunks are already here. They will pick you up at half past two sharp on Monday and drive you to the Facility to witness—and take part in the creation of a historic first. Joanni has already have your ticket ready fer 'ee, and you'll be stayin' in your usual favorite hotel wi' da pool-side seat. Lot's off luff and lotsa duff! Don't be late, Mon ami!'

Darius Mortimer said he recognized the tone o' my voice, which was my own trademark, couched in a half-apology, the nuance of which my friend readily understood. There was also, an undertone, he said he detected that this project was supposed to be hush-hush, and da media people were not supposed to know what we are up to;—until we were ready to announce it to da wurl after its completion. He said he thought, I wasn't like him since I wasn't a cool hand, like him; but, also, unlike him, I wasn't about to get arrogant, boastful or egoistical—like he, Darius Mortimer,—would get, under a similar circumstance!

Doctor Mortimer boarded a trans-continental flight from Kennedy Airport and all the time during the flight, he read funny magazines, and ordered cocktails after cocktails, smoking like a furnace, and making a general piss-head o' himself, da which, he enjoyed doin' after a tough day at the office—since he was ready fer play; but, on this flight out, the waitresses he had set his ticker on weren't too much interested in him. When Captain Paul Eros announced that they are cruising at 50,000 feet, he was looking out da window from his window-seat with an air o' melancholic imbecility bec'os she wouldn't flirt. He eyed da milk shake that whipped past the aircraft's flaps astern; and waited to be told they had crossed time zones,—but which information, was as interesting to him, as a dull lump of cold potato. Doctor Mortimer was ever a hyperactive adult, and, when under-stimulated, he was in pain; and liable to be one—in someone's behind; as though, cut off from the attention he craved for, da limelight he hogged, his intellectual powers, to wit his brains,—had grinded to a dead halt. Nevertheless, in an office party, wearing his new suit, fancy tie, and funny hat, an' newly pomaded and cologned, he would be lookin' sharp as a new pin, he was da life o' it. For him, the ideal life: ah, the good life, this gotta be, c'est la vie, babe: is one great Saturday Night Party that niver ends, but rolls him forward, to even greater pleasure, and even less responsibility, until, he woke up wi' da rude awakening upon him, and realized he had been a great pig!—He would say, 'Darius, 'ee great pig! Wot a great whoppin' hawg 'ee have been!'—Nevertheless, despite being contrite, the pattern would repeat itself, 'I am not crazy . . . da whole wurl is . . . !!' he would thus defend himself. Inside the plane, he earned the acrimony of some of his fellow passengers; an' da scorn of a blond bombshell, an' soon left to his own devices, an' feeling bored and down, he vegetated. In short, without running his mind over Humphrey's summons, or anything important at all, he felt into a deep snooze with a pillow between his knees,—while listening to the plug-in music which was then Beethoven's Sonata in C Minor, Op 10, no:1, his favorite piece o' music . . . but, before he came to da recapitulation phase he was out like a cold fish; what with da heavy drinks sloppin' an' sloshin' inside o' him!

Flight 322 touched down in Pasadena slightly behind schedule. Still with the cobwebs in his head, in his checkered suit and Hawaiian tie, Doctor Darius Mortimer walked down the gangplank and caught a glimpse of da bright Californian sunlight. He was surprised to find that it was only Ronnie Roper—who was on hand to meet him. 'The baggage of our gizmos and apparatus has already arrived,' said Mr. Roper without preamble, 'We are going to my stepbrother's apartment where you will be staying in to—cut back da costs! This year our profits have gone down drastically, so no V.I.P treatment dis time around.—I'll take your luggage, suh.—You do travel light, doncha, Doctor Mortimer?'

'Sez who?' he snapped fuming. 'I am not going to your stepbrother's apartment.'

'Humphrey sezs so!'

'All right, you are da boss! Lead the way!' he grumbled and muttered something unsavory under his breath.

'Doan be crass-headed, Darius!' said Ronnie Roper as he brought Darius to their parked automobile and by this time, things had cooled down somewhat inside o' 'em and Mr. Roper said, 'I apologize fer Doctor Humperdinck, Doctor Darius Mortimer! Shake hands, suh?'

'Tell Humphrey, I think dat #$@* much o' him!' and then he laughed, grinned like an ape rather, and slapped Mr. Roper on the back. 'Let's git outta here! Let's go! I'm sick of gude ole Pasadena already . . . too hot fer me today! I need a long cool one already.'

They talked, smoked, chatted, and traded stories and anecdotes wi' each other all the way to Mr. Roper's brother's house, as Ronnie drove his beat-up Chevrolet, but Ronnie, Darius said, seemed to be preoccupied; as though there was more on his mind than that. His grayish sideburns, for all that, seemed to have been tingling with a sort of weird excitement. Intimations of me or Humphrey, Darius thought!

Darius said, he thought Mr. Roper thought I, Humphrey Humperdinck was a great man, a great hero-savant, a leading light in the American Academy of Psychic Science an' Research into da Paranormal; and it was at that time before my breakdown in Somerset, England, which only came about two years later. Anyway, Darius said he make a few helpful comments about the Pasadena City Council's committees' style of doing things, da Reagan Administration—which our cadet member (a true Republican!) had to pretend to concur to,—to save them both the blushes, and at last the car swung up the drive of a quiet suburb with its wide streets lined with palm trees. Compared with the much anticipated hotel stay, it made a great impression, Darius said. For, when Darius saw the semi-wooden structure, he almost shouted, 'Give me what I want, babe!' The man was licking his wounds.—Poor Darius Mortimer!

'Hey, cool dude, aren't you staying here, too?'

'No! I have got my own small, select place. Ta-ta! Until tomorrow, and early, sir! Au revoir! Early afternoon, two o'clock, suh!'

Darius said, he felt Humphrey was a no good guy—and felt like he was abandoned at his Grandpa's when he was eight years old. He hardly knew Anton de Bois, and I will not introduce da fellow into these pages, except to say, he was a very obliging an' kind host. As far as I could tell, Darius got on middling well with da cameo,—but it wasn't Darius's attitude or nature to feel he had to say, 'Please' and 'Thank you' without da correct amount of grumbling . . .

The visitant to Pasadena overslept, ate a couple of Danish, and after he showered it was already two-fifteen PM. He was finished with pulling up his zippers and putting on his boots when he thought he heard a car horn! As quick as a jackrabbit,—pitter-pattering up to his room, he went—to fetch his gear that had to be brought to da research site, for he knew, the rest of the gang was waiting for him outside, in front of his temporary lodging. The picture of the threesome, real men, real team-players, giants an' colossi all rolled into one; as they stood there, similarly dressed like him, he said,—struck him, just then;—bec'os they looked so self-assured basking in their noontide of their greatness, their hour of fame,—and being famous, so divinely at ease, 'twere, as if their names, DOCTOR HUMPHREY HUMPERDINCK, DOCTOR STANISLAUS OWEN, DOCTOR DARIUS MORTIMER, RONALD ROPER, were igniting everything like dynamite da wurl over, all over again! If, as they say, thought is da enemy o' perfection, there was nothing resembling anythin' like thinkin' in me, Doctor Humphrey Humperdinck, at that moment,—Darius told me. How we hailed, hallooed, cheered, and patted Darius on the shoulder, when he joined us.

Darius continued wi' his observation, by saying, 'Nothing ruminatory about you, you know, Doctor Humperdinck . . . ?' and filled me in on New York, as I took out a parcel of chunky broiled beef and began to eat it, hastily. 'I wish I have extra salt and some vinegar . . .' I observed. Darius smiled while I maneuvered my jaws around and bit into the meat because I was very hungry. 'Flying down was very excellent; as my relationship with the KERXB anchorwoman is getting—er—rather stymied: I thought it might be—,' said Darius,—as the others were giving him da thumbs-up signal. 'You will be of very material assistance to me, Doctor Mortimer,' I said, between bites,—'now, Darius, 'ave you followed my explicit instru—?'

Darius said he duly noted my formidable grin and how his heart swelled with joy and pride at my words. Indeed, after mumblin' something babyish incoherently, cleared his throat, and looked at us as if he were stone-blind,—his pale cheeks wobbled. He had a strange tendency to be nervous when being handed a compliment by someone he really looked up to. Strange for a man o' such stature as Darius! It was as though his feet was a long way down, as he tottered in da front seat a little for half a second. His eyes grew misty—as if he had fallen in love all over again with his first love.—Science!

'Cocky Darius Mortimer!' laughed Mr. Roper.

'Quite so!' said Darius, 'of course . . . !'

'Let's remove to the site now—we're nearly there; and remember no snide remarks about the set-up theer!' warned Stanislaus. 'Have Ronnie told you the latest about our preparations?'

'I daresay, not! As if—'

'As if what, Darius?' rejoined Doctor Stanislaus Owen coldly.

'As if I was about to blab. You know, I niver do blab, Stan. You know that.'

I ignored his last remark and cut short their conversation by saying evasively, 'Good on you, Ronnie!'

'What's that song on the radio? Isn't that Dolly Parton?' said a dignified Darius, switching to another subject—also.

'Dolly Parton and Ricky van Shelton, it's Rockin chairs, rocking babies, rock-a-bye, Rock of all ages,' said the black man, smiling broadly at him, 'I know da song well—a countree chart-topper, suhs!' Then, when we were gettin' outta da car, Darius was talking about Marsha and his wild adventures, in which he did mentioned he was slightly emotionally stunted, bec'os of his bad childhood. 'There's da Facility: the National Science Laboratory fer da Research into Paranormal Activities: ready to rock-an'-roll, babe?' said Ronnie with a wink.

'Love to,'—said Darius;—smiling just as broadly at him, 'Babe!' 'But, heef anythin' goes awry—horribly awry, tell 'em, I bain't to be blamed, Humphrey . . . !'

'Oh, doan be such a silly pessimistic ass, Darius!' Mr. Roper told him.

'I bain't silly! Hey, look at that crazy dude!' Darius suddenly cried, when he caught sight of a rock-and-rollin', longhaired type o' young person; stumbling about drunkenly in front o' us.

A word about Darius, bec'os as a psychologist, you would not like him, Doctor Tanischi.—Be however as it may, as we say in our own circles, Darius is our Darius, and there is only one like Darius in da whole wide wurl! Period!—We had underwent many changes in our lives, but he had remained the same, the same expensive men's aftershave, the same checkered suit, the same tan, and the same appellation, "babe" constantly on the tip of his tongue and niver quite get outta it. He sported an ivy-league look, which was, of course, a bogus one; and it seemed that in his relationships outside his professional ones, da map he has made for himself had not been updated for years; he had not larned to accommodate the growth of his significant others: their spiritual, mental, emotional growth,— and therefore, his tended to be a rather stultifying presence in these circumstances an' social interactions . . . Anyway, here we were at the National Lab. and I was determined to get my money's worth outta him . . . 'Come on, this way,' I said. 'Let's go. Take out your passes.'

We were now in a secret laboratory, amid tight security and round-da-clock hallway patrols by uniformed an' well armed guards, and Darius was reading through and checking the procedure list;— doing some ongoing calculation, rechecking and collecting the incoming data, doing the binary numbers,—as though he was stalling to cover up some temporary slowness of his mind, and so, I said,— 'Come! Come on! Do hurry up a bit, Darius, can't you?'

'Yes, it's work-time, play-time, and time to kick ass!' rejoined Darius with a sly grunt. 'Wait a minute here, Humphrey! Blah-blah-blah . . .'

The clock was striking five when an impatient hour had passed. 'All of you, stop gibbering and stop larking about!' I called out. Then, Darius started chuckling an out-and-out belly-roar,—'Stop! Listen, Humphrey; I tink I've got it sorted out at last! I've put my heart an' soul into it an' tinker wi' it. I tink I've got it at last, by golly!—Rock-n'-roll, babe!—Ha, ha, ha!'

'What, ho!' we said, 'Good on you! Very good, an' articulate, Darius!'

And he began humming a tune, and called out, 'All, systems go, Humphrey!'

'Starting subroutines number one and two, all booting sequences complete! Proceed electronizin' procedures accordingly,' I said, muttering under my breath,—seeing the strained look on their faces,—being silenced by their mounting tension, as the seconds passed. We would know whether step one had been a success and we could proceed to step two. 'I should have listened to my Mother and studied to become a rocket scientist,' I quipped suddenly . . . The instrument panel had lit up like a Christmas tree and the wires were feeding the equipment in a sequential, prearranged order according to Stan's ingenious an' cleaver programmin'. On a steel table, in the center of the room, da glass panels slid open and a kind of robotic arm with a plier-shaped hand began to pick up something, a silver glass bead-like pellet, from some kinda of snuff-box and deposited it in a petri-dish, which was filled to the brim with a kind of bluish gel. When the pellet was dropped, being released,—there was a flash of brilliant light, bursts of X-rays, an' da pellet disappeared. We were watching this through our visor, but da feelin', while this was happening (what can I say?), defied all description. Then, I called out softly,—crooned rather, scarcely above a whisper, 'Ron, ole boy, where art thou?—Ron babe? Time for 'ee to go beddy-bye. Papa Humphrey will put 'ee to sleep. Did 'ee bring his Theodore Roosevelt with 'ee, Darius?'

The, big black buck shrugged his shoulders nervously: 'Come, come!—Swallow down your promise!' I said.

'Me no sabbee, wot 'ee wanna o' mee! Catchin' 'em, and lockin' 'em up is all very good; but making a ghoastee, nu siree! Nu, nu, suh! It's outta question! Hask Darius! Darius kin volunteer! His is one-quarter Cherokee, and he understands dhat mumbo jumbo stuff! Dat's final! It's plump loco!'

'You can be spared Ronnie,' said Darius, 'What if I'm needed in a real emergency? Where would you be then? You have da high distinction o' being the cadet of our team; here's your teddy bear! So say you,—it's downright hoochy-spooky! Spooky! Now, in point of fact, butthead, if you choose to renege on da deal—didna Doctor Stanislaus Owen stuck his neck out in the interest of the group, da last time? So, Ronnie, numbskull, ye just have to do it! That's all!'—and Darius folded his arms across his chest wi' a gesture of obstinate and bullying finality.

'Oh, just leave him alone!' said Doctor Stanislaus Owen quietly, still busying at da controls.

Ronnie Roper made his last desperate bid, 'I'll toss wi' you fer it, Darius! Wotduhyasayeh?'

'No need,' I interrupted finally . . . 'We do not want to put Ould Darius here in the least bit of danger, do we? Not above the odds of a thousand to one;—but, as you niver know, it's best not to take chances. You refused Roper, and wanna back out? Well, I'll do it. I will volunteer myself! Proceed to strap me in! and be very careful wi' da hypodermic, Stanislaus!'

(They told me when the drug was having its full effect, I was singing and roaring like a drunken lord, yo-ho-ho; and a bottl' o' rum—and all that! Darius anticipated all da probable effects, checked and rechecked da data, troubleshot all possible glitches, and swore at his esteemed colleague, myself, who had put him to this;—and that old demmed piece of technological junk they were using at da Facility. 'Dem—this is supposed to glow red now—according to Humphrey's notes—why doesn't it glow red? Hey, dude, Ronnie, stop fiddling with that thing, an' twiddlin' your thumbs makes me nervous—ease up this lever, theer! Toss me my bubblegum! Come on, come on!

There should be some subtle variations in Humphrey's alpha, beta and gamma waves, reet about now! It's way overdue . . . Stupid machine!— You know, Stanislaus, I could kick it hard like that! Can I?' Ha—the residue—the residue has appear'd in da most beautiful petri dish. Ha! Humphrey: here's your unresolved fears and stunning, beautiful emotions!' The two opposite him rubbed their hands together as Darius shouted gleefully. Suddenly there was a flash of lightning through the high double barred window, and da alarms down the hall went off for fifteen seconds. Then icy drops and da noisy crackle of static followed da congealed stuff in da petri dish—and Mr. Roper said, 'It's Humphrey's fear!' 'Divided by the inverted square root . . . . Multiplied by . . . da width of a single strand of his hair to the nearest mili-micron and divided by . . . to the last gram-atom,' said Doctor Stanislaus Owen,—with a sweet, cadaverous smile.

'Wow, that's not Natur'-like!' said Mr. Roper, sweat dripping from his face. 'I have 'eard of . . . of . . . but dis is ridiculous!'

'Are 'ee afraid? gives you da sheer adrenaline jolt, doan it?'

'Yes, suh,' said Mr. Roper and he piously crossed himself. 'Gut-busting, suh!'

'It's more sanitized, sane—done with much clinical precision,' I said weakly, waking up, 'There is no more state o' da art . . . than this . . . but da Space Shuttle Program . . . but, ho hum! What a frightful dream I had! Most frightful! Ho hum!—But, how did da singular experiment go?'

'Without a hitch!'

'This new thing has my psychological an' psychic imprint on it, now,' I said, 'Stand clear gentlemen! Ronnie, Stanislaus, let's have a peek at the beginnings o' this thingamabob!'

'Let's enhance it fer just a bit—da psychic plasma in its tiny whorl: look it's expandin' an' contractin'!' I said.

It wasn't like anything we had ever seen that was ever invented before. The beams of highly concentrated electrons revealed what it looked like, its shape, which was, like a two-kilogram pinkish pear, and its lineaments, which was, like an ageless old man; a face bearing singular resemblance to a Chinese or Japanese chef,—and, it made us sheerly amazed; as we interjected with real delight—looking, at this timeless, and nameless thing—like a bloated human heart,— a-beating an' throbbin',—but crying and sobbing at da same time! How it bawled an' howled! On reflection, it wasn't surprisin' that a life thing should cry at suddenly being flung into existence as two contrary instincts pulled it wide apart: thus, it must have been a great shock! Here was my psychic babe a-crying and a-sobbing!—Feeling da pure burden of being summoned into life! It was existential pain! Every single thing that pricked its senses, would have felt like death,— not knowing what it was, and where it had come from, and having no means to figure this out;—being driven to distraction, no doubt, bec'os of this . . . ! It was still pristine and had no knowledge or contact with evil . . .

'Is it evil . . . ?' Darius wanted to know, with an unholy soundin' chuckle.

'What?' I mumbled. 'What?'

'Humphrey's babe?' said Mr. Roper, shaking his hoary head; his sideburns tingling wi' amusement.

'You niver know,' Darius sharply observed.

'You are evil, Darius!' said Mr. Roper, 'So evil.'

'Sush!' we whispered . . .

'On second thoughts, it might become corrupted,' said the black man, thoughtfully, scratching his lumpy chin . . . 'Arter it gits a chance to mingle wi' da common 'uns outta theer,—'ee know'd what I mean, suhs?'

We were gathered all on one side and peering at it with intense curiously,—trying to anticipate what it would do.

'Look it has dozed off, it seems! Let's use the probe to wake it up, lightly, lightly!'

We opened the second partition a bit and with the first whiff of it as the ectoplasm mixed with air, astral gases from our electron accelerators: a genesis of a smile came to what answered for its mouth, and we reciprocated this. Then the ghoast uttered faint gobbledygook. It sounded both funny and cute, as though from afar (thus, picked up by the voice detector)—and even Darius Mortimer couldn't help smiling back at it.

'What should we do?' he said shrugging his shoulders.

'Lordy, send us an answer . . . !' muttered Mr. Roper. 'Yes, er—we must exclude mucho good vibes, create a clean environment; so ees feels us as safe and secure people to be with,—and make it understands us . . . We, simply put,—mun loves it, sahs!'

'Huh?' we all exclaimed with surprise. 'Well done this time, Roper, buddy; your perspicacity amaze us!' Humphrey said.

The babe ghoast, said, giving an Oriental expression, 'Ga, ga, ga!' and Humphrey said, 'I love you, infant ghoast!'

'It's beautiful, isna he—?'

'Goo,' said the ghost, as the partition was being opened, emerging in into the main container. There was a pink and yellowish tint about its forehead and it spread down to its cheeks,—being what was particularly striking, now. Then, it slid like a balloon up the bell jar (which had a tiny snout-like mouth, like a monster kettle's) and then—moving up the psychic pipeline to da physical world, as it were, one could say, it would be finally released into da wurl; wi' vapor running down, like a mountain, spillin' ice—da lid was lifted automatically by da press of a button and da new-made ghoast, at last,—vacated its birth chamber. It was moving about, fighting wi' its rudimentary instincts of fear and cautious desire . . .

'Hey, stop that!' cried Stanislaus suddenly, whose potato wedges was being snatched by da Pink Ghoast; as it suddenly dashed up an' pinched his left ear. 'Hey, da critter poached muh chips!' cried our Stan. Then, looked up to us, it challenged us, to remonstrate with it, or to disapprove, or scold it. Additionally, it was also gibbering, squeaking,—and a-questionin' itself so incoherently that,—the well-read Doctor Stanislaus Owen—was moved to quote Jules Verne, (da Father of Science Fiction ya know?)—'"When science had uttered her voice let babblers hold their peace"! Git it? I tink . . . we've made . . . a monumental mistake . . . making this live ting . . . !'

I was now talking at a rapid pace, talking at the ghoast, and both it and I, began gesticulating wildly, trying to communicate,—trying to cement a bond of friendship, but when suddenly Mr. Roper, not able to restrain his curiosity, made an attempt to touch it, it shot back an' squeezed itself back into da giant bell-shaped jar through the jar's snout, squealing a mousy squeak—terrified. The black man cried, 'What?—shit!'—bec'os now, he had gunk bespattered all over his brand-new Swatch; that he had been extremely proud of . . .

'Serves you reet, Stanehead!' said Darius Mortimer, scornfully.

'Tetchy, bain't it?' grimaced da black man with a glint in his eye.

There was another moment of silence as each of us pondered what we should do. The Negro then, smiling at the others, picked up a pencil and wrote down PINK GHOSTE on his perfumed notepad. "Type down his name of the project as, operation pink ghoast: successfully completed! Again, to be hailed a historic first!" Pretty wraps it up—I'm going home to hev a cold shower . . . Let's call it a day. Doan reetly knows why it should be pink though, suhs . . . !!!'

'Me, neither.'

'Nor I.'

We all grinned at each other. 'The jab of the syringe—was rather painful,'—I remarked ruefully to 'em, 'Now then, to recuperate after the fatigues of all this hard work, and my strangest o' dreams. Tell you about that some other time. But let's transfer—this thingamabob— into our portable unit. We shall take in to New York, with us, under some tight security, and perform further experiments on it; there might be a social usefulness in to-day's hard work,—and it might help us understand the nature of da TRANSIT between spirit-matter and physical-matter,—and what ectoplasm is; but make sure all our secret scientific information an' data and our equipment are safe, Doctors Owen and Mortimer.—Okay?'

'The critter might make us millionaires!' Darius burst out, unable to control himself, beaming broadly at me . . .

Chapter Twenty-one

FAREWELL TO DOCTOR HUMPHREY HUMPERDINCK

One of the last sessions proper we had together took place in the fall of one year in the early-nineties. We sat in my office, and over a cup of coffee, we talked about Humphrey's plans for da future an' about his family relationships—especially his Mother's attitude towards him; and he said he will not let his temper git in the way of making her last years as comfortable as she could be made to feel. You see her Mother's map of her relationship, like da pattern, she used to make her dresses, had not changed for forty-eight years, and he was still a six-year-old boy to her, in her mind; and had continued, to relate to him this way. Maps of personal relationships, as has been said, by a number of people, time and again, needed to be updated just like a map of a town or city needed to be upgraded as the city grows and new buildings are put up, especially, in the light of, and in places where there are rapid urban development. One can't just hang on and conduct one's affairs based on an old map of a hundred or even twenty years ago! But for Humphrey there was no helping it, he must make da best of his situation as best he can. He asked me eagerly about his writings, and I told him, to continue to pursue his literary ambitions, by all means, and he admitted, with a quick sense of his sharp mind, his works being published, was bound to happen: but, had he determined it years ago, the impact, however, would not be as great, as when, he allowed it to happen this way: which was, until he had perfected his own style. 'You know, Professor, the mind is an eye that never shuts or sleeps; and God's MIND is a divine eye that never shuts or sleeps! If nobody wants to read me, I must tighten my belt and girt my loins, and make muh next book or da next sentence I write better!'

'You have showed a natural propensity for da language, Humphrey, my friend! But where is the boy who walks through walls now:—you know, Stevie Applecross; and where is that Pink Ghoast, as well?'

'Thank you, sir, for sayin' those kind words to me . . . Well, first . . . da Pink Ghoast is housed in our headquarters, it is still our liddle cute mascot. Its talismanic presence so valuable to us serves to alert us of dangerous customers and evil forces lurkin' around da old building; those that have nuffin' to recommend themselves to themselves; in case, da fort ever comes under a siege! As far as it goes as it was created by us and laboratory-made in artificial conditions, you know, it still is sumptin' of a Cro-Magnon's ghoast compared to other normal entities that abound everywhere around us; a pure, complete innocent! Stevie Applecross from Wales on da other hand, is still somewhere in London, England or Paris, France or Bonn, Germany at different times o' da year; and topnotch physicists and expert doctors an' biological-engineers are conductin' their classified experiments on his altered genetic makeup an' magnetic aura (most valuable o' properties, indeed!), what, not only a few national governments, including our very own United States o' America, have a huge hand, and vested interest in.'

'What should you like to do, my good sir?'

'I should like to do anything in the world,' Humphrey answered candidly.

'Such as?'

'Travel a bit, study some more, invent more things, have children.'

'Are you going to actively catch ghoasts, anymore?'

'Maybe. I don't know. I will have to think that over.'

'Anything else, you would like us to discuss today?'

'Well . . . there is one thing. Pleez tell me, how do I get out of da HURT TRAP?'

'Pay attention to your auto-suggestion mechanism, which is sumptin' factored into your mind-body equation. D' you know what I mean? You are often tempted to tempt the fate to do its worse, relishing in the chaotic swirl of chemicals, in your brain, when you do that! Last time, I often catch you with a heightened tension in your face, especially your lips. I want you to see, Humphrey, it is the Tempter, tempting you, to tempt fate, or God or da gods or whate'er! And you often take da bait like a silly mouse nibblin' about a mousetrap and finally got ensnared, and into deep trouble an' hurt. Cut that out! D' ye hear! Once you stop this roller-coaster ride, you preempt the HURT TRAP from coming into operation in your mind more n' more! Do I make sound sense to you? You are addicted to da adrenaline rush! Is what I said an accurate description of the mind games you play with yourself that might involve da bad 'Uns, as you always say?' It is going against your own good sense that a person sins; not that he refused to listen to this or that person who has something important to say or who has authority; you shouldn't go against you good sense, which tells you, "BE SENSIBLE!" but most people would choose to be rebels, we are all rebels under da skin, every one, sometime or other, and we are always rebelling, ever da rebel, as having the REBEL'S imprint upon us! You should also chalk down human stupidity an' cupidity as ORIGINAL SIN. That helps!'

'Yes, yes! You are right: what you say is true.'

'Anything else I can help you? You know life IS playing the game. To live well, of course, you have to play well. And play to win. Do not do things unilaterally, but seek to get cooperation from others, negotiate and renegotiate! What is negotiation but getting what you want for in return for what you are prepared to give up. If things do not work out, do not get angry, do not lose your temper! Always be prepared to negotiate, so that there won't be tears or one side and laughter on the other; but laughter on both sides—if you can help it!'

'Yes, Professor John Wyndham Tanischi,' said Humphrey humbly.

'Once again, Humphrey, all the best to you! You have tried out some Ayruvedic Medicine and it has pared down your anxiety to nothing. Come around to my house and visit us during Christmastime, and I think you'd have more stories written down by then to show me. I'd be glad to read them, then. But you can still drop in here, anytime, if you need to see me urgently and if it's an emergency. That's just for da sake o' contingency you know . . . ?'

'God bless you, my dear John Tanischi. I don't know how I could have made it without you, let me make so bold as to say . . .'

One day, during the period Humphrey had made the firm decision to be brave enough to be a thoroughly good and healthy man, saying yes to Him, and no to His opposite number, it became the fulcrum in which his rapid healing turned. He was no more seeing faces, which were da top part o' da body above da torso, an' that might be an indication that he had lost his head, a subtle indication, since, a face is closely associated, an' like to a head. I advised him to loathe and avoid sin and told him, also, to resist temptation, as the Bible exhorts us; and that lust makes a person "fuddy-duddy" (Bec'os he said he sometimes had a wrong amoratory air about him, at times)! 'You are superior and not inferior to these base feelings, although they might have leaked from some psychic pipeline, or bec'os o' sumptin' had screwed you up inside your brains, Humphrey,' I had said this often enough. 'There is wetness in muh eyes every time I heard a Melissa Manchester song . . . !' Doctor Humperdinck replied . . .

'Do you know what our famous American Philosopher said? "On the other hand the law hold with equal sureness for all right action. Love, and you shall be loved. All love is mathematically just, as much as the two side of an algebraic equation . . . (hmm, he must be a very mathematically-minded man!) The good man has absolute good, which like fire turns everything to its own nature, so that you cannot do him any harm; but as the loyal armies send against Napoleon, when he approached cast down their colors and from enemies become friends, so disasters of all kinds, as sickness, offence, poverty, prove benefactors." Then, train yourself, to breathed a rarified air; for your gains has infused, in you, a sharp talent to live and work, an appetite for justified living, that has ripened slowly; through years of deep adversity an' much pain,' I said with much solemnity. Then, I added, with a judicious little appeal, 'Now, at last, it is up to you to sue for her patents. I mean, Miss Rolland's—seek your happiness in her, and have confidence to stand at the altar before Him, with her by your side. It is His bespoken Will that you live an upright and moral life, before all else. You will think about that won't you?'

'I cherish no fond hope of success, but, indeed leave it to a higher POWER—'

Even before that, he tried to be good and in an honest, unhypocritical way, to love his neighbor; devout, in his anxiety-breeding way, due to his upbringing. But, for a long time, he had great bitterness o' heart, I suspect; and, as his false self, had gained ascendency, which climaxed in the crisis in Canterville Chase, therefore, he had taken a long time to rebuild himself.

'Heart, lie still in my bosom, lie still, be still, in my breast:
Lodge thou and rest here, and take thy sweet respose:
Black Vesper's Pageant or my Pathological Morbid Feelings
Do not rear thy awful corpsed Shape
Uncoil now unto stillness and deepest peace:
Thou tranquil be, lie in soundest slumber!
The Bard is right: the brains' armies are a-fighting!
Fearsome combat, waged & dinned—see I am paid back soon!'

Chapter Twenty-two

DOCTOR HUMPHREY HUMPERDINCK AN' SATIN, BOOKS AND BASIN

Some people might hope to be somebody else, but this, I say, was not a nature of Doctor Humphrey Humperdinck. The public had had its perfect scoop o' da headline news; da culmination of the savant's most cherished hopes and desires already; but I should like to augment these newspaper reports, and refresh people's memory once more; and 'twas with great happiness that I am able to pen da last chapter but two in regard to Doctor Humphrey's perverse vicissitudes. The music had started: Steve Windwood's Higher Love has begun playin'; and with Humphrey's own realization he was a galant homme, and his history would become an inspiring story to many people, who come to know about it, being a bona fide hero, hence, he was glad to tell me all about it: how he got his darlin' girl he wanted most of all at long last! He was entitled to get his reward. At last, when he felt the timing was right, true to his new form, he confidentially put forward his claim, or otherwise he would bring everybody down, and hence, he made his gentle speech to Helen, the creature he desired most in all Ephemeral earth; askin' for Miss Rolland's hand in Holy Matrimony. Doctor Humphrey had niver desired to be some other person else and had always been persistent in pursuing her, by stickin' to his guns! Despite certain embellishments that he treated himself to: despite da occasional big and small mistakes and setbacks, he was moving speedily towards a divinely-assisted, God-willed conclusion of his affairs! In the savant's life as in men of good will, the fire of love, God's inextinguishable fire spur us onwards; to lead us roundly home. It was slightly more than seven-and-a-half years since da breakdown, and a long an' dolorous time he had o' it, and this time around anyway, he would not let anything lead him astray. Helen Rolland, an equally shy and modest person, had nursed and stood by him while he was tucked away at Poole's Sanatorium: a potential dreg and washout o' a highly critical society. With Helen Rolland's patient love and nursing experience for a time he had been thoroughly dependent on her, but she had not despised his weakness. She had sustained his broken mind, and stopped him from deteriorating into a morbid and permanent condition—by her companionship that went far beyond da call of duty, and not infrequently—this had been the trumps that kept his center together when his days were cold an' dark. After that, they had remained, good friends, and true ones, to each other! Missy Ho's wild, warrior heart, conversely—had always been cap-a-pie and inaccessible to him.

Helen was his extraordinary if not ordinary girlfriend. She seemed to have understood the depths of his character and what made him tick, and was not inundated or overwhelmed by what she saw or sensed. Her sacred profession made her eminently suited to take good an' wholehearted care of him, for she was a kind, good and holy person—with—what is rare—a pure mind and a pure heart! He had hoped, and prayed, before she made it with someone else, though she was chaste, hoped rather, that he would have recovered before that, and she was not grabbed by someone: and not on the matrimonial market anymore! There were times when, hoping against hope, he felt he were racing against time, because it was incredible that someone canny has not snapped her up. It might be due to grace; and to the all-powerful operative POWER of HIM! HE was always arrangin' da affairs of those who He loves in such a way that their heart's desires were being fulfilled, no matter what, in such circumstances, as made 'em entirely grateful to HIM! It goes without saying that Humphrey Humperdinck loved Helen Rolland, very much. Her love, to him, was special and a higher one, than the love of any woman or girl he would have considered looking at, because she took him into her heart—joyfully, kept him there—when he seemed no longer a sane person or complete human being. He was nuffin'!—but she filled him with longings to pull himself up by his bootstraps! And reestablishin' relationships of normalcy with himself, and, a healthy spirituality, through da restorative power o' Jesus Christ's Redemption. Because he was loved in his straitened condition when the chips were down, though they were unevenly paired as lovers they had brought da treasures o' their heart into this therapeutic encounter, at last he found the thing missin' all his childhood. He found Helen Rolland really loved him as a man, with a love that had strength of character that was not dishonest; or an affectation, or a cheap fling—but, which, was rooted and sprang from the center of her being! Helen he had always known was quiet and peaceful, unlike his fuming Mother. His Mother would be like an eagle when they were together, even when they were only sitting an' not talking an' before he did anything wrong or anything she might disapprove of (sich as makin' a comment that hurt her, though, it was not his intention) she would jump all over him, "fumigate" him, lash out at him with her woman's tongue. She preempted him from making any mistake because, for one, she thought he was weak-spirited; and when he was going to Pre-school many, many years ago, he thought ruefully now if she had a choice she would have spared him the agony if she could, and gone fer him in his place an' in his stead. She could sense what he was about to do or what he was going to say, from living together for so long an' from long usage. But it was a funny kind of love. Well he promised himself he shall be his Mother's solace from now on, no matter what! I'd only mentioned this here to contrast and compare with Helen. For there is no togetherness or da feelings of togetherness (one of the states of mind we human beings have; others are: when one is laughing, crying, sleeping, working, playing, being alone, etc.) is bogus when there is stress; and stress is featured and factored in territorial conflicts. When somebaddy has sumptin an' somebaddy else wants that thing but the first somebaddy refuses to give it to him; that is when da troubles in this wurl start! When there is stress, because of the proximity of the stressor or stressors to the one feelin' da heat, there could be no real togetherness: it is completely bogus altogether! (If a wise child, seeing that it is not all right in the family situation says, 'Hey, Mom and Dad—be careful, you might lose your soul?' what do you think his Mom, at least, would do? Wouldn't she wallop him gude, and so I ask you; but, who triumphed in da end? Pareints are given by God to punish children, but who's to punish 'em if they go wrong?) That was why he valued and loved Miss Helen very much; she was as warm and peaceful, quiet and soft-spoken a spirit there ever was, and not a fiery, oratorical one! With her, even in his dubious or less than impeccable moments, he always felt comfortable and secure with her. Missy had not wanted him and had had no patience to wait fer him. So he had to forgit about her! In addition he wasn't sure of her heart as he had been sure of Helen's . . . He could imagine himself as being less than honest with Missy in some circumstances, but not wi' Helen. With Miss Rolland, the better or the righter choice it was to be something that no eye had seen, no ear had ever heard . . . the perfect bliss of heaven that no leaps of the imagination can penetrate or fathom, and it was only then he realized she was da God-appointed one. Hadn't he been wearied to the depths of bone-rattling despair because of the deadening trauma to his normal affections, that had concussed his brain but after such a long time this was the momentous raising of the new man, having kicked his troubles, mind, body and soul? Having taken Ashwagandha and garlic hawthorn, his brain an' heart no longer doubled up with fear or elbowed like some plastic straw, his coiled up healthy energies was at long last straightened and properly released.

Humphrey had been seeing her lately quite a lot. It was on the tenth or eleventh date that she immediately realized a difference in him. 'You look so very wonderful and strange tonight,' was her immediate comment to him as he was passin' her some endearin' tender compliment. And her heart swelled like a thrilling song, the sensation of which she never would have felt possible. 'I want to hold you—and reach out and touch you. Humphrey! you have become completely renewed, a new man, has emerged, I feel, and know it, now! a Man walking in gentleness, truth and beauty!' And they were like reagent and reactor! Water and carbon dioxide!'—hush, now. After all that time she had seen him through da worst o' it an' havin' been through it supporting him, she was thus prepared to know and taste da best in him, knowing having come back to life, he would not take her for granted: no, not by a long chalk . . . !

They parted after exchanging a passionate kiss; the exploration of one o' da other's desire, and the unveiling of their personalities, a fulfillment of a blessing that reverts back to God's Promise to his obedient Children—Children who reverenced da Father's LAWS. Just one kiss and da pressin' o' their bodies, it became a new beginning that wiped da slate clean of all of his life's bitter disappointments; and all of her years of waiting for the right man to come along; and all of their heartaches and loneliness! 'Goodnight!' he whispered sweetly in her blushing ear; then louder, as he played wi' her hand, 'Goodnight, Miss Rolland! Yes, Miss Rolland! No, Miss Rolland! I will remember, Miss Rolland!' in answer to her solicitous questioning and her injunctions to take good care of himself. Finally, they both called out, 'Goodnight!' simultaneously to each other (the love that beckoned 'em was restorative of the inward qualities of each other's mind an' spirit; for they were involved in a search, all their lives; and Helen, especially, had been resolutely giving up casual romances and casual entanglements for one exclusive relationship she was hoping for in da future; that being, her bargain with her good Lord). That future has come! They had obeyed the dictates of their deep hearts; and the conviction grew that the other was the right person. Truly, da right one! The music they heard when they kissed, just now, was, which, someone nearby had switched on, A World Without Love: by Peter and Gordon and then, Cliff Richard's The Best of Me. The convulsion, which started, grew perceptibly, in the depth of each other's natures, and, all at once, they surrendered and accepted the fact that they cannot live without da other—after that moment. Their fates were sealed—with a kiss! After a wurl of aggravation, trouble, fear and anxiety,—they were being rainbow'd after being chained in the bowels of perdition (at least, for Humphrey)! It seemed the debbil's spells that were woven over him were shattered; since he had found someone to take that final step with him in a man-woman relationship, by walkin' down da Aisle wi' him . . . And, thus, havin' broken the jinx; Humphrey Humperdinck found his one and only! And it reminded him o' Shania Twain's song, 'From this moment on . . .'

'What . . . I thought I'd never . . . I know now,' said Humphrey, belaborin' to breathe, 'I know now; I love you!'

Helen lowered her eyes and it seemed to bring back their self-possession, of captivating him with demure femininity; her heart soaring—thus filled, brimmed, with overflowing awed love; da justification o' her faith in her being attracted to him whilst he was still a broken man. She attributed to God, her findin' this gentle, loving man who had for a long time seemed to be an improbable life partner and co-benefactor of His blessings: her Everything, whom, she was made for. So, with a kiss, delicious, loving, and tender—they had fallen for each other all o'er again! Yea, to da utmost measure they must, henceforth, be with each other in a celebration that would fill the entire span of their lives: a relationship secure an' warm tasting of honey and honeycombs as each other plighted their troth!

'Stay a while bec'os I love you so, too!' murmured Helen misty-eyed with an ardor that made her white throat catch with an aching, delicious pain. Her features soft and serious, a-trembling she said they should get married as soon as possible. Although they had already said their goodbyes fer da night neither made any move to go. She was still in his arms, her eyes breathing him in the knowledge he was in heaven, he, fondlin' her fingertips. 'Oh,' she said, as he leaned salubriously against her; 'oh!' 'So—you will have me?' he asked in a tone of genuine humility at last. 'Yes, I will have you,' she answered deeply, full o' trusting.

'And stand by me?' said Humphrey.

'Yes!' Helen made reply.

'Forever n' ever?'

'Yes! Oh, yes! Forever n' ever!'

'Amen!' You'll be a Catholic, of course?'

'Of course I will, ay, my only love.'

She smiled, very much pleased, and she followed up with 'You don't mind children, do you?'

'Oh, I love kids very much!' cried Humphrey, 'No, I don't mind havin' a few o' 'em. That's what an ideal husband should do, of course! A whole tribe o' liddle Humphrey Humperdincks!'

'And you'll always love me tenderly and passionately, and as much, you shall love our children? Regardless how they turned out?'

'Yes I promise with all my heart.' He looked her full in the face now, 'Ah!'

'Dearest darling, my soul's true friend—my own sweet snow-white turtledove! Sometimes, when my hopes and dreams were upside down, I thought I'd niver see this day! And now my eyes have seen God's very greatness!'

'Hush, it will be all right forever: it shall be: forever!'

Humphrey Humperdinck had occupied her thoughts a great deal up to that moment, and when they plighted their most true and completest love, it seemed that somehow their love had grown in their absence from one another; and the loneliness of many nights had awakened a deep feeling in her, that she, knowing that he had surmounted his troubles, his declension to such a greater degree, had she wanted to fill in the rest for him. Helen knew Humphrey was ever looking for his dream life-partner, and she was glad she should be the one. She would be the one to love him, and to hold him, for the rest of his life; and she was right glad she was now engaged to him, after such a long time of watching and waiting for him to "come around" and recover from his ocular troubles: help him the rest of the way in his emotional disorder,—if this ever came round again. It seemed their their faith together had moved mountains and they will be together always from now on; and his wish had come true at last. Helen, on her part also, had taken deeply to heart all that had passed between them these last six years, and she had treasured each moment of tenderness they shared together, in knowing him, and in sympathizing with him, although at that time she had not completely given her heart.

I was one of da main honored guests at their wedding when it was solemnized in Helen's hometown, down Connecticut way; and Humphrey's bald head, neatly shaved and polished, gave him a distinction of maturity:—with a few noble curls around the region of his temples. His round bifocals were so transparent that there seemed to be a jovial fire in his eyes; showing him to be a man who had balanced his various parts to perfection! Yes, it was all true! The Bride wore a fleecy gown, with orange buttons, and a gauze veil of purest white was thrown over her head; on that day, after da ceremony, of which, they would be husband and wife onwards. It was not a dream, and nothing was going to spoil it for 'em! She was refulgent—gown, skin, lips, with a brilliancy which made him proud o' her love and o' her consent to be his partner for him to reciprocate her love. The fusion o' hearts was symbolized by the exchange of rings; and after that he was so moved; he said to me, he thought he would just die with sheer bliss . . . 'I pronounce you man and wife,' da wonderful priest intoned . . . Now, when they kissed it sent reverberations down every strand and particle of their being (and that o' da entire congregation o' friends an' well-wishers' spine-tingly backs as well!) Fer a scientist:—this would be nuclear fission! Later, as Mr. and Mrs. Humphrey Humperdinck, in each other's arms, they exchanged another prolonged kiss, and he said, 'First, the lace which I will always give you! It will adorn and set off your adorable femininity! And, keep it intact! The books are to be shared, to study to please, to satisfy, each other's needs without me relinquishing my role as humble leader . . . And lastly, the basins, a symbol of humility, meekness and service! We are to wash each other's feet, after the example of our Lord at da Last Supper . . .' As I put the last final changes into this book, tweaking a sentence and slottin' and takin' out a word there; a round baker's dozen o' commas; the radio had been playing He's So Shy . . . You've Got a Friend in Me . . . Going Back . . . and da perennial Kenny Roger's, 'You Decorated My Life . . .' and I tink, God had discovered me when it aptly plays—very aptly to cap it off—We're All Alone, by Rita Coolidge, and, yes, it must have been LOVE: God's ENDURING LOVE . . . !!! While, in Hound of Heaven, it says, 'Everything sooner or later betrays him who betrays Christ,' the converse is true to those who are true to Him to da last; an' da healing energy o' HIM have brought everything to the exceedingly good, finally. Another quote from Emerson, Ralph Waldo is in order, 'Our strength grows out of our weakness. The indignation, which arms itself with secret forces, do not awaken until we are pricked and stung and sorely assailed. A great man is always willing to be little. While he sits on the cushion of advantage, he goes to sleep. When he is pushed, tormented, defeated, he has a chance to learn something; he has been put on his wits, on his manhood; he has gained facts; learns his ignorance; is cured of the insanity of his conceit; has got moderation and real skill. The wise man throws himself on the side of his assailants. It is more his interest than it is theirs to find his weak point. The wound cicatrices and falls off from him like dead skin, and when they would triumph, lo! he has passed on invulnerable . . . !' Words of wisdom from da great homegrown American Plato, indeed!

'You know, Professor John Tanischi in most of the latter half of my unfortunate experience, which seared my consciousness except for da brief period when I didn't pray for da repose of muh Father's soul (or my Grandfathers' and Grandmothers', either) da darkness had been NOT without a sort of light, especially, when I am unconscious, in my sleep. I must say, legitimate mental pain and psychic adversity, after all, is very good! It helps you to grow in leaps and bounds, to be heads and shoulders above da others . . .' Such were the inspiriting words Doctor Humphrey Humperdinck gave, which I will carry with me forever in muh heart to muh very own grave!!

Hence Humphrey Humperdinck larned to skirt or confront every imperfection and defect, withstand every discomfort to gain strength and maturity of soul, to be perfectly attuned to God's MUSIC, through his willingness to suffer interminably, and though there is no return to yesterday's golden clime, he looked forward to greater intimacy with Him and with Helen, his newly married wife, by building up their faith together, and attuned to da harmony within God's universe . . . After a lapse of two years Helen gave him a fine son, and they named him Humphrey Humperdinck the Third, after da family tradition; and after that, when I came to see him in Vermont, after some little time, I asked him, 'Which would 'ee like to prefer, by da way, to be on your deathbed: to say "There my loves; what availeth my gold!" or "These are my monies; what availeth my dear ones?"' However, he laughed quickly and said, 'I will say, "Pareints beware of children. Children beware of pareints. Older people beware of young people. Young people beware of older people." I love my son very, very much, and he is a good boy . . . However, it is inconsistency and not anything in the parent or parents that a child utterly abhors! My writings will mostly go towards muh own Foundation fer da alleviation of hunger, disease and poverty in da wurl . . . ! The method I have hit upon is to give your progeny ninety-five percent of what it needs (not what it wants!) and make him sweat for the other five percent; make him run fer da money fer da rest! Then you give the hundred percent to him, but to give more is wastage. I am also encouraged to think the percentage I should give him; of what he wants, but I think, a wise parent would say it varies with the situation an' da season.'

About da last o' him, I heard, he was doing some studies on the nature of mental processes, the genesis o' thoughts, and relishing the chaotic mental situations, because, he said, that is the point of growth, being fastest and the greatest area of growth. 'If you were allowed da final word, Doctor Humphrey Humperdinck, what would that be, then?' I asked him, very interested, and laughing. 'Oh,' he replied, grinning broadly, 'doan rub it in. YES, doan rub it in; without a single doubt . . . ! There's not everybaddy, which has a chance to be holy in this wurl; an' so, one should be more understanding, kind an' patient.'

And later, as I partook of his roast beef, seated at his table decked out with immaculately white napkins amid da silver and da crystal, I bethought mysel', 'Didn't Mrs. Humperdinck look so fine in her Chantilly lace and satin wedding gown and Doctor Humphrey Humperdinck Junior so handsome and grand in his off-white suit and black tie four years ago? It was Humphrey's greatest coup, and what a magnificent occasion to remember fer always an' always! Mrs. Helen Humperdinck is still as trim and neat of figure as before; and Humphrey Humperdinck the Third is two-and-a-half years old now, a chubby rosy babe, who is thriving exceptionally well on da love, kindness and tenderness shown by both parents.'

Chapter Twenty-three

THE GOOD SIDE O' THE
HUMAN HEART!

'Half to forget the wandering and the pain,
Half to remember days that have gone by,
And dream and dream I am home again.'
James Elroy Flecker ("Brumana")

'After all my bitter an' enlightening experiences,' said Humphrey Humperdinck while we were having strong port an' a liddle light sherry beside the fireside table about the last time I saw him, 'If I have a Master word to share with you, Professor John Wyndham Tanischi (are 'ee dreamin' o' home?), it's this: love an' cherish da turbulent storm within your mind and heart; it's da cutting edge of things, and so, happily, go to da fringe of da storm, where da storm is at its fiercest, until the eye of the storm had passed (but pick your battles) and you would have won against da bad spirits; as the wurl is slowly being healed an' constantly, renewed . . . I wish all the best fer da wurl! Ever since I was a teenager, I was always deciding to take a line different from my brothers, which was more beyond da common lot. I was da Phoenix; that legendary Arabian bird which was so beautifully described, by Hans Christian Andersen in his short sketch of the same name. To stand at the periphery of da buffeting storm when everyone else is losing his head an' have da patience to wait till the eye o' da storm passes, is da Phoenix, carryin' wood for its funeral pyre an' Christ, my Lord, is quelling the tempest at the command o' his WORD, in the midst of tearful and frightened disciples . . . For if, one is able to do that; da law of da flesh is supervened, and da "afflatus materia mundi" is changed . . . ! That is when lousy experiences become ecstatic ones, when, there is a cheerful willingness to suffer the buffets of outrageous fortune; which then become outrageous no more! That was what Humphrey Humperdinck's spectacle o' spectacles had taught him fair, by far, muh dear Professor Tanischi. Bottom's up. Cheers! When I have muh share o' troubles, I praise da Lord, throw my weight behind my enemy, and wait graciously an' cheerfully fer da eye o' da storm to pass by. Then, my troubles are at an end and then, I'm restored, to myself. Pass da port, dear sir.'

It was a peach day in winter and it was blowing sleety rain, and the milky sun came slow up afterwards.

'But I should add that between guidelines one and two, "Praise and thank God (for yer pains)" . . . and . . ."throw your weight behind your enemy's (its) attacks"(against yersel'), there should be inserted sumptin else, sich as, "Watch what your enemy (it) is goin' to do or is doing to 'ee" . . . don't you think? Well, I have to leave pretty soon, I think I'll take my little rest; and thank you, Humphrey!'

'I, also, when I go to sleep in a happy mood, use my dream state as a powerful resource to solve life's problems,' said Humphrey. 'The psychology of Evil is that it's very cagey and skittish—it attacks wi' an element of surprise; once you take the pains or trouble, yet not kicking against the goad, to notice what it is doing, it immediately backs down or go away. There is always an element of surprise when I saw those rapacious faces bristling with rapacity, yes, you are right, the problem of Eyes and all mental illness or spiritual troubles is solved if one patiently follows these few simple rules, with the added rule of praying and watching for the eye of the storm to pass you by. "It"—does not have to be your enemy, it might be your partner, your opposite number, or any other person, say, another driver on da road, that is, the wurl at large.—I have become a believer in Ayruvedic Medicine, thanks to you. I also take garlic hawthorn to calm my heart. Yes, always praise and take the trouble to thank God too, on top of everything else at every moment; and that would preempt irritation and bad feelings from surfacing because all these guidelines make it nearly impossible, with constant vigilant effort.'

And I said: 'You represent the good side o' da human heart!'

'I am glad you said that. I am in no pain,' he replied. 'My Dad wants the very thing he could not give us, and this thing I am not going to deny him—unconditional love. I am going to give him that always. And if I ask God does He regrets it for creating me: I am sure His answer would be, "No, a thousand times no, a hundred thousand times no!"'

'Good on you, Doctor Humphrey Humperdinck. It was due to his unresolved childhood problems that made him unable to love his own children unconditionally; but you are grown up with facing all your problems and you have learnt to depend on God's Unconditional love, so you had been able to break the curse that has been the plague of the Humperdinck family. Good on you.'

'I, Professor John Wyndham Tanischi, then said, to Humphrey, 'The task of human beings being put on earth is to know God. The true test of knowing God is whether we will thank Him and praise Him for our sufferings and pains or not (that comes from His hand). The pleasure He denies us and the pains and sufferings He gives us, whether we will curse Him to His face, be deflated with depression, desperation or disappointment, or whether we will praise and thank him for them, thus,—is that ultimate test! If I am determined and I promise him to praise and thank Him for every pain and suffering as soon as it is received (whether from family members, accidents, animals, nature, diseases, stupidity which is the top part of pride, the devil, laziness, circumstances, neighbors, ennui, foreigners, countrymen, the world), I would do well to pass the test! Although the Son of God may be excused for crying 'My God, my God, why have you forsaken me?', and it showed, due to the extremity of his pain he lost his focus, though he might be excused, we have no such excuse! We who are supposed to continue his work and do greater things than Him have to do our part to help humankind. If you can praise God and thank God, for every ounce of pain and suffering you endure, something double clicks and something is etched in your consciousness! Firstly, the key to the trauma in your heart is unlocked; and secondly, the key to the trauma in your mind and brain an' feelings is unlocked! Going beyond that if you can thank God for the hurts and sufferings and disappointment other people give you, as understanding God's purpose, as well as the hurts and sufferings and disappointments you gave them, (if you are sensitive enough, you'll know this will return to you),—then you truly know God and you are truly blessed, and it will set you free completely from your predicament: this I as a Christian psychologist would like to tell you, Doctor Humphrey Humperdinck! Do not let any god or anything: blasphemy, anger, hatred, unforgiveness stand before God, for wasn't it writ, you shall not have any strange gods before Me? For, if we know God, we would automatically want to serve Him and do His will because He is a triumphant God (He doesn't give rise to depression and a deflation of our healthy spirit) and a triumphant God is a winner! (Other gods are idols in relation to Him; it is only when the true God is known that the other gods are known as idols, and not before that . . .) Now, who are the people who know God? Maybe, not mostly those who are known as saints . . . Heaven is no eye has seen, no ear has heard, you will never know who you will find there, for it is for those whose faith is known to Him alone, git it? People who know God are those whom God has given a job to do, and do it well, by His grace; who says, like the prophets of old, "Here I am Lord. I come to do your WILL!' This is a natural response because we would like to be a winner on the last day as well and He would make us into winners! So do not have evil spirits and bad thoughts before God and before yourself. At the last analysis, only the pure in heart can see God, you concur Humphrey . . . !'

Lastly, Dear Reader, you suffer yea? Yet, suffering is often with joy mingled, and sometimes they are often viscerally connected. Let this be the groundwork of knowing God, truly knowing Him, as Job did, thousands of years before Christ, and his is an oft forgotten message: you must not only worship your God but you must know God, if possible know Him inside out (with effort) . . . What you know you must not 'unknow' again; just as true knowledge cannot return to ignorance without detriment. And, like me, if you are in God's service, there isn't time to "rest on your laurels" as the saying goes, for He will not allow that, and you will have more on your plate at any one time than you could possibly handle. 'Now then, Humphrey, goodbye; I am to take my leave . . . but before so, read more about

Charles Bonnett Syndrome and Phobias as we have discussed, and learn from other people who have similar experiences . . . make time to read masterpieces of literature and use other people's words to fuel your own by using their productions as your notebook . . . and write an autobiography of yours. You were pretty conceited once, you know; but you, as Helen's husband are now steady as an oak, and use your talents now well in all humility,—and all will be well wi' 'ee. God bless!'

Chapter Twenty-four

LAST CONVERSATION AND CONSULTATION

Finally, I would like to report that there was one last time we met, and that was to find out if all was well, and things were as it should be. In a nutshell, I would also like to summarize the Case of Humphrey Humperdinck, who made a startling observation about himself on that occasion.

'Vision is emotion expressed by the heart, guided or misguided by the brain, so that vision is steered along its path in the course of daily living, to be what it is,' said my client, during our consultation.

'How about thought, Humphrey?' I wanted him to inform me.

'Thought is emotion expressed by the brain, and informed by the heart, Professor Tanischi. As you know, I was messed up for a long time—and why was I messed up for a long time?—it was as if I was under a spell, and a great percentage o' it is just stupid, plain self-hypnotism! That was why my throat got all clammy and constricted, and itchy, and I feel pressure in my temples! When I am out of sorts! I'd auto-suggested to myself; that I should suffer for a long time bec'os I was brain-washed by the things I read and somehow I suggested to myself that I should atone for the sins of others and of the world! I was perfectly an idiot! I had for a long time, since my youth, discounted my feelings; and I often wondered why God created human beings with emotions, thinking it is so much better if he dispensed with bestowing emotions on men and women. If they have no feelings but intellect alone, so much the better!'

'You suggested it to yourself? Who told you to suggest it to yourself?'

'I couldn't say for sure; I think it has something to do with the spirit of the times.'

'You mean you tried to be good too much and your mind turned in the end?'

'Yes!'

'But most of us modern folks deny our feelings, I must say, or relegate them to be of secondary importance; or we think they are counted of no consequence one way or another!'

'Yes, I have fitted myself in a strait-jacket, to the detriment of my own self and mental health. I come lately to realize feelings are the most important thing to a human being and the most enduring; at least, for someone like myself'

'What do you mean by that? Explain yourself!'

'I was a dead ringer for da hang-dog look, purty always tryin' to stifle my own feelings! I was always a sort of very religious, and when I plunged the nozzle (in Canterville Chase), I thought I was saving the world. Only, I panicked the split-second the stream of ectoplasmic matter touched my skin; and then I thought to myself, "Oh-oh!" but by then it was too late, of course.

'You never told me this before.'

'Somehow, I must have blocked it from my conscious mind for a long time.'

'Why was that, do you know?'

'I blocked it along with my massive guilt! I didn't think I have saved the world, and it was because I messed up and did not front the demons properly, having flinched, that I felt I have to be in a wretched state of mind for a long time, to make up for my failure in not facing up to the mob from hell. That is why I later realized it was self-hypnotism, and my guilt and fear held the declension in place inside myself.'

'You want to repair your chance—that's what spurred you on in your seeing faces:—together with your guilt of wasting your chance?'

'YES! And, the unknown evil that I always felt when I closed my eye is always more real than the evil I see with my eyes opened. I did not realize that it was my own auto-suggestion that caused me to see those faces, and I thought mostly I was stuck with it, maybe, for the rest of my life, as I have to endure my lot as a failed "savior of the world." I felt a lot of pathos together with false consolation, I must say.'

'Are you really all right Humphrey Humperdinck?' I commiserated: 'That is being hysterical.'

'You are right. Do you know what my friend, Ronnie Roper said to me the other day. "Man, do not be hysterical, man, and you are all right."'

'You are right, Mr. Roper—I was being hysterical.'

'"How is your life now, suh?"'

'"It's hysterical; but doan git me wrong—in a good way!" And we had a good laugh.'

'Yes, thank God, that part of my life is behind me now. Helen taught me a snippet o' a prayer, "Jesus, propitiation for sins" and this prayer has done me a whole world of good, never greater good has a single prayer done for me! And it was opportune too, because I suddenly realized that it was Jesus that atoned for sinners, not me; and I don't have to do it. I also realized, furthermore, that it was EASY not to see faces at all; all I have is to say, 'It is easy!' and then, feeling this is so; and so the pressure in my head began slowly to relax and the self-hypnotism that it is supposed to be hard to be free of (my problem) is beat! BEAT! BEAT! It is really that simple and easy! I had been laboring under the notion it is almost impossible to get well and be restored to myself again; but after taking Ashwagandha and garlic hawthorn, and realizing with utter conviction that it is EASY TO UNSEE THOSE FACES; and it is easy to have a normal mind and a healthy body, too—the thing was achieved in a day or two or three!'

'So you tell yourself, "It is easy not to see faces! Everything is really easy," and lo and behold! It is easy not to see those faces? And the stress and tension that you once felt, but slowly diminishing, the fear, and the anxiety—they are all gone? You say, "It's easy for my mind and body to be normal—better than normal—and healthy"— and it is so? You have pared down the fabrications of your brains, as you purified your conscience, and the dastardly question-mark doesn't trip you up no more?'

'Yes, right, the shadows that were cast once over my life are gone; and I don't think they will ever come back. The anticipation that I get of coming out of my own auto-suggestion is pleasurable and a great relief:—I can report this to you; they are wholly good. That is to say, the unspeakable horrors are the same as the speakable horrors in my life now—and things that go bump in da night are the same things you see, one not more than the other; because you see, I have fronted them all—and although it is the brain that is seared, it is the heart that restores the equilibrium—because the things you see wi' your eyes wide open have become those you see with your eyes wide shut, being no different or are no different and both don't shock or injure your heart and brains, and so I suppose you'd better get used to it, bud. It is due to the fear of the dark shadow with the long tooth that grips one, but now, there is a cascading light in the summer breeze, in the flight of the swallow's wings; a light that seems to grow on everything and unbinds the musty earth not so long ago corseted by winter's constricting dress, my, ah—how August undulates between July and September upon summer's joyous cries—!'

'Good, good! And I suppose, you repeat that it is easy to unsee those faces for some time, even after that?'

'Yes, I am amazed by the clarity of my mind now; and I constantly remind myself to keep alert and not to come under the spell of anybody or anything; and now I am in the tip-top of my health, yes, the very tip-top of my health, as you can see, Professor Tanischi. I have waited for morning like waiting for the dawn of time, living a life composed of inauspicious small beginnings and always building on that to the limits of that perhaps inimitable end.'

I fixed my eye on him; and my gaze confirmed everything he had said about himself. Then clasping his hand and shaking it firmly, I said, with gusto:

'Then I must say, goodbye to you Doctor Humperdinck Humperdinck, for it is true that da sometime "prophet" has succeeded in self-curing himself completely! Goodbye, and God bless, once again! There is no need to keep any more appointments, and I shall see you to the door. Hang loose and see there are no more sads in your life.'

'God bless you, too, Professor John Wyndham Tanischi!' said he, as he hugged me.

Thus, everything is told and explained; and here is my bread, kneaded and shaped, still in the dough, this novel of mine, that I hope some time to get published, and dear reader, whether I get my double-due is all up to you, I think! And, just then, Matt Monro's voice, singing The Impossible Dream issued from my stereo, coming through clear and strong, as it behooves:— to afford a closure to Doctor Humphrey Humperdinck's story, with a meetness:—swelling my heart—an aptness,—with regard to its resounding words, beat, and melody. For, after all, these late years,—in looking back, the game of life is analogous with Reality-Tee-vee Shows, or Contest, and so be prepared to fail: —sometime, bec'os the rewards are immense and sure, and great,—for it is a dangerous game for one like him; —because the director or producer o' dat show is a devilish being: nay doot; and, to be a winner one has to surmount all the odds—I say,—bec'os if you want to play at life, you must not forfeit, fail, break contest rules, or the country's laws,—bec'os evil will have you stuck, or, in its clutches in less than no time at all if you do. So play this game to win for goodness' sake! Win!

Even in the long-lasting nadir of Doctor Humphrey's predicament—his connection to the world and up to the affableness of God was always strong—even though he was skewered, and it was peace of mind for himself and da world that he had been hungering forever for—until his marriage to his Beloved who consented to give him her hand. That was the fulfillment of his deepest hopes and desires—after being wounded by God's musical knife—at last relief and relaxation soothed his whole being—the culmination of the fulfillment of his deepest hopes and desires—when it was peace of mind he was hungering after; when he was among the children of men.

And Jesus Christ's Words shall mark the last minute of your reading of this book before putting it down:

(JOHN 11:4:7-9)

Then he said to his disciples, 'Let us go back to Judea.'

'But Rabbi,' they said, 'a short while ago the Jews tried to stone you, and yet you are going back there?'

Jesus answered, 'Are there not twelve hours of daylight? A man who walks by day will not stumble, for he sees by the world's light. It is when he walks by night that he stumbles, for he has no light.'

END OF NOVEL